CHAPTER 1

HATTIE

Hattie stood at her kitchen sink, her hands dabbling in the hot, soapy water as she searched for the elusive teaspoon which she knew was in the bowl somewhere, and paused, her head cocked to one side as though she was listening to something faint and distant.

The raucous chatter of hungry birds squabbling over the seeds in the feeder floated in through the closed window and a chill November wind made the bare branches of the bushes in the garden tremble and bend. The sky was grey and lowering, the threatened rain holding off for now, and even though it was gone nine o'clock in the morning, dawn had only just come and gone. But it wasn't the signs of the fast-approaching winter which made Hattie stop for a moment – it was something else, something sensed rather than seen or heard. Things were about to happen, change was afoot; she didn't know how she knew, but she did. And it made her restless, excited, and a little uneasy, all at the same time.

Shaking her head at her own silliness, she finally caught the spoon and dropped it on the draining board with a clatter, then wiped her hands on her pinny and checked that the hob was off. She'd made herself scrambled eggs on toast for breakfast and thoroughly enjoyable it had been too, but now she needed to get ready for work or else she would be late. Considering she couldn't stand tardiness in other people, she wasn't about to be guilty of doing the very same thing herself. Besides, Maddison depended on her more than ever now that the coffee shop side of the business had taken off and her only full-time member of staff, Rhea, was occupied with her new-born baby girl.

Gladys was such an odd choice of name for a wee baby, Hattie had thought the first time she'd heard it, and she hadn't changed her mind since. The name reminded her of her aunt, her mother's sister, a cantankerous old lady who had never married although she'd come close to it once or twice. As Hattie thought about Aunt Gladys from the perspective of being an old woman herself, Hattie gradually realised how much like her aunt she'd

The Ticklemore
Christmas Toy Shop

LIZ DAVIES

To Catherine,
thank you x

become – cantankerous, grumpy, and opinionated, although she had been married, unlike Aunt Gladys.

A persistent purring and a warm, furry feeling around her ankles brought Hattie back to the present. Puss was a large, laid-back ginger tom who she had adopted a few years ago, although he did tend to take off from time to time – either mousing or looking for a lady friend, Hattie guessed. To be honest, she wasn't entirely sure who had adopted whom – despite his half-starved and mangey appearance, he had demanded food, a warm comfortable place to sleep, and attention – in that order. She hadn't had much of a say about him moving in. It was lucky he was home this morning she thought when she saw the time, to stop her from daydreaming. Goodness, she was going to be late if she didn't get a move on, and she wondered what had got into her today to make her so dreamy.

Hastily she unhooked her purple cloak from the hat stand near the door, flung it around her shoulders in much the same way she imagined a Tudor princess might have done (Princess Elizabeth was her favourite, or was she thinking of Elizabeth Taylor?), called goodbye to Puss and hobbled out of the cottage (she would have strode, but her arthritis was playing her up in her left knee), letting the front door slam shut behind her, but not before the cat had shot through it nearly tripping her up.

'Puss!' she cried crossly. But the cat took no notice, trotting jauntily ahead of her along the little lane which ran in front of the row of cottages, its fluffy tail in the air. Hattie hurried after it. But she still couldn't shake the feeling that something was afoot.

When she reached Bookylicious (which was all of a five-minute walk away) it was to find Maddison up to her armpits in the morning rush, and only having time to throw a quick smile in Hattie's direction. Her employer didn't look any different, Hattie decided after studying her critically as she unswished her cloak and hung it up.

Whatever she'd felt this morning, she was pretty sure it didn't have anything to do with Maddison. Although, come to think of it, the girl had been married for a while, and with Rhea having recently given birth, it might be about time Maddison started thinking about babies. Hattie made a mental note to gently put the idea into her employer's head; after all, she wasn't getting any younger. Hattie was referring to herself, of course, not Maddison. She'd be eighty in a few months, her life nearly done, and it would be nice to see Maddison with a family before she breathed her last.

How had it happened? Where had all those years gone? One minute she'd had her whole life in front of her, full of promise and sunlight, and now here she was with the vast majority of it behind her. It hadn't lived up to its promise, either, the sunlight having gradually given way to shadows and lost opportunities.

With an annoyed shake of her head, Hattie drove the morbid thoughts out of her mind and dived on the nearest customer.

'What can I get you?' she asked, pen and notepad poised. She didn't need the prop (her memory was as keen as it had always been) but she'd learnt that customers seemed happier to believe she'd get their order right if they saw her write it down. It did irk her a little that those same customers didn't have the same need to see either Maddison, Rhea, Kim, or Teresa scribble down their cake choices on a scrap of paper. It was as though they assumed old age automatically meant a loss of one's marbles, rather than the gaining of more as a result of experience. Wisdom often came with age, if only people recognised it.

Hattie busied herself with pouring just-boiled water onto loose Earl Grey tea leaves, and slicing the scrummy looking lemon drizzle cake. If there was any left, she'd treat herself to a piece later.

For the next hour or so she was too occupied with taking orders, clearing tables, and serving, to think about odd notions and premonitions, and when she finally had a chance to catch her breath for a second, she found herself gazing around the little café-cum-bookshop with a sense of pride. She mightn't own it, but she felt as much a part of it as the shiny coffee machine or the stacks of shelves filled with all those glorious books, and she took great pride in her work. She loved the banter with the customers, enjoying the look on their faces when they bit into a piece of cake and the flavours exploded on their tongues.

She particularly enjoyed helping Maddison out with stocking the shelves and helping customers find that perfect book. For such a long time Hattie had felt unneeded, redundant, and past-it. Maddison had befriended her over the latest Jodi Picoult novel and the result had been the offer of a job at Bookylicious. It had given her a new lease of life, a new purpose in these twilight years of hers, and she loved every minute of it.

'Good morning,' Maddison said to her later when there was a lull. 'How are you today?'

Hattie paused. 'I honestly don't know,' she replied, then seeing the sudden look of concern on her friend's face, she added, 'Don't worry, I'm not ill or anything. It's just...' She hesitated, unsure how to describe it. 'There's a disruption in the force,' she finished, for want of a better explanation.

Maddison burst out laughing. 'You sound like Yoda,' she teased, 'but without the weird way of speaking. What do you mean, "a disruption in the force"?'

Hattie shrugged. She couldn't explain it to herself, so how could she expect Maddison to understand? All Hattie knew was that there was something slightly off with the day. And not necessarily in a bad way, either. It wasn't the first time she'd experienced such a thing, and hopefully it wouldn't be the last, but she had learnt to listen to her instincts. She wasn't experiencing a sense of doom or anything so dramatic, but a change was coming and she could feel it in her water.

Talking of water, she took the opportunity to nip to the loo while it was quiet. Just because all her mental faculties were still intact, it didn't mean old age had bypassed her entirely, and her bladder was one part of her anatomy that frequently reminded her of her advancing years, along with her dodgy knee. The knee could be ignored to a certain extent – her waterworks were a different matter.

While she was in the loo, she did a quick check on the status of the toilet paper and the nice-smelling hand-wash, replenishing both from the cupboard under the sink, so she was in there a little longer than she anticipated. By the time she emerged the café had filled up again.

At first, she didn't notice the elderly gentleman sitting on his own at one of the window tables. Mrs Hamilton was busy telling anyone who would listen, about her latest trip to the doctor, and the story drew Hattie's attention.

'He said it was sciatica. That's in your back, you know,' Mrs Hamilton explained to the room in general, her remarks not aimed at anyone in particular. She had a fork in one hand and was waving it around, sending gobbets of buttercream flying across the tablecloth. 'He looked all right to me,' she added indignantly.

Hattie knew she shouldn't, but she couldn't resist. 'I should hope so. He is the doctor, after all.'

'Who is?'

Hattie rolled her eyes. 'The doctor.'

'Which doctor?'

'The one who told you you've got sciatica.'

'I haven't got sciatica.'

'Who has then? Do you mean to say, the doctor has?'

'No, the man in the surgery.'

'Which man?' Hattie wanted to know.

'The one with sciatica,' Mrs Hamilton said triumphantly. 'But he looked all right to me!' she repeated.

'I give up,' Hattie said, wishing she hadn't stopped to chat in the first place, but as she turned on her heel and began to walk away, she gave the tables a quick once over to see if anyone wanted anything, and it was then that she spotted the man. Elderly, with almost-white hair, wearing a tweed jacket, and looking forlorn. He was alone and not just in the physical sense of the word. She could feel the loneliness radiating off him like heat from a fire.

The air left her lungs in one long drawn out sigh; she knew immediately that this gentleman was what her water had been trying to tell her about all morning, and her heart fluttered – something she hadn't felt it do in a terribly long time.

'Right,' she muttered to herself. 'Bring it on.'

CHAPTER 2

ALFRED

Alfred was trying to work out when he'd gone from being Alfred and had become Alfie. He'd been Alfred all his life, but at some point during the past couple of years, Alfie had begun to creep in.

He didn't feel like an Alfie. He still felt like an Alfred, although what he felt like on the inside and what people saw on the outside appeared to be two different things. They saw Alfie, and he wasn't happy with the change.

But then, he wasn't happy with a lot of things, beginning with his enforced move to live with his daughter. Neither she nor those damned social workers knew what they were talking about. Of course he could still look after himself. He'd been doing it for most of his adult life, hadn't he? What was so different now?

That lot had no idea. A couple of little falls and the odd forgetful moment was all it took for them to decide it wasn't safe for him to live on his own. Which was why he had to move in with Sara. It was either that, or a nursing home, and there was no way they were putting him into one of those. Nursing homes were for people who were bedridden, and who couldn't wash and dress themselves. He was perfectly capable of doing both, thank you very much.

He glanced down at his neat brown trousers with the crease down the front, just the way he liked them, his checked shirt, brown cardigan, and loafers. Because he was only popping out to the shops to have a sneaky cuppa and a slice of cake at Bookylicious, he hadn't bothered with a tie. Even if he did say so himself, he looked as smart today as he usually did. He'd had a shower this morning, had shaved, and had made his own breakfast. He'd not even expected Sara to wash up after him, because he'd done that himself too, although she would have given him hell if she'd caught him.

So why on earth did everyone think he was incapable of looking after himself, when he was so clearly demonstrating that he could?

Hope flared briefly in his chest, only for his heart to sink back down to his boots again when he remembered he was being forced to sell the house, the one he'd shared with Dorothy, who was dead now, bless her; the one in which they'd watched their daughter grow from a tiny baby into an independent woman. Sara had a home, a husband, and a daughter of her own, now. The last thing she needed was her old dad hanging about. He didn't think it was fair on him or her, but she'd given him no choice in the matter. It was either come and live with her and David in one of their spare rooms, or go into a nursing home.

He knew which he preferred.

But neither option was entirely to his liking. He was simply having to make the best of a bad job.

What he missed most, besides having his own house with the wonderful little workshop at the far end of the garden, was his independence. Not since Dorothy had passed away had Alfred reported to anyone. He'd pleased himself, had done what he wanted to do when he'd wanted to do it, without being answerable to anyone else. Now, it was "where are you going, Dad?" and "what time will you be back?" Usually followed by, "you'll be careful, won't you?" and "make sure you take your stick; you don't want to fall again, do you?"

No, he damned well didn't. Not only would it prove them right, but he wouldn't hear the end of it. Sara would be even more reluctant to let him out on his own, and he didn't think he could cope with that.

When the issue of moving in with his daughter was first mentioned, Sara had still been working full time, and although he hadn't had much enthusiasm for living with her and her husband, the one thing which had kept him going was the consolation that she would be out all day. Except, she wasn't out all day, was she? She was at home because she'd decided to take early retirement, and was watching him with the same intensity as a hawk watched a sparrow. Therefore, one of the few enjoyments left to him, was to ruffle her feathers a bit. Nipping into the village for a paper and coming home later than promised was one such way.

It was petty, he knew, but a little devil inside him drove him to do it. He wasn't being deliberately awkward, just trying to push back a little, to feel a bit less of the burden she undoubtedly saw him as. It didn't help his mood today, that he'd overheard a conversation in the newsagents. Two youngish women had been talking about their elderly parents. One of them had been comparing her mother to a small child, complaining that the old woman was regressing and becoming more like a determined toddler every day.

To his dismay, Alfred found he could relate to that. His behaviour towards his daughter was reminiscent of a little child pushing the boundaries. Except in his case, Alfred wasn't little, and he had a horrible notion he'd be having more and more restrictions placed upon him as time went on.

It was a depressing thought.

Scowling, he glanced up at a woman hovering by his elbow, who was waiting to take his order.

'Have you decided, or do I have to guess?' she asked. 'My name is Hattie. What's yours?'

He wanted to say, "mind your own business", but he was too polite.

'Alfie,' he replied, without thinking. He was utterly sick of being Alfie. Alfie allowed himself to be pushed about, to be told what to do, to be ignored, to be patronized. He'd had more than enough of being Alfie, but the name slipped out of his mouth before he had a chance to think about it.

Anyway, what did it matter? It wasn't that far from Alfred. If he tried hard enough, he could convince himself it was a term of endearment.

'Short for Alfred, is it? Nice to meet you, Alfred,' the waitress said. 'What can I get you?'

He'd only been in Bookylicious once before and that time he'd had an Eccles cake and a cup of tea. Nice, safe options. Expected options.

'I'll have a slice of that over there, please,' he said, pointing to an item in the chilled cabinet beneath the counter.

'The red velvet cake?'

'If that's what it's called, and an espresso, please.' He knew he was being grumpy, but he couldn't help it.

'Coming right up,' Hattie said, and strode off towards the counter.

Alfred watched her go, his eyes narrowing behind his glasses. He guessed she might be about the same age as him, but it was difficult to tell with women. She was dressed like a cross between a teenager and an old biddy – red plimsolls on her feet, yellow tights, a grey skirt with what looked like orange bats on it (although he supposed they could be birds) and a purple jumper. This interesting combination was completed by the addition of a green apron with the word 'Bookylicious' embroidered on it. She also had her hair in a bun, and wisps of white-grey tendrils framed her face. It wasn't the sort of hairstyle often seen on old ladies, and he wasn't sure what to make of it.

If she was in her late 70s or early 80s as he guessed she might be, then she was quite sprightly, and he envied the fact that she had a job. He wished he was still working. Work gave you a purpose, a reason to get out of bed in the morning, and not just because you had to pee.

It also gave a person a sense of self-worth, and that was probably what Alfred missed the most.

On the scrapheap, that's what he was. A nuisance, a burden, and useless.

Sara wouldn't let him do anything around the house, probably because she didn't trust him to do it right. But since Dorothy died, he'd become so used to doing things for himself that he found it difficult to be waited on hand, foot, and finger. These days he didn't even get to wash his cup up, and on the few occasions he'd tried, Sara or David had taken it from him and gently explained they had a dishwasher to do that for them. This morning's successful attempt had been a small victory.

Dishwasher, indeed. In his day, the only dishwasher in the house was whoever happened to be stood by the kitchen sink when the washing-up needed to be done. Not some machine that ate money and which you often forgot to switch on.

The old way was much better. When you used something, you washed it up, then you put it away. There was none of this swilling it off under the tap first, or arguing over who was going to load it, or getting into a tizzy because there was still a load of dirty dishes in there from the last time.

'Here you go.' The waitress, the one called Hattie, slid a plate containing a generous portion of red velvet cake on the table and popped a tiny cup of rich strong coffee down next to it, along with a glass of water, the way they served it abroad.

Alfred expected her to leave him alone to enjoy his treat in peace. Instead, the woman pulled out a chair and plonked herself down on it.

He stared at her in confusion. Was this normal? Had he said something or done something to warrant this kind of attention from a complete stranger?

No, he didn't think so. But then again, sometimes the world had a tendency to slip away from him, and he lost bits of it. He didn't think it had happened just now, though. Which meant there had to be another explanation which didn't involve him thinking he was losing his marbles.

'What can I do for you?' he asked.

'It's more what I can do for you,' the woman retorted.

'I don't understand.'

'You don't need to. You can leave that up to me.' She nodded at his plate. 'Try your cake and tell me what you think.'

Alfred continued to stare at her for a little while longer, then he did as he was told (like he so often had to, these days) and picked up the fork.

The waitress was watching him intently. Maybe the cake was a new recipe, and she was waiting to see what he thought of it.

'Delicious,' he mumbled, his mouth full of glorious sweetness.

'I know. It's my favourite.'

'If you know,' he said, swallowing, 'Why did you ask what I thought?'

'Ooh, aren't you the snipey one? Got out of the wrong side of the bed this morning, did you?'

'Mind your own business.' He wasn't usually so rude, and especially not to a woman, but this one deserved it.

'It is my business when you're sitting there with a face sour enough to scare small children.'

'I have not!'

'You have, too.'

'You're rude.'

'And you're miserable, but don't worry, we'll soon snap you out of it.'

'What if I don't want to be snapped out of it?' Alfred asked.

'You do want to, I can tell. Come back here this time tomorrow, and I'll have a little surprise for you.'

'What is it?' Alfred peered at her suspiciously.

'If I told you, it wouldn't be a surprise, would it?'

'I suppose not.' He scowled again. 'I don't like surprises.'

'And I don't like grumpy old gits.'

'I might be old but I'm not grumpy,' Alfred retorted.

'Have you taken a look in the mirror lately? You look grumpy to me.'

'I don't have to sit here and take this.'

'No, Alfred, you don't; but you *need* to.'

With that, Hattie got creakily to her feet and wandered away, leaving Alfred to stare after her in puzzlement.

What an odd woman, and quite rude too. But she had called him Alfred, even though Alfie had slipped out of his mouth, and for that he was pathetically grateful.

He wasn't entirely sure whether he wanted to visit this little establishment again though, not if the staff were this strange. To be fair, the last time he was here, the young one with fair hair and a sparkle in her eye had served him, and she'd been pleasant enough from what he could remember.

It was just the old woman who was obnoxious.

All he'd wanted to do, was to sit there in peace with a cup of forbidden coffee (it was bad for his blood pressure, according to his daughter) and a naughty slice of cake (which was also bad for him, but for his cholesterol this time). It was getting to the point, where there was very little he could eat or drink which was enjoyable. One by one, the little pleasures in life were being eroded away, and soon there'd be nothing left but bare bones and the hope it would all end soon and he shuffled off this mortal coil to join Dorothy.

Dammit, now look what she'd done. The woman had made him cross and morbid. He'd find another coffee shop from now on, one that didn't have rude, opinionated, elderly waitresses. Which was a pity because he liked being able to read the free newspapers in this one, and he also liked being surrounded by books. There was something soothing about them, with whole other worlds hidden between their pages and the wonderful ability to be someone else for a while when you dived into them; someone young, with a whole lifeful of love and adventure before them.

With a wistful sigh, he polished off the last of his cake, drained his tiny cup of coffee, placed enough money on the table to cover his order, and stalked out of the door.

At least, he'd *wanted* to stalk.

What he'd actually managed was little more than a quick shuffle while gripping onto his walking stick with all his might with white-knuckled hands.

Old age had a lot to bloody well answer for, and nothing whatsoever to recommend it.

CHAPTER 3

HATTIE

As soon as there was a lull, Hattie said to Maddison, 'I need to speak with you. It's important.'

'Oh, God, I'm pregnant,' Maddison cried, clapping a hand to her mouth.

'Are you?' Hattie looked at her friend closely. 'How did I miss that?'

'You mean to say, I'm not?'

'Make your mind up.' Hattie frowned. 'I thought you said you were.'

'I thought that you were going to tell me I was.'

'Eh? Why would I do that? Look, can we start again?'

'I didn't start anything,' Maddison pointed out. 'You did.'

'I didn't. All I said was, we need to talk.'

'Yeah, I know what happens when you say things

like that.'

'I don't know what you're wittering on about.' Hattie stuck her nose in the air.

'Yes, you do. You tell people things.'

'Do I?'

'Stop acting all innocent, you know you do.'

'Give me an example,' Hattie demanded.

'Rhea.'

'Ah.'

'Yes, ah,' Maddison said. 'You knew she was pregnant before she did.'

Hattie *had* known, hadn't she? She had gone and put her foot in things, and had asked Rhea when it was due, with the added awkwardness of saying she didn't realise Rhea had a boyfriend. Rhea had been three months along, boyfriendless, and mortified. The rest of the family had been a bit shocked, too. If pushed as to how she'd known, Hattie tapped her nose and gave the person who'd asked an enigmatic smile.

She quite enjoyed adding to the reputation she already had of being a bit eccentric and mysterious. In reality, her knowledge had come from years watching the glow that pregnant women got, and envying it. She would have given anything to have had that glow herself.

'So, am I pregnant, or not?' Maddison wanted to

know.

Hattie squinted at her. 'Not that I can see.'

'Oh, OK.'

The girl was disappointed, Hattie could tell. She needn't worry though, it would probably happen for her soon enough.

'What did you want to talk about?' Maddison asked, busying herself with removing a soiled tablecloth and replacing it with a fresh one.

'Say what?' Hattie loved that phrase. She'd got it off the TV. For a second, she couldn't remember what it was she'd wanted to talk about… Oh yes… 'Who was that man?'

'What man?'

'The elderly gentleman sitting on his own.'

'Did I serve him?'

'No, I did.'

'Sorry.' Maddison shook her head. 'If I didn't serve him, I'm not likely to remember him. Anyway, I don't tend to remember faces – I usually remember what they ordered and where they were sitting.'

'Red velvet cake and an espresso,' Hattie said. 'And he sat at that table.' She pointed to the table concerned.

'No, he still doesn't ring any bells. Why do you want to know? Did he run off without paying, or did he have a complaint?'

'Neither.'

'Why the interest?'

Hattie shrugged. 'I'm not sure.'

'Are you having one of your *feelings*?'

'I heard that.'

'Heard what?'

'You said the word "feelings "in italics.'

'How can you tell?'

'You'd be surprised.' Hattie hoped she had an inscrutable look on her face and didn't simply look constipated. She had a reputation to uphold.

'Sorry, I can't help you. I didn't notice him.'

That's a shame, Hattie thought. Knowledge was power and at the moment she felt totally powerless. The man, Alfred, had been put in her path for a reason.

All Hattie had to do figure out what it was.

She was a firm believer in a higher power, was Hattie. Call it destiny, fate, karma – whatever. It wasn't a coincidence that Alfred had been in Bookylicious today. She'd felt it in her bones this morning, only she hadn't recognised what it was that she was feeling until she saw him sitting there.

Alfred was her destiny. She didn't know how, or why. She just knew.

For the second time that day, she muttered, 'Bring it on.'

Then she shoved all thoughts of Alfred to one side and got on with serving the next wave of hungry customers.

CHAPTER 4

ALFRED

'Where have you been?' Sara demanded as soon as Alfred walked through the door. 'We've been worried sick about you.'

Alfred scowled. He seemed to be doing that an awful lot lately. 'I don't know why you were worried. I only popped to the newsagents, and then fancied a bit of cake and a cuppa in Bookylicious.'

'We were worried about you,' his daughter repeated.

'This is getting ridiculous,' Alfred grumbled. 'You're treating me like a child.'

'Dad,' Sara's voice softened. 'Have you forgotten we're supposed to be going to your house today, to sort things out?'

'No, I haven't forgotten,' he muttered. But he had, though. In fact, he couldn't remember Sara telling him anything about it in the first place, and a trickle of fear slid down his spine. He was doing this more and more lately, forgetting.

It was nothing to worry about, he was sure of it. Show him someone who never had one of those moments when they walked into a room and couldn't remember why they were there; or they spent half an hour looking for a pair of glasses which were sitting on top of their head all along. Everyone's done it, he said to himself. It wasn't anything to be alarmed about.

But you are alarmed, aren't you, a little voice whispered in his head.

He scowled again and pushed the worry away.

'Well, are we going?' his daughter wanted to know. 'The sooner we get this done, the better.'

Better for whom? Alfred felt like asking, but he kept his mouth shut.

He didn't want to go. He loved his house. He missed it terribly, and everything it stood for and everything that went with it. It would be far too painful to return to it, but return he must. There was just so much stuff to sort out, and he didn't trust Sara or David to do it properly. Knowing Sara, she'd want to get rid of everything, and Alfred wasn't prepared to let certain things go. He'd brought the most important things with him last week, when he'd finally bowed to the inevitable and had agreed to move in with his daughter. Things such as all his important documents, his photographs, and the memory box he'd kept since he was a boy and had added to throughout his life. The last thing he'd put in there had been a printout of the memorial service which had been held when his wife died. He'd not added anything to it since. There didn't seem to be any point.

He'd brought his clothes, toiletries, and some of his books as well, but little else.

There wasn't any room for much more in his daughter's house. She had no use for his furniture, and even if she had needed a dining table or another chest of drawers, his stuff would have looked glaringly out of place. It was too old-fashioned for her.

So he'd left everything else, including most of his memories, because he'd been able to picture his wife in a room whenever he'd walked into it and her presence was still very much in the house and had been right up until the point where David had taken the suitcase out of his hand and walked him to the front door.

No one had heard his whispered, "goodbye my love". No one had noticed the tears gathering in his eyes. No one had noticed his heart breaking, as he left the home in which he'd spent all his married life.

And now he was being forced to go back in order to pick through the rest of his and Dorothy's possessions, to decide what, if anything, he would be allowed to keep. It was just too cruel for words.

'David!' Sara shouted up the stairs. 'Dad's back — we can go now.' She sounded cross and impatient, as usual. It seemed he couldn't do anything right in her eyes, and he felt he'd done nothing but inconvenience her since he'd arrived.

Even the stairs in his daughter's house were a bone of contention, with Sara and David making noises about having a stairlift put in. How daft was that? He didn't need a bloody stairlift; he could get up them just fine, thank you. He might be a bit wobbly now and again, but it was only to be expected at his age. As long as he was careful and didn't try to dash up and down them like a teenager, he could negotiate them well enough. To prove a point, he popped upstairs to use the family bathroom, instead of using the cloakroom near the front door.

He could feel Sara roll her eyes at his retreating back, but at least she didn't say anything for once and to his relief she remained quiet throughout the journey.

Alfred was also silent during the drive, becoming more morose the closer he got to the town he'd once lived in and the house he'd once called home.

When the car pulled up outside the three-bed semi, it was on the tip of his tongue to beg Sara and David to turn around. He couldn't face this, he wasn't ready.

The problem was, he didn't think he'd ever be ready, so he might as well do it now and get it over with, rather than postponing it and having it hanging over his head for days or weeks. Besides, Sara would only nag him about it.

Stiffly and with great reluctance, he slowly got out of the car. His daughter already had his house keys in her hand and was striding up the path with determination.

For her, this was simply another task that needed to be done. She'd always been too practical for her own good. There wasn't an ounce of sentiment in her. She'd got that attitude from her mother. Dorothy had been a practical woman, too. Alfred, on the other hand, had enough sentiment for the whole family. Hence the memory box. Dorothy had known not to touch it, and the shed had also been out-of-bounds to her.

The shed had been his domain. The rest of the house had been his wife's. The arrangement had suited them perfectly. Then the cancer had taken her, and there had no longer been a need for any arrangement.

God, he missed her so much, and he'd give anything to have her back.

He wandered from room to room, running his fingers over the backs of the chairs, stroking the tabletop, blowing dust off the sideboard. This place wasn't a home anymore; it was a shell, a memory of what had once been. There was no longer anything left for him here; he could see that now.

He left his daughter and son-in-law to their rummaging and went and stood by the window. The view was as familiar to him as the lines on his wife's face, and just as dear. It pained him to know that he'd most likely never see it again. However, the pain of not seeing Dorothy again was a far, far greater one. If he could survive that, he could survive anything.

David's voice called faintly from the bottom of the garden, 'Sara, come and have a look at this.'

Alfred knew exactly where David was and what he'd found. His guilty secret. Not even Dorothy had known what he'd got up to during all those hours he'd spent in the shed. She knew it was something to do with wood, because she'd complained bitterly about the sawdust he'd tracked in on the bottom of his shoes and the wood glue which had clung stubbornly to his clothing and had refused all of her attempts to remove it.

But she didn't know what he did in there. What he made.

While Dorothy had potted around the house, and was busy with church activities and the Salvation Army, Alfred had pottered in his shed.

They'd never spoken about it. Alfred guessed that Dorothy had assumed he'd show her when he was ready. But he'd never been ready, had he? Besides, it wasn't as though he was going to do anything with any of it. He'd made those things for his own amusement, to give his hands something to do and to keep his mind busy after he'd retired.

He'd always enjoyed woodwork...

'What?' That was Sara, sounding impatient yet again. 'I'm busy. Can't you just tell me what's in there?'

'No,' David called. 'You've got to see this.'

Alfred heard her mutter under her breath, 'I bet it's that old push-along lawn mower that was in there when I was a child.'

No, Alfred was tempted to say. Guess again.

Instead he said nothing, just pulled a chair out from under the kitchen table and sat in it, waiting for his daughter to suggest hiring a skip for all the things he and his wife had so lovingly collected.

He watched Sara march down the narrow garden path and come to a halt in front of the open shed door.

He saw her poke her head inside. After a moment the rest of her followed.

Still Alfred waited.

Several minutes later, he watched her make her way back up the garden path. He wasn't able to read her expression.

When she came into the kitchen, she went to the sink and swilled her hands, then she turned to him. 'All that stuff, Dad. Mum never said you made toys.'

'She didn't know.'

Sara blinked. 'What do you mean, she didn't know?'

'I never told her.'

'You must have spent hours down there. Didn't she ask you what you were up to?'

'No, never. The same way I didn't ask her what she was up to in the Sally Army. We didn't need to live in each other's pockets.'

'But telling Mum you were making toys was hardly living in each other's pockets. You've got a shed full of them,' Sara added, as if he didn't know what was in his own shed. 'What on earth were you planning on doing with them?'

'I've no idea,' Alfred replied, mildly.

'You must have planned on doing something with them, else why make them in the first place?'

'Because I could,' was his simple reply.

'David says you've done a good job.'

Alfred looked away. David was a decent enough fellow, but Alfred didn't care for his opinion one way or the other when it came to the contents of the shed. Anyway, what did his son-in-law know about hand-made, wooden toys, when kids these days were given the latest this and that, all plastic and garish colours and more packaging than you could shake a stick at.

Alfred's toys were made from scavenged wood and lovingly brought to life with little more than some woodworking tools that he'd found in a second-hand shop and a ten-week course in woodworking aimed at giving pensioners something to do.

So, no, David's opinion was mostly irrelevant. The only opinions that would matter to Alfred would be those of the people the toys were intended for – children.

But Alfred had never found the courage to show them to anyone, let alone allow anyone to play with them. So there they sat, shelf upon shelf of them, in his shed, and now they faced being thrown away like so much rubbish.

'Right then,' Sara said. 'All this furniture will have to go. I'll see about getting a house clearance company to take most of it, but there are some things which will have to be taken to the charity shop.' She tore off a plastic bag from a roll and shook it open. 'I'll start upstairs in your room. Mum's side of the wardrobe is still full of her clothes.'

Alfred walked back out of the house and went to sit in the car, unable to watch his daughter emptying the remnants of her mother's life into bin bags.

He had an awful feeling she wished she could do the same with him.

CHAPTER 5

HATTIE

Hattie handed the parcel to Barbara in the post office and waited for her receipt. It was a darned nuisance buying stuff off the internet, because more often than not she ended up sending whatever it was she'd ordered back. In this instance it was a felt hat. It had looked lovely on the model (wasn't that always the case?) but not so good on her. She liked the idea of hats, but she didn't have the head for anything more fancy than a knitted one which she could pull down over her ears.

It seemed that her bun was the problem with anything that wasn't stretchy, because most hats, this one especially, tended to balance on the back of it. She tried wearing her bun up higher on her crown but she'd ended up looking as though she had a grey, hairy egg on her head, and she'd quickly rearranged her hair so it coiled neatly at the nape of her neck once more. Thankfully, these days any wispy strands which escaped and floated around her face, were considered fashionable. Years ago, they'd have been regarded as scruffy.

'Been buying again?' Barbara said. 'What is it this time?'

'A hat.' Hattie's reply was short – she didn't need to be quizzed every time she came into the post office, but that was the problem with living in a small place like Ticklemore – everyone knew everyone else's business, and what they didn't know they made up or asked outright.

Speaking of which…

'Has anyone by the name of Alfred, or Alfie, been in here recently?' she asked, softening her tone.

'Who wants to know?' Barbara eyed her suspiciously.

'I do. That's why I'm asking.'

'Oh, right, I see. Who is he?'

'I'm not sure. He was in Bookylicious this morning. Face like a slapped arse. Old. Grumpy. White hair. Uses a walking stick.'

'That description could fit most of the old codgers around here,' Barbara said.

'Watch it,' a voice from behind Hattie piped up. 'Those codgers are your customers.'

'If the cap fits…' Barbara said.

Hattie sniggered – that was why she was sending this one back, because it didn't. She took her printed receipt, folded it neatly and put it in her purse. 'Well? Has he been in or not?

'A stranger, is he?'

Blimming' heck, Barbara was on form today. 'If he wasn't, I'd know who he was,' Hattie pointed out.

Barbara huffed. 'He may have done. But I get a lot of people in here.' She leant forwards and hissed, 'Tourists.'

Hattie rolled her eyes. 'What was he doing?'

Now that the dam had burst and she'd admitted the old gent had indeed paid the post office a visit, Barbara let it all flood out. 'Drawing money out. He waited for ages in the queue and when I pointed out the cashpoint outside that he could use next time, he told me he didn't trust those things. I tried to tell him that the process was the same, but he wasn't having any of it.'

'Do you know his name?'

'Alfred, or Alfie, that's what you said.'

'His surname.'

'I didn't see his bank card. I don't handle them, they just pop it in the machine.' Barbara pointed to the card machine on Hattie's side of the counter. 'They put their PIN in and I give them the cash. Why the interest?'

'I'm not sure.' And she wasn't. But she trusted her instincts. There was something not quite right with the old fella. She felt the same way about Alfred as she'd done about Puss. Not that she was comparing the man to a half-starved battle-worn moggie – but then some scars weren't physical.

'Shall I keep a lookout for him and let you know if he comes into the post office again?' Barbara asked.

'If you wouldn't mind.' It wouldn't hurt, and it would be a backup in case he failed to visit Bookylicious tomorrow.

With the parcel duly dispatched, Hattie popped along to the little Co-op to pick up a few bits. She didn't need much, and she could probably manage without doing any shopping at all, but she spent enough time on her own in the cottage, and if she could delay returning to it for half an hour, she would.

'It's going to get colder towards the end of the week,' Mrs Acker said, and Hattie gave her a smile. Poor love, the woman's family lived halfway across the other side of the world and she felt their absence keenly, always wanting to stop and chat with anyone who'd talk to her.

She had appeared at Hattie's side whilst Hattie was debating the merits of a tin of baked beans versus a tin of baked beans with sausages. She fancied a fry up for tea and having the sausages in the tin meant that she wouldn't have to go to the trouble of cooking any from fresh. On the other hand, the tinned ones did alter the taste of the baked beans slightly.

It was a big decision.

'It is November,' Hattie replied, 'So a bit of cold weather is only to be expected.' Which was one of the reasons Hattie had treated herself to a new hat. Never mind, she had a collection of knitted ones that would do, until another one caught her eye.

'Bought any Christmas presents yet?' Hattie asked the elderly lady, knowing that she had to shop early in order to post them off soon if they were to reach the Solomon Islands in time for the big day.

'I've made a start, although I'll have to go into Hereford for most of it.'

Ticklemore was quaint and pretty, with a village green, a small river running through it, an arched stone bridge, and a selection of small independent shops, as well as a pub, the post office and the Co-op. Bookylicious was complemented by two other cafés further along the road, a baker, a grocer, one of the best butchers for miles, a florist, an antique shop, and a handful of other businesses aimed at visitors and tourists. Ticklemore also boasted the Ticklemore Emporium, which sold everything from pins to elephants (one of her mum's expressions, God rest her soul) but not the gaudy plastic toys so beloved by children these days. In fact, the Ticklemore Emporium didn't sell toys at all, but it did a fantastic range of gardening implements. Not much good for a kiddie's Christmas present, though. Unless the kid was into weeding.

'Ow!' Hattie was knocked sideways into one of the shelves, and her arm tingled as someone barged into her. Why was it called a funny bone? It sodding hurt. The woman who had so rudely pushed past her, had caught that tender spot on the elbow with the edge of her wire basket. 'Watch where you're going.'

'Sorry.' The woman barely glanced at her and the apology was perfunctory to say the least.

Hattie bristled. She hated bad manners; but she hated being brushed off as though she was of no importance even more. What was it with the younger generation? Did they not realise they would get old one day? This lady ought to slow down and smell the roses – she was no spring chicken herself (Hattie estimated her to be in her late fifties) – and old age and invisibility were just around her snooty corner.

With narrowed eyes, Hattie watched her disappear around a stack of shelving and into an adjacent aisle, a man of roughly the same age as her close on her heels.

At least he had the decency to stop for a second before following his wife, look Hattie in the eye and ask if she was all right.

'I'm fine, thank you for asking,' Hattie replied as he hesitated.

'I'm sorry, my wife's a bit distracted. We've only been in the shop for a couple of minutes and her father has already wandered off.'

Hattie didn't think being distracted was an excuse for rudeness and she was just about to tell him so, but decided it wasn't worth the bother. It wasn't the man's fault he was married to an ill-mannered, inconsiderate—

'There you are! We've been looking everywhere for you.' A strident voice carried around the shop and Hattie guessed it belonged to the rude woman. Instead of sounding relieved that she'd found her father, she sounded irritated, and Hattie winced. It was times like these she was grateful she didn't have a family – because the saying that you can choose your friends but you can't choose your relatives had never been more true.

'You couldn't have looked very hard,' a man's voice retorted. 'I've been here all the time, in this aisle.'

Hattie frowned; she'd heard that voice before and recently, too. Its gravelly tones sent a shiver through her. Or was it that her water was playing up again? She wanted to tell it to pipe down, but she supposed that right now wasn't the best time to be seen talking to herself.

Edging to the end of the aisle, she peered around the shelves and down the next, then she froze – rude woman was speaking to the grumpy old man who had been in Bookylicious earlier.

Curiosity riding her hard (some might call it nosiness) Hattie moved a bit closer, not wanting to miss any of the conversation, although that didn't seem likely considering the rude woman appeared to have a megaphone inserted into her gob.

'What's so fascinating about biscuits?' the woman demanded, tugging at the old gent's sleeve. 'We've got plenty of biscuits at home.'

'Not the ones I like. I like pink wafers.'

'They're nothing but air and sugar with a bit of food colouring thrown in,' his daughter said.

'So? I like them. Your mother always used to buy them.'

'Mum isn't here anymore, Dad.' The woman's voice had softened a little, but Hattie could still hear an undercurrent of annoyance running through it like mould in blue cheese.

Poor bugger, she thought; fancy having a harridan like that for a daughter.

'I do realise she's no longer with us. I'm not senile,' Alfred retorted.

The silence went on for a little too long for comfort, and Hattie frowned. He'd sounded as though he had all his marbles when she spoke to him earlier, but that was the problem with dementia; it was difficult for a stranger to tell whether anything was wrong if the person was having a good day. Hattie inched a little closer, pretending to be fascinated by a slab of cellophane-wrapped walnut cake.

'Come on, Dad, let's finish this bit of shopping and get you home, eh? You must be tired.' His daughter turned away and Hattie looked up – just in time to see Alfred mouth, 'Yeah, tired of you.'

She bit back a smile but let it loose when she caught Alfred's eye.

'You again?' he grunted.

'Just getting something for my tea. What's your opinion on a tin of beans with sausages?'

'That's cake you've got in your hands, not beans.'

'I know, I've still got all my marbles, too.'

'You heard, did you?'

'Couldn't help it.'

'Her mother always used to say she had a bell on every tooth.'

'Dad! I thought you were behind me.' The woman's head appeared from around the end shelving unit, quickly followed by the rest of her.

She marched up to him and took hold of his arm.

Hattie stepped forwards. 'I'm Hattie. Nice to meet you. What's your name?'

'Er, Sara.' She looked at her father. 'Dad?'

'We've already met, so there's no need to introduce us,' Hattie said, oblivious to Sara's discomfort.

Sara's husband appeared, clutching a loaf of bread and a carton of milk, a look of vague concern on his face.

'Don't worry, I'm not having a go at her,' Hattie told him. 'I'm just saying hello.'

'Yes, hello, OK, right.' Sara said, her mind on more important things than Hattie.

'I work in Bookylicious,' Hattie forged on. 'Are you still popping in tomorrow, Alfred?'

That got his daughter's attention. 'What's Bootylicious? Dad?' Her eyes had widened, and Hattie could imagine what she was thinking.

'A bookshop in the village with a café attached to it, so you can get your mind out of the gutter, lady,' Hattie said. 'And it's Bookylicious, not Booty.'

Sara's mouth dropped open, but she soon collected herself. 'I was thinking no such thing,' she protested.

'Yes, you were. You had an image of Beyoncé in

your head, didn't you? It's a play on words; you know, Booky—'

'I'm fully aware what a play on words refers to, and no, my father will not be "popping in" tomorrow. Or any time soon, for that matter.'

We'll see about that, Hattie thought, catching Alfred's eye again, and an almost imperceptible nod passed between the two of them.

Hattie treated Sara to her widest grin. She probably looked a little manic, but she didn't care. She intended to get to the bottom of what was going on between Alfred and his daughter, because something was. The poor bloke was obviously deeply unhappy, and having a child of his loins (she always considered the expression to be rather naughty) remonstrate with him in such a fashion wasn't acceptable, as far as she was concerned.

'Nice to have met you,' Hattie said to the woman, still grinning. She replaced the walnut cake (not a patch on the cake sold in Bookylicious) and walked away; she still had the issue of the baked beans to consider before she returned home.

There was one thing she'd made her mind up about though; something had to be done about Alfred. He was clearly lonely and unhappy.
And Hattie intended to make it her mission to relieve him of both states of mind.

CHAPTER 6

ALFRED

Seething couldn't begin to describe how Alfred felt. How dare Sara make such a fool of him in public? And especially in front of that extremely odd old woman who worked in the café attached to the bookshop. If anyone needed to restock their marbles it was Hattie, because a fair portion of hers were most certainly missing.

She *had* shared a moment of recognition with him, though, acknowledging that no matter what his daughter had told him, he'd do as he wanted; so she couldn't be all bad.

And he was still fuming about it the following day; until, that is, Sara told him some news which gave him something else to think about.

'Morning, Dad,' she chirped when he wandered downstairs and into the kitchen, his mouth as dry as a camel's backside. 'Had a good lie in?'

Hardly. Last night had followed the same pattern as almost every night for the past twenty or more years – he dropped off to sleep easily enough (too easily, as his regular snoring in the armchair proved), woke up in the middle of the night and then spent several hours awake, only to fall asleep again when the rest of the world was stirring.

When Dorothy was alive, he used to go downstairs, make himself a cup of tea, and sketch out his latest idea for a toy. Then when he was done, often after only an hour or so of wakefulness, he'd take himself off to bed, slip underneath the covers, pull Dorothy into a spoon, and go back to sleep.

He could cope with being awake for an hour in the middle of the night. What he couldn't cope with was being awake for three, four, or, on one memorable night, five and a half. Five bloody hours of staring at the ceiling. For pity's sake!

The first few nights after moving in with Sara and David, he'd ventured downstairs for a cuppa, only for Sara (she must have ears like a sodding bat) to traipse into the kitchen demanding to know why he was up at such a Godforsaken hour and insisting he returned to bed. She'd pulled her trump card of telling him that she wouldn't be able to rest if she knew he was prowling around the house. Did she think he was going to purloin the silverware, and slip out into the night to meet a fence?

The likelier explanation was that she was worried he'd go wandering down the middle of the road in his pyjamas.

The thought had crossed his mind that maybe he'd do that one night, just to see the looks on the neighbour's faces – but knowing his luck, Sara would think he had really lost the plot and she'd try and stick him in a home.

Over his dead body, he thought, quickly followed by another – if that's what it would take to avoid having to go into such a place, then so be it.

'Dad, I asked if you had a good lie in?' Sara was standing there with her hands on her hips and her mouth in a thin line.

'Yes, thanks.' There wasn't any point in telling her the truth; she had enough ammunition as it was.

Just as he was worrying that it was an awful way to think of his only child, the only child said, 'That's good. I've arranged for the contents of the house to be taken away by one of those house clearance companies. I doubt you'll get much for it, but you never know, some pieces might be worth a pound or two. The sooner we get it done the better, as a house full of rubbish might put potential buyers off.'

Alfred dropped onto the nearest chair, and rubbed

a shaking hand across his face, the sound of skin against stubble loud in the sudden silence.

'Did you hear what I said?' Sara threw a teabag in a mug.

'I heard.'

'Of course, I'll have to make another trip to the charity shop – I never knew Mum had so many clothes. Where on earth did she go to wear them all?'

You'd be surprised, Alfred wanted to say. Into town, of course; coffee with "the girls"; church; meals out; day trips with Byron's Coaches – he and Dorothy were hardly in. Which Sara would have known, if she hadn't been so wrapped up in her own world.

And Dorothy used to like to look nice – she used to have her hair done every week, her nails done once a month, and she never, ever went without make-up, even if it was only a bit of rouge on her cheeks. She had been a proud woman, had his Dorothy.

'Will I have to be there?' he asked, hoping to God that he wouldn't. He didn't think he could face seeing the treasures he and his wife had accumulated over years of careful selection, being pawed over by strangers who were only interested in how little they could buy them for.

'I don't see the point, do you? It'll only upset you.'

His daughter had got that right. Her acknowledgement of his feelings was a first, because up until now, she'd been quite happy to ride roughshod over them.

'And you'll only get in the way,' she added.

Ah. That's what she'd meant. It figured.

'When have you arranged for them to come?' he asked.

'Next Friday. I wanted them to come sooner, but they've got a lot on. If we can agree on a price, I'm hoping they'll take everything there and then. I'll try and get the most I can for you, Dad.'

Alfred very much wanted to swear. As if he cared a fig for the money. What was he going to spend it on? He'd prefer to keep his possessions. To think that the old wooden bed he and Dorothy had slept in all their married life, might become nothing more than kindling, made him want to weep. He knew it wouldn't be worth much to anyone else, but to him the memories it held were priceless.

He was just about coping with living in his daughter's house because he knew his own was still there, ready and waiting for him. He was pretending he was visiting, that he was only staying with Sara for a few days and he could go back home whenever he wanted.

But once all his and Dorothy's things were removed and the house was an empty shell, it would make his situation all the more real.

Six days.

That's all he had left.

Six days in which to save all those things he wanted to save.

Six days to save *himself.*

CHAPTER 7

HATTIE

It was Saturday before Hattie spotted Alfred sidling into the bookshop side of the business, and she hurried to put a peppermint tea and a hot chocolate in front of the customers they were intended for before following him around one of the central bookcases.

'I was expecting you yesterday. I thought we had an agreement,' she said to him.

'You might have – I didn't agree to anything.'

'No need to be mardy – I was just being polite and making conversation.' When he'd failed to show, she'd guessed that his witch of a daughter had grounded him. Crikey, it was worse than being a child.

'I'm in a bookshop,' he said.

Hattie narrowed her eyes at him. 'I know. I work here.'

'What I mean is, people come into bookshops to look at books, not to talk.'

Hattie raised her eyebrows and sent a pointed glance at the people in the café area who were chatting away. He was being incredibly silly. Or rude. Or both. 'You realise Bookylicious is a café, too? You've had coffee and cake here before.'

'I'm old, not senile. I do realise I've been here before.'

'I was being facetious,' Hattie retorted. He kept mentioning the "senile" word, which made her think that there might be something to his daughter's concern after all.

Alfred harrumphed and ignored her.

'What's up with Mrs Bossy-Boots? She's a bit headmistress-ish, isn't she?' Hattie asked.

Alfred smiled for the first time since she'd met him. 'That's because she is a headmistress. Or, used to be; she's retired now.' He pulled a face.

'And you're cross about that because…?'

'Are you always this nosy?'

'Pretty much.' She leant a little closer to him and said, 'Go on, you know you want to tell me.'

'What I want is for you to go away and leave me alone.'

'No chance.'

He heaved a heavy sigh. 'I thought not.'

'What are you looking for anyway?'

'A book.'

'What on? I mean, are you after fiction or non-fiction?'

'Non-fiction, not that it's any business of yours.'

'I work here, therefore helping you find the book you want *is* my business. Fishing?'

'Pardon?'

'Are you after a book on fly fishing?'

'No. What gave you that idea?'

'You're standing next to the shelf on fishing.'

He glanced to where Hattie indicated. Then he glanced at the shelves above and below. 'I'm also in the game shooting bit, and the bee-keeping section, and I'm not interested in any of those, either.'

'What are you interested in?'

'Storage.'

'Cabinet-making?'

He shook his head. 'Cabinet storing.'

'I don't follow.'

'I don't expect you to. Now, will you leave me alone? Please.'

Hattie snorted. 'I'll be over there, if you need me.' She pointed at the counter where the till was located.

'I won't,' he said.

'I think you'll find you will,' she muttered as she walked away. Cabinet storing, indeed. What was the daft old coot on about?

It took fifteen minutes before he gave in; she'd been counting. She looked up from the online ordering system, and smiled as he walked towards her. One nil, one nil, she chanted silently.

Her smile faded as he carried on past her, heading towards the door.

Hattie dashed around the counter and trotted over to him, thankful that she was nimbler than him. 'You didn't, did you? Find the book you wanted,' she added, in case he'd forgotten their earlier conversation – with this fella, it was more than likely. 'Tell me what you are after, and I can look it up for you.'

Alfred stopped. 'Look it up?'

'On the computer. I can tell you if any of the wholesalers have it, and whether it's still in print.'

'You use the internet?'

'Er… yes?'

'To look for books?'

'Yeah…' She narrowed her eyes at him. 'You do know what the internet is, right?'

'Of course I bloody know. I wasn't born yesterday.'

'You'd probably have a better grasp of the concept if you were,' she replied wryly. 'Kids today can use an iPad before they can walk.' She shook her head; she was all for teaching kids about technology, because that's where the future lay, but some of them were going to school without ever having held a book in their hands. It was a crying shame, that's what it was.

'Can you look *anything* up?' he asked.

'Mostly. If it's ever been published, there'll be a record of it somewhere.'

'I'm after the Yellow Pages,' he announced.

'You want to purchase a copy of the Yellow Pages?' The poor bloke wasn't all there, was he?

Alfred looked sheepish and chewed his bottom lip.

Ah, maybe he didn't want to buy it – it was fairly common for customers to use the non-fiction section of a bookshop as a reference library. 'You want to look up a listing in the Yellow Pages?' she guessed.

'Yes. Please,' he added. 'Do you happen to have a copy?'

'I've not seen one of those for years. I didn't think they printed them anymore.'

'See, you don't know everything about books!'

'The Yellow Pages is hardly a book, it's a telephone directory. I believe they do an online version, though. What are you looking for?'

'Storage.'

'Let's don't start that again. I was confused enough the first time around.'

'I need a storage facility, like the ones on the

adverts you see on TV. I've been keeping my eyes peeled, but you know what it's like – the minute you want them to show an advert, you'll never see it again.'

'Until you don't want it anymore?' she cackled.

'Exactly.'

'OK, I can help with that. What sort of storage? How much space do you need? And for how long?'

'Enough to fit in the contents of your average three-bed semi. And I'll need it until I die.'

'Is that going to be anytime soon?' Hattie asked, leading him towards the till.

He snorted, but she noticed he didn't answer her and her heart dropped straight into her purple Doc Marten boots. So that's what her water had been trying to tell her, and that's why he was grumpy (who wouldn't be when faced with the prospect of one's own demise?). It also went some way to explaining his daughter's attitude. *Explain*, she noted, not *excuse*.

Hattie perused the computer screen for several minutes before she found something that might interest Alfred, who was patiently waiting with both hands clasped on top of the walking stick which was planted firmly in front of him.

'It might take me a while,' she said, 'but I usually get there in the end. I'm not as quick as the youngsters, but what do you expect? If you calculate it on a percentage basis, I've only been doing this computer stuff for about ten per cent of my life. They've got an unfair advantage.'

Alfred didn't look at all interested. He was staring intently at the back of the screen and she could see a "hurry up" expression in his eyes.

'There are a couple of places in Hereford,' she told him, 'and more if you are prepared to go further afield. The cheapest prices start at about eleven pounds per week, but it depends on the square footage and the length of time you want to rent it for. You get a discount if you rent for a year.' Hattie winced. Perhaps she shouldn't have mentioned a year…?

'A year will be fine. What sizes do they do?'

'Here.' She turned the screen around. 'Take a look for yourself.'

She studied his face as he read the details, and he didn't look thrilled by what he was seeing.

'Eleven pounds will get you little more than a cupboard. I need something about the size of a garage,' he said, with a sigh. 'That's going to cost. Oh, well, if that's what it takes, then so be it. It's not as though I've got a lot else to spend my money on.' He hesitated. 'Can you see if you can find the phone number for a man with a van?'

Hattie nodded, curiosity burning so hot inside her,

she thought she might spontaneously combust.

'There's a local man,' she said, her attention on the screen. 'I'll write down his phone number for you, and the ones for the storage units.'

'Thank you. You've been very helpful,' he said, his tone somewhat stilted.

'It's my job.'

He went to walk away, then stopped. 'Can I ask you something? The last time I was in here, you told me to come back tomorrow because you had a surprise for me; what was it?'

Bugger, she'd forgotten she'd said that, and she had no idea what she'd meant. Her only thought had been to get him to come back into the shop.

'Black Forest gateaux,' she blurted. 'A real blast from the past.'

'That was the surprise?'

Hattie didn't blame him for looking sceptical, but she carried on trying to big it up. 'Maddison doesn't make it very often, but when she does people go mad for it; especially pensioners. It takes them back to the 1970s.'

'I'm glad I missed it – I don't like cherries.'

'Do you like pub grub?' she burst out. 'I, um, won a raffle for a free lunch at the… er… Ticklemore Tavern. For two. For today.'

He frowned and she could see he was about to

refuse.

'I won't go if I have to go on my own,' she added, putting a woebegone expression on her face.

He sighed again. 'I suppose it won't hurt. I can't be long though.'

'You'll be missed?'

'Something like that.'

Hattie clapped her hands. 'Goodie! And while we eat, you can tell me all about why you need a storage unit and a man with a van.'

CHAPTER 8

ALFRED

What the hell had possessed him to agree to have lunch with this woman, Alfred grumbled to himself as he watched Hattie speak to her employer, who gave him a smile and a little wave.

He waved back, a small motion with his hand, and his answering smile was hardly more than a twitch of his lips.

Maddison turned her attention back to Hattie, and Hattie briefly glanced at him and patted Maddison's arm. Whatever they were talking about, they both seemed rather earnest, and Hattie's expression bore more than a hint of determination as she ended the conversation and walked over to him.

'Let's go,' she said, linking her arm through his and guiding him out onto the street and along the pavement.

The gesture was far too familiar for his liking, hinting at a closeness which wasn't there, but the unaccustomed contact felt good so he let her arm stay where it was.

'I wonder what's on the specials board today,' she said, smacking her lips. 'It's ages since I've been out for a meal – a panini or soup at Bookylicious, as lovely as it is, isn't the same as a proper meal.'

He let her chatter on, not listening; his mind was on getting back to Sara's house before she did so he could use the phone. How long will he have to live in his daughter's house before he called it home, he mused, suspecting it would be a long time indeed, if ever. He was also fretting about Sara seeing the itemised phone bill, wondering who the strange numbers belonged to, dialling them and discovering—

'Do you own a mobile phone?' he asked Hattie, who was in full flow chuntering on about the merits of proper home-cooked chips over oven ones. Apparently, the Ticklemore Tavern served real chips.

'Of course, I do,' she replied.

As far as he was concerned, there was no "of course" about it. He didn't own one, did he, and neither had Dorothy. Sara had been on at him to get one for years, but he hadn't seen the point. Until now.

'Can I borrow it?' he asked.

Hattie came to a halt outside the pub's door and dug around in her handbag, producing her phone with a flourish. 'There you go,' she cried, handing it to him.

He handed it straight back, before opening the door and ushering her through.

'Oh, silly me, I need to unlock it for you,' she said, walking ahead of him and aiming straight for the bar. She poked a finger at the keyboard several times then gave it back to him. 'You go and sit down, and I'll fetch us some drinks and grab a couple of menus. What would you like? A pint?'

'Yes, please, but let me buy these. I don't expect drinks are included with the meal.'

'Er, I'll get these, you get the next round in; I need to let Logan know I'm claiming my prize.' She shooed him away, and he headed for a table in an alcove near the log burner. It was lit, the yellow glow and the warmth adding to the cosy atmosphere. It seemed like a decent enough place, and he couldn't recall the last time he'd seen the inside of a pub. It was before Dorothy was diagnosed, that was for certain, and the novelty made him nostalgic.

He put the phone carefully down on the table and stared at it. Hattie unlocking it for him was all well and good, if only he knew how to use it. What were all those colourful little things on the screen?

Alfred slipped off his winter anorak. Meh, he'd wait until Hattie sat down. He didn't want to press anything he shouldn't and break the damned thing.

While he waited, his gaze wandered around the room. The pub had looked nice from the outside, with its stone walls and little windows – a typical olde worlde pub. And it was just as nice inside. There was the log burner for a start (a good idea on a winter's day), comfy cushions on the seats, a polished bar with a decent selection of draft ales, and a barman pouring his pint, whilst Hattie chewed the poor man's ear off. She could talk for Britain, but he supposed there was no harm in her, and she had helped him find the phone numbers he needed. Plus, she'd invited him to share her meal with her.

Besides feeling a little beholden to her for her help in the bookshop, he suspected she was lonely, so he was glad he'd accompanied her. He hated to think of her eating a meal on her own. And a decent pint of beer wasn't to be sniffed at, either. It was worth listening to the woman's constant chatter for that alone.

'There you go. Get that down your neck,' Hattie said, placing his drink on a beermat. She kept hold of hers and took a decent swig, then gave him one of the menus she'd tucked under her armpit.

Alfred wondered what was in her drink. Gin,

possibly? Vodka? He hoped she slowed down, because if she carried on the way she was going she'd be half-cut by the time their meals arrived.

Picking up his pint, he sniffed appreciatively, the aroma of hops filling his nose. 'Ahh,' he said, then he sipped at it, rolled the liquid around his mouth and swallowed. Holding his glass up, he examined its brown depths. 'Not bad, that.'

It was actually very nice indeed. And it was more than nice to be sitting in a pub and feeling like a grown up again. He was sick and tired of being treated like child, and if he wanted to go out for a pint then Sara couldn't stop him. So there.

'I fancy scampi and chips,' Hattie said. 'Did I tell you the chips are homemade?'

'You might have mentioned it. I'll have the same.' He closed the menu and put it on the table. Scampi was probably another one of those things which was on Sara's list of foods he wasn't allowed to eat; and chips most definitely were.

As if it mattered what he ate at his age? The only enjoyment he had left in life was food and the occasional pint, and his daughter was doing her level best to take that away from him. Since Dorothy had died there hadn't been much worth living for, and since he'd moved in with Sara, there had been even less.

Today though, this tiny act of rebellion was sitting well on his old shoulders – and the plan he was hatching sat even better. If Sara thought she was going to have things all her own way, she had another think coming.

Seeing her phone on the table, its screen dark, Hattie picked it up. 'Did you make your calls?'

'Um, no, I couldn't.'

'Strange.' She turned the device over in her hands. 'There's usually a decent signal in here.'

'I didn't actually try,' Alfred admitted.

'Why not— Oh.' There was a pause. 'Would you like me to ring them for you?'

'You can if you want.' He knew he sounded churlish, as if he was the one doing her the favour, not the other way around, but it was embarrassing to admit he didn't know how to operate one of those things. Maybe he should have bought one when Sara first mentioned it. If he'd have got one ten years ago, he'd be au fait with it by now.

It was too late now, of course. From what he gathered, they were as complicated as hell, and although he knew there were some more basic models on the market, he was too old to learn new tricks. Anyway, he chuckled silently to himself as a thought struck him – if he owned one, it would mean Sara could contact him whenever she wanted, and he was quite enjoying being AWOL.

'Do you want me to dial the number, then you speak to them? Or would you like me to talk to them?' Hattie was asking, and he looked at her in confusion.

What should he do? Either way, she'd know his business because she was sitting right there and he could hardly ask her to leave when it was her meal he was about to eat and her phone he was about to use.

He shrugged. 'Don't care.'

'Yes, you do. Now, how about you tell me why you need storage and a man with a van, and I'll see what I can do to help. Oh, and while we're at it, are you going to be pushing up the daisy's anytime soon? Because if you are, it'll make a difference to how long you'll want to rent a unit for.'

'Not many of us have the privilege of knowing when we're going to snuff it,' he said. 'I wish I did.'

'So do I! I'd know how much time I had left, so I could cram all those things in I still want to do.'

'Like what?'

'Ride a horse. Drive a Lamborghini. Learn to speak another language…' She ground to a halt.

As far as Alfred was concerned, she already spoke another language and it was called gobbledygook. 'That's an interesting list.'

'What's on your bucket list?'

68

'Nothing.'

'Go on, you can tell me. I won't laugh, I promise.'

'I'm serious – I've not got a bucket list.'

'Are you telling me, you've done everything you want to in life? You lucky sod!'

Alfred wished someone would come to take their order and give Hattie something else to think about for a minute, because she was starting to get on his nerves. He looked at the barman hopefully but failed to catch his eye.

'There's only one thing I want to do,' he replied quietly, realising his lunch companion wasn't going to shut up, 'and that's to stop my daughter from disposing of everything I hold dear.'

Hattie sank back in her seat, a startled expression on her face. 'Is that why you think you're going to die soon, because she's going to bump you off for your money?'

'No! Whatever gave you that idea?'

'You said you'll need the storage unit until you die.'

'That doesn't mean my demise is imminent. It means that I don't want my daughter getting rid of all those things Dorothy and I bought together whilst I'm still alive. After I'm gone, she can do what she likes with them.'

'Was Dorothy your wife?'

He nodded, the ache of her loss spreading through him.

'When did she die?'

'Two years ago, last July.'

Hattie nodded. 'I lost my Ted years ago, so I know what you're going through. If you need a friend, I'm here.'

'Thank you.' He took a fortifying mouthful of beer.

'Does your daughter want to put you in a home?' she asked.

'No, I've moved in with her permanently.'

'That's sensible if you've got a house to sell and you don't want the nursing home to gobble up all the proceeds.'

'It wasn't my decision. Apparently, I'm a danger to myself.'

'And are you? Logan?' she yelled, twisting around in her seat. 'We're ready to order. We're not getting any younger, you know!'

'Scarlet will be with you in a tick – I'm just about to knock off for the afternoon.'

'Part-timer,' Hattie called back, good-naturedly.

'I've had a couple of falls and I've also been a bit distracted lately,' Alfred muttered. 'And I forget things.' There, he'd said it.

'Hmph! Don't we all. How long have you been

distracted?'

'A couple of years, I suppose. It's getting worse.'

'Who says? You, or that daughter of yours?'

He didn't say anything. It was Sara who'd first pointed it out, and he knew she'd become increasingly concerned about him since her mother's death. But maybe she and the social workers were right?

'You know what it is, don't you?' Hattie asked playing with her almost empty glass. 'You're lonely, you're grieving, and you probably haven't got enough to do. It's easy to get confused when all the days blur into one and the only thing to occupy you is the telly and your memories.'

He realised she was correct on all three counts, but that didn't prevent him from worrying that Sara had a point and that he was in the early stages of dementia.

'Sara is putting my house on the market,' he announced abruptly.

Hattie tipped the last drop of her drink into her open mouth. 'Can you move back in?'

'I don't think so. I live – *lived* – on the other side of Hereford, closer to Worcester than to Ticklemore. It's too far for her to be able to keep an eye on me.'

'Do you *need* her to keep an eye on you?'

He shrugged. He didn't want to admit it, but the house had been getting a bit too much for him to cope with. And at least he didn't feel as lonely as he had been, now that he was living with Sara. Quite the opposite.

What would be ideal, was if he could shrink his house and move it closer to Ticklemore – then he'd have the best of both worlds.

Hattie was staring at him, and he shifted uncomfortably in his seat. 'Why are you looking at me like that?'

'I've got an idea… Logan!'

CHAPTER 9

HATTIE

'Bloody hell, are you sure you want to keep all this?' Hattie asked, gazing around Alfred's living room. No wonder he needed a bloody great big storage unit. She'd been imagining that most of his stuff had been cleared out, and that he just wanted to keep a few of his more treasured possessions.

But this was a fully furnished house, even down to the dead plant in a pot on the coffee table.

'Can you move it all?' Alfred asked, and Logan scratched his head.

'I can, but I don't think even a third of it will fit in Hattie's shed,' Logan said.

Hattie blew out her cheeks. 'Are you sure you want to keep *everything*?' She gave the dead plant a pointed look.

'Not everything obviously,' Alfred replied, picking

up the pot the poor plant was in and taking it into the kitchen.

Hattie and Logan followed.

There was nearly as much stuff in there, most of it covered in a film of dust and disillusionment. Was there anything as sad as seeing a dead woman's apron still hanging over the back of a chair two years after she'd passed on?

Alfred looked at his watch. 'We can't be long – I need to get back.'

He'd said the same thing when he got into Logan's van, and that had been three-quarters of an hour ago.

'You're going to have to decide what to keep and what to let Sara deal with,' Hattie pointed out, 'Unless you want to go ahead with the storage unit idea.'

'I don't know…'

'When has she arranged for the house clearance people to arrive?'

'Friday.'

'That's less than a week away, so you've not got long,' Hattie said. 'You need to make a decision today.'

When she saw him starting to look flustered, Hattie said 'Have you got any tea bags or coffee?'

'There should be some in the cupboard.' He pointed. 'I doubt there's any milk, though, Sara threw out all the fresh stuff. No doubt she'll be doing the same thing to the rest of my things.'

Hattie filled the kettle with fresh water; she could drink her coffee black if she had to. She hoped that they could take a few minutes out to think logically about Alfred's options. She understood where he was coming from, but the logistics would be a nightmare.

'You're never going to move back into this house again, are you?' she asked him, as she leant against a kitchen counter and waited for the kettle to boil.

Alfred pulled a face. 'I doubt it.'

'What if you were to move into somewhere smaller, like one of those granny flats? Do you think that's a possibility?'

He shrugged.

Logan sent Hattie a look, and she could tell he was thinking that Alfred would be unlikely to live on his own ever again.

'Let's run with that scenario, shall we, and maybe you could have a think about what you could keep in order to furnish a one-bed flat.'

Alfred brightened a little.

'Why don't you show Logan what you want to store in my shed – I could let you have my garage space as well,' she added, feeling generous. 'And while you do that, I'll see if I can find us a biscuit to go with our coffee.' She was absolutely starving – and she'd been looking forward to her scampi and chips. But when she'd asked Logan how he was fixed for driving them to Alfred's house, then maybe shifting the old man's stuff into her shed, he'd suggested they go there for a recce right now. So that's what they'd done.

And now that Alfred was here, he was getting worried that Sara would be on his case, Hattie guessed. Which is exactly what his daughter would do. At least he could honestly tell her that he went to the Ticklemore Tavern for a meal with a friend. He just needn't tell the woman that he didn't get to eat his meal, and that he'd ended up back at his old house instead. Technically, he wouldn't be lying.

Hearing Alfred and Logan (such a lovely young man – if only she was forty years younger…) clumping about upstairs, Hattie slipped into the living room and had another look around.

Apart from the dead plant and a selection of ornaments and other knick-knacks, there wasn't much in the way of personal items like photographs, and she guessed Alfred must have taken anything like that with him to his daughter's house.

Unable to prevent herself, she climbed the stairs, desperate for a gander. She could see Alfred in the bedroom at the far end of the landing, his back to her, so she took the opportunity to have a peep in the first door she came to. It was a box room, containing a single bed, a wardrobe and a chest of drawers. Another, larger room was next to it. This one had a double bed, hideous pink patterned wallpaper, and a collection of cuddly toys which stared balefully down at her from the top of a rather grand and very large wardrobe.

A fairly ordinary family bathroom was next, which meant that Alfred and his wife's bedroom must be the one at the end.

'The kettle's just boiled,' she said, and when Alfred turned to look at her the desolation in his eyes made her want to cry. 'Is any of this going into storage?' she asked, and gave out a startled yelp when Alfred pushed past her and tottered across the landing, heading for the stairs.

Her heart was in her mouth as she watched him stumble down them far too fast for his own safety, but when she heard him reach the bottom without incident, she let out a relieved breath.

'What's happened?' she asked Logan.

The man shook his head and pulled a face. 'The majority of the stuff in the drawers and the wardrobes has gone. It upset him a bit to see them empty. He knew his daughter was clearing out his wife's clothes and whatnot, but seeing it for himself made it more real.'

'Poor bugger.'

'I think he's also realised that most of the furniture probably won't fit into a granny flat – and that's if he gets to live in one. It sounds to me that he'll spend the rest of his days in his daughter's house.'

'Yeah, that's what I'm worried about,' Hattie said. She squared her shoulders. She mightn't be able to do anything about that, but she could help him store some of the things he wanted to keep. The garage was lying empty, at the end of her garden. The shed didn't have a great deal in it, either, just a bit of gardening equipment, so he might get quite a few bits and pieces in there – but whichever way you looked at it, there wasn't enough room for this lot. And there wasn't even any flat-packed stuff that could be taken apart. Logan was going to have to rope in some help to get anything larger than one of the bedside tables down those narrow stairs. It was a miracle the huge walnut sleigh-bed made it into the bedroom in the first place, and she half-suspected that the removal of a window and a winch had been involved, as well as several burly men.

'Let's go find him,' she said. 'We can have a chat in the van. If he isn't home soon, I wouldn't put it past that Sara-woman to call the police.'

'She's not that bad, is she?'

'Hmm. Not sure. I suppose it all depends on Alfred's mental health. He seems fine to me, but I might only be seeing him on the good days. On the other hand, he's probably depressed, he is definitely lonely, and he hasn't got anything to do all day. I'd probably go off my rocker in that situation, too.'

'You already are,' came Logan's dry response.

'Cheeky git.' Hattie had to chuckle, though – she knew people considered her eccentric. At least it gave her some character and she rather enjoyed playing up to it.

When they got downstairs, Alfred wasn't in the house.

He wasn't in the van either, as Logan informed her when he went to check.

Hattie was beginning to worry that he may have wandered off, and she was about to panic when Logan said, 'The door to the garden is open. Do you think he's in there?' He pointed to a large outbuilding roughly the size of her own, at the bottom of the garden.

'I suppose we'd better check before we send out a search party,' she said, and led the way down the concrete path which dissected two overgrown lawns with bare-branched shrubs lining their edges.

The garden was probably lovely in the summer if it was being looked after, but left to run wild and with winter harrying at its heels, it looked rather sorry for itself.

Much like Alfred was looking, she observed, when she pushed the shed door open to find him standing at a workbench and absentmindedly stroking a clamp.

Logan came to a halt close behind her, and she flinched as he whistled in her ear. 'Bloomin' heck, take a look at all this. You could open a shop with this lot.' He gently moved her aside and stepped over the threshold.

Hattie tore her gaze away from Alfred and scanned the inside of the shed. Except, it wasn't a shed in the traditional sense of rusty lawnmowers and snow shovels; it was more reminiscent of a well-equipped and extremely neat workshop. And there was more…

'It's like Santa's grotto at the North Pole,' Logan said. 'I'm expecting an elf to appear at any minute.'

Shelves lined most of the available wall space and nearly every one of them was crammed with toys. Wooden toys, in all shapes and sizes.

'Where did these come from?' Hattie asked, her eyes darting everywhere as she tried to take it all in.

Alfred ignored her. He continued to run his hand over the clamp, and his attention was fixed on a partly-constructed train which was covered in dust. The whole place had an air of abandonment about it.

'You made these, didn't you?' Logan asked gently, as he picked up a pull-along-cat and blew the dust off it. He barked out a cough, then gave an almighty sneeze.

Alfred finally looked up. 'Yes, I did.' He lifted his chin and Hattie was pleased to see the pride that flared in his eyes. But all too soon it was gone, and the only expression on Alfred's lined face was incredible sadness.

'They're beautiful,' Logan said, turning the toy cat over in his hands and running his fingers over its surface. 'It's so smooth and polished, and the detailing is exquisite. It must have taken you ages.'

'It did, but I enjoyed making it,' Alfred said, slumping against the workbench. Hattie thought he might be close to tears.

She made a mental note to make sure he brushed the dust and grime off himself before they dropped him off at his daughter's house.

'What…? I mean, why…?' Logan scratched his head and frowned.

Alfred said, 'Can you leave me on my own for a minute? I want to say goodbye.'

Hattie frowned. There were far too many sharp tools lying around for her liking. What sort of goodbye was he thinking of? She shot Logan a warning look.

'I'll come out to the van when I'm ready,' Alfred added.

His assurance didn't make her feel any better.

'Does that mean you've changed your mind about storing your stuff at my house?' she asked.

Alfred slumped even lower against the workbench and nodded. 'It was a stupid idea; I can see that now.'

'Say goodbye, take as long as you want,' Logan said, grabbing hold of Hattie by the elbow and steering her towards the door.

'But what if he—?' she hissed at him.

'He won't.'

'He might. Did you see his poor little face? The man is devastated.'

Logan manoeuvred her through the door and pulled it shut behind them. 'I saw and I've been thinking about what you said about Alfred not having anything to do, and I've got an idea,' he said, glancing over his shoulder. 'How good are you at picking pockets?'

Hattie narrowed her eyes at him. 'Why, what do you have in mind?'

When he told her, she began to smile.

CHAPTER 10

ALFRED

Everyone was right, including his bossy daughter – never again was Alfred going to live in the house he'd called home for most of his adult life. It was too big for one man on his own for one thing, and for another Alfred had to admit that he'd let things slide a bit. There hadn't seemed much point in dusting skirting boards if Dorothy wasn't there to witness the result. And once he'd started letting the little things go by the wayside, it had become increasingly easier to ignore the bigger stuff, like the washing up and the hoovering. Shamefacedly, he conceded that if Dorothy had seen the state of the bathroom, World War Three would have broken out.

The fact that his own lack of interest in anything to do with the house (or life in general, if he was honest) had been partly responsible for Sara and the social workers declaring that he could no longer cope on his own, was a bitter pill. He'd brought it all down on himself and he only had himself to blame for being in this situation.

However, he also had to admit that not having to think about anything domestic, including shopping and cooking, was a weight off his mind. If only Sara didn't fuss around him so much and worry about him all the time, then life in her house wouldn't be so bad. He did miss having his own things around him though, and his own space. He'd become far too used to solitude to easily fit in with living with his daughter and her husband.

Oh, bugger. Why was life so difficult?

Then there was the last fall he'd had. The previous two had been minor and he might have got away with a couple more years living in his own place, if he hadn't slipped on a wet tea bag. He'd been lucky not to have broken a hip. The bruising had been bad enough, and the expression of dismay on Sara's face when she'd arrived at the hospital and had seen the state of him, would stay in his mind for a long time.

Bloody nosey neighbours! He hadn't needed the ambulance that Mrs Snelby had called. He'd been a bit winded, that was all. Another hour or so, and he'd have got up off the kitchen floor by himself. Trust her to notice that he'd not fetched his milk off the doorstep that morning. Dorothy always used to complain that the woman spent most of her life twitching the net curtains.

With a final look around the shed, Alfred brushed the tears from his cheeks and shuffled to the door. For some inexplicable reason, of all the things he was leaving behind the toys were the most difficult to let go of, and he had no idea why. It wasn't as though they reminded him of Dorothy (she never even knew he'd made them), or Shelley (his granddaughter had been too old for toys). It had just seemed a worthwhile thing to do – to make something out of scraps of discarded wood – and had kept his hands and his mind busy.

The contents of his shed represented years of loving work.

In a couple of days, it would all be in a skip.

God, what a waste. Not only of the toys themselves, but of the time he'd spent making them. Time that he should have spent with Dorothy; but then, she'd had her own interests and she'd have resented him hanging around her all the time.

Alfred tapped his coat pocket to make sure his keys were safely inside and snapped the padlock shut. He supposed he'd have to hand them over soon, but for the time being it gave him comfort to have them about his person. The key to Sara's house was on there too, and he thought about it hanging all by itself from the keyring he'd bought in Margate more than thirty years ago, and he felt incredibly sad.

It took him longer than it should have to wander around the rest of the house, and he was conscious of the afternoon rapidly slipping away. No doubt Sara would be frantic, but she would have to learn to get over herself. She couldn't keep an eye on him twenty-four hours a day, and despite what she thought (and what he secretly feared) he wasn't totally ga-ga yet. And, in spite of what was happening to his home, during the past couple of days he'd felt a bit better in himself – a bit more *with it*. Especially today, the sadness of leaving here notwithstanding.

His final act before he left his house for the very last time, was to pat the newel post at the bottom of the stairs. As he recalled, it had been the very first thing he'd done on entering the house when he and Dorothy had bought it, after the estate agent had handed over the keys all those years ago.

'Goodbye and God bless,' he said to the house, feeling the wood slightly pitted under his hand due to years of being knocked and bumped. 'I hope your new owners will love you as much as we did.'

His eyes were still damp when he clambered into the van, Logan giving him a gentle shove, and he settled into his own thoughts, ignoring Hattie, who seemed desperate to give him a hug.

'Get off,' he muttered, after she threw her arms around him and tried to bury her face in his shoulder.

'Are you OK, my lovely?' she asked, when he nudged her away with his elbow.

'I would be if you'd stop mauling me. Keep your hands to yourself, woman.'

Hattie huffed. 'I was trying to give you a cuddle because you looked like you needed one, but if you're going to be snooty, then I shan't.'

'Good.'

'Fine.' She folded her arms and stared rigidly ahead.

Logan kept shooting them odd looks, but when Hattie stopped being silly, he seemed to settle too, and concentrated on the road rather than his passengers, to Alfred's relief.

'Where do you want me to drop you?' Logan asked as they took the turn-off for Ticklemore.

'At the end of Castle Lane, please,' Alfred said. He'd walk the rest of the way, as he didn't want to run the risk of Sara seeing him getting out of the van – she'd only keep on and on at him until he told her where he'd been.

'Ooh, do you live in one of those posh big houses? I remember it when it was nothing but fields.' Hattie was already craning her neck for a good look – the nosey so-and-so.

He nodded.

'How come I've never seen your daughter in the village? Ticklemore is hardly a big place. I thought I knew most of the residents.'

'I dunno.' He didn't care, either.

'Has she lived here long?'

'A good few years.'

'Where did they live before that?'

'Stop being so nosey,' Alfred said. 'Talking to you is like talking to the Spanish Inquisition.'

'Well!' Hattie huffed again and folded her arms, her elbow digging into his side. 'If you don't want to be friendly…'

Logan said, 'Leave the poor man alone, Hattie. I'm not surprised he's not feeling very talkative.'

Alfred shot him a grateful look. It wasn't that he didn't want to be friendly, it was more that he wasn't used to being asked so many questions or to have anyone take such an interest in him.

Logan brought the van to a stop and jumped out, hurrying around to the passenger side to let Alfred out.

'Thank you, Logan, for your help. And you, too, Hattie.' He was grateful, despite how he appeared. He couldn't remember the last time a stranger had been as kind. It wasn't their fault that his idea had been a pie-in-the-sky one. At least they'd tried, and he wouldn't forget that.

He was aware that Logan had pulled the van up a bit to make sure he got home safely, and part of him was touched at how thoughtful the publican was. A smaller part of him was slightly irritated that Logan thought he needed watching to Sara's front door. He might walk with a stick, but he was steady enough on his feet.

Before he had a chance to get his keys out of his pocket, Sara yanked the front door open and cried, 'Where have you been?'

'You've got to stop asking me that every time I walk through the door,' he grumbled, resisting the urge to look over his shoulder to check whether Logan was still at the end of the road. 'Out, that's where I've been.'

Sara tutted as she stood to one side to let him pass. 'You sound like a teenager.'

'Maybe that's because you treat me like one?' he retorted.

His daughter heaved a sigh. 'I worry about you, that's all.'

'I know you do, but I can look after myself.' He ignored the sceptical look she gave him. 'I've been to the pub, and before you start, it was for lunch. With a friend.' Her scepticism turned to astonishment and it emboldened him enough to add, 'And I might go again next week.'

'Dad, I don't mind you having friends; I'm glad about it. I don't mind you going to the pub, either. I just wish you'd let me know where you are.'

'What if I don't want to?'

Sara frowned and shook her head. 'There's no need to be difficult.'

'I'm not the one being difficult, you are.'

'For f—' She snapped her mouth shut.

'You nearly swore,' Alfred said, feeling rather pleased with himself. His prim and proper headmistress of a daughter never swore.

'I was going to say, "four fat snakes".' Sara lifted her nose in the air.

'No, you weren't.'

Another deep sigh was followed by, 'I don't suppose you'll want much more than a sandwich, considering you had a meal at lunchtime.'

Bugger. He was starving, but if he ate a full meal, she might smell a rat. 'I could manage a small portion,' he said. 'What are we having?'

'Chicken yakitori.'

Alfred wasn't any the wiser. 'Chicken what?'

'Chicken with a teriyaki sauce.'

'Right. Will I like it?' He still had no idea what that was.

'Probably.'

'I'll have some then, please.'

Sara narrowed her eyes. 'I'm going to see about getting you a mobile phone. I know you don't like them, but it'll give me peace of mind.'

No, it wouldn't, he thought, not if she knew what he'd been planning today; she'd have had a hissy fit if he'd told her where he was. He didn't like the idea of his daughter being able to keep tabs on him, and he didn't know if it was possible for her to track his movements through one, but he wasn't prepared to take the risk. If she'd realised he was in the Ticklemore Tavern, she'd have winkled him out of there quicker than a blackbird pecking a snail out of its shell.

He wilted at the prospect of having a mobile phone foisted on him – it would be akin to being on remand and having one of those anklet things on your leg, he mused. Then he brightened – even he knew that mobile phones could run out of charge, be switched off, or be forgotten. And it might come in handy. Plus, he didn't want to admit it, but if Hattie had the wherewithal to work one of those things then he should be able to, and if it meant that Sara was less likely to panic, then maybe it wasn't such a bad idea after all.

He decided to pick Hattie's brains, the next time

he saw her. Failing that, Logan seemed a nice enough bloke. He'd give Alfred the lowdown on the ins and outs of modern technology. It was ironic, though, he thought – his daughter didn't trust him to walk down his own stairs, yet she'd happily let him loose in the big wide world if he had a mobile with him.

Chicken yakitori was rather tasty, he discovered a short while later, and he polished off two skewers' worth as well as a portion of rice and salad.

At least his daughter was a decent cook, and that was one thing he didn't miss about living alone – making his own dinner. The weight that had gradually slipped off him since Dorothy had passed away, was now creeping back on, and when he gazed at his naked self in the mirror as he was changing into his pyjamas later that evening, he noticed that he didn't look as frail as he once did. There was a bit more flesh on his old bones and he felt stronger in himself.

It was hard to concede that Sara might have been right about him having not coped too well over the last couple of years, but it was even harder to have to leave everything behind.

Growing old was a bitch.

CHAPTER 11

HATTIE

Hattie waited on the pavement, excitement twisting her tummy into knots of anticipation. It couldn't technically be classed as breaking and entering if you had a key, could it? Thinking of keys had her patting her chest to make sure Alfred's keys were still safely stashed in her bra.

She was travelling light, without a handbag, and she didn't trust putting them in her pocket – things fell out of pockets. Therefore her bra was the safest option, and she had been known to hide a whole raft of objects in its depths, from her lipstick (which had been a disaster because it had melted into a mushy mess), her mobile phone, money (although coins tended to slip and drop out), hankies, and, once, a spare pair of knickers.

Ah, there he was, the delectable landlord of the

Ticklemore Tavern. He was right on time, and when he pulled over and opened the van door for her, she saw he was dressed all in black, like a proper cat burglar.

Hattie didn't own anything black. She didn't see the point in wearing a colour which should only be seen at funerals or on bankers' suits. Therefore, she was dressed in the closest shade she could find in her eclectic wardrobe – grey patterned jogging bottoms (ignore the sparkly bits) and a purple jumper. Over the top she'd shrugged on a combat jacket in army colours, and concluded she'd be just fine if she needed to blend into the undergrowth. Not that there had been a great deal of undergrowth to blend into along the road Alfred used to live on, but his garden was quite wild. Maybe she should have daubed some warpaint over her face – she could have sworn she had an old palette of eyeshadows in one of her drawers which would have done the trick.

'All set?' Logan asked as he helped her up the step into the van.

Hattie patted her bosom. 'Yep,' she said and chortled when she saw Logan's face. 'Who's covering you behind the bar? I've never known you take a Saturday evening off.'

'You've heard of the saying "all work and no play makes Jack a dull boy"? That's me, according to my mother. She agreed to stand in for me when I told her I was taking a lady out for the evening.'

Logan's mum, Marie, was a mere babe in arms what with only being in her late fifties, but she knew what she was talking about. Logan was a fine-looking man, but he had yet to settle down, and Hattie knew that Marie was hankering after grandchildren. Hattie would have thought that running his own pub would put Logan in the firing line for meeting a decent selection of young ladies, but the clientele were mostly couples or the elderly. The Ticklemore Tavern was far more country pub than city bar. Marie feared that if he spent all day every day pulling pints then he wouldn't be pulling the woman he was destined to fall in love with. Hattie suspected that heisting wooden toys from a shed in Shorbrook with an octogenarian wasn't quite what Logan's mother had in mind. Nice of him to refer to her as a lady, though, and Hattie simpered at him, ignoring the slightly alarmed expression on his face.

'What if we're caught?' Logan asked, when they were nearly there.

'This was your idea; you should have considered the consequences before you dragged me into your life of crime. I could go to prison, you know, and at my age, I'll probably never get out.' Hattie saw him swallow nervously, and she chuckled. 'We won't be caught. And if anyone challenges us, we've got a key, remember?' She patted her boob again. 'How many burglars can say they've got a key?'

'Some of them must have.'

'You're being silly. That Sara-woman would only throw the whole lot in a skip anyway, so we're doing her a favour. Pull up here; we'll go the rest of the way on foot and scope the place out.'

'You've been watching too many police thrillers,' Logan accused her, but he drew the van to a halt.

'At least it's dark,' she said.

'If we're not doing anything wrong, that shouldn't make any difference.'

'I just don't want some busybody sticking their nose in. I want to get in, get the job done and get away without being seen.'

Logan rolled his eyes. 'Shall we synchronise our watches?'

'Ooh, do we need to? I wish I'd known – I haven't got mine on.'

'No, I don't think we need to. I was being sarcastic.'

'If you don't behave yourself, I'll tell the rozzers that you coerced me into doing it.'

Logan snorted. 'Rozzers? Do people still call the police, rozzers? And I thought you said we won't be caught?'

'We might unless you stop faffing around and get a move on. I want to be in bed by ten.'

The street was quiet and deserted. Not even a dog walker was in evidence and Hattie grunted in approval. This was going to be a walk in the park. 'Shit, I didn't think to bring a torch – we can't go turning lights on left, right and centre or someone might see.'

'I've got one in the van,' Logan said, scanning the drive. 'You stay here, and I'll bring the van closer. I thought we could fetch everything from the shed and stack it along the side of the house and—' He slapped a hand to his forehead. 'There's a lane behind the garden, and I noticed a gate set into the fence. We don't have to lug it all to the front of the house – we can load it straight into the van.'

'I knew I brought you for a reason,' Hattie said, nudging him with her shoulder. 'You're not just a pretty face.'

'You brought me because one, it was my idea; two, you don't know anyone else with a van; three, no one else would be daft enough to do this; and four, I have muscles. Can you give me the keys? My best guess is that the gate will be locked from the inside.'

Hattie fished around in her bra and drew them out, handing them to Logan, who grimaced.

'They're warm,' he said.

'So would you be if you'd been down there for the past hour.'

'Gross. I'll be as quick as I can.'

Hattie watched him sneak down the side of the house and disappear around the back. While she waited, she shuffled between a couple of bushes and tried to blend in as she scanned the windows of the nearest houses. Most were either in darkness or had their curtains drawn, and the light they held in was muted and faint.

So far, so good, she thought, breathing a sigh of relief when Logan reappeared. 'Let's go.'

They climbed back into the van and Logan drove to the end of the street, turned right onto another, and right again almost immediately. He killed the lights and inched slowly down the alleyway. Light spilt from the houses on either side, and although Hattie kept her eyes peeled, she didn't see anyone peering out of their windows at them. Many of the houses had garages or other outbuildings butting up to the lane, so she surmised that it wouldn't be too unusual for a vehicle to be trundling down it.

'This is it,' Logan said coming to a stop and craning his neck. 'If you start putting things in boxes, I can carry them out to the van.'

'You brought boxes? Good man!'

It took the pair of them well over two hours to

transfer all the toys from the shed to the van, along with as many tools as they could find. It wasn't easy working in semi-darkness, Logan making sure the torch was angled at the floor, but finally, it was done, including the contents of an old bookcase on which jar upon jar of odds-and-sods had sat, all of them neatly labelled, along with pots of paints and brushes.

'I can't get the workbench in,' Logan told her. 'I'm not going to be able to lift it on my own, and even if I could there's no room in the van.'

Hattie studied it. It looked like an old farmhouse table, rather than a purpose-made piece of kit. 'Would he be able to use any old table, do you think?'

Logan shrugged. 'I don't see why not, as long as it's sturdy enough. Why? Have you got something in mind?'

'I sure have, but I can't do anything about the shelves; although I have a couple of shelving units in my shed I don't have enough, so most of this will have to stay in boxes for the time being.'

'Can we talk about that later? I think our work here is done.'

With a final check around to make sure they'd hadn't missed anything important, Hattie gave a cry. 'The clamp – can you remove it?'

He could, and after that they were ready to leave, and Hattie let out a long slow breath. Relief coursed through her, making her feel a little light-headed. Despite her bravado, she had borne a very real fear that they might have been caught.

She was also knackered. A day in the shop (admittedly not all day), two trips to Shorbrook, and an evening spent packing boxes was more than her old bones could take, and she sank into the passenger seat, feeling far less sprightly on the return journey than she had on the outward one. She hadn't been joking when she'd said she wanted to be in bed by ten o'clock.

But the night wasn't over yet, and there was still much to be done before bedtime.

One thing she was looking forward to though, was seeing the look on Alfred's face when they showed him what she and Logan had done.

Despite her exhaustion, Hattie clapped her hands together and laughed. They'd done it, they had bloody well done it!

CHAPTER 12

ALFRED

Alfred might need glasses, and he might need a stick to help him get about, but there was nothing wrong with his hearing, thank you very much. Which was why he was standing stark naked in his bedroom, wondering what the hell that noise was. It sounded like someone tapping on the window, but considering the bedroom which Sara had allocated him was on the first floor, that would be mighty tricky.

There it was again, but not so much of a tap, more of a splatter of something hitting the glass. Maybe it was hailstones. Rain was forecast for later tonight, and it had been quite cold of late, so it could be.

The sound came again.

'Goddam it,' he muttered. That wasn't hailstones. It sounded like someone was throwing something at his window.

As hastily as he could, Alfred yanked on his pyjama bottoms and shrugged his arms into the shirt-style top. Then he shuffled to the window, pulled the curtain aside and peered out.

There, standing in front of Sara's ornamental fern, was the mad woman and her side-kick. The side-kick, aka Logan from the Ticklemore Tavern, must have imbibed too much of his own beer, because he was holding a handful of gravel and was preparing to lob it at the window.

Seeing him staring down at them, Hattie clapped her hands together then waved, bouncing up and down on the soles of her feet. The yellow streetlamp backlit the pair of them perfectly, and mist from their breath clouded the air around their heads.

Alfred wrestled with the catch for a moment before releasing it and pushing the window open. 'What are you doing?' he hissed.

'Trying to attract your attention,' Logan hissed in reply.

Alfred pulled his head back a little and listened hard. He could hear the TV in the living room, but that was all. 'Do you know what time it is?'

'Yes, I bloomin' well do!' Hattie cried.

'Shhh!' He glanced over his shoulder and eyed his bedroom door, praying it stayed shut, before turning his attention back to the pair of idiots on Sara's drive.

'It's ten-thirty.' Clearly Hattie *didn't* know, else she wouldn't be here.

'I *know*. Were you asleep?'

'No.'

'Can you come down? We've got something to show you.' This was from Logan, who should know better, Alfred thought, pursing his lips.

'No,' he repeated.

'Please? You'll like it,' Hattie said. She'd stopped bouncing, and although it wasn't easy to tell in the dark, he thought she looked tired as her shoulders sagged and she leant against Logan.

'Go away,' Alfred whispered, as loudly as he dared.

Neither of them moved.

He huffed. They weren't going to go away, were they? And the longer the pair of them loitered on the drive, the greater the chances that Sara or David would see them.

'This had better be good,' he warned, then he closed the window and pulled the curtains across. Stuffing his feet into his slippers, he drew on his dressing gown and opened his bedroom door. The sound of the TV increased slightly, but he could tell that the living room door was still firmly closed.

Creeping as quietly as he could, he tiptoed across the landing.

Then he had a thought and tiptoed back to his

room. He'd better take his keys with him, in the off chance that whilst he was outside playing silly buggers with the terrible twosome, Sara or David locked up. He didn't fancy sleeping under a bush.

Back in his bedroom, he stood in the middle of it, his mind blank as he tried to remember what it was that he'd come back for. Ah, yes! Keys.

Now, where were they? He usually put them on top of his chest of drawers, but they weren't there, so he must have left them in the pocket of his coat. He tried to think… He always took his coat off and hung it in the closet in the hall after he came in, and he always kept his keys in his hand for fear of popping them down somewhere and being unable to remember where he'd left them. At home, he used to keep them in a bowl on the hall table, but Sara didn't have a hall table, so he always took them upstairs and put them on top of the chest of drawers.

So why weren't they there?

The spatter of a handful of gravel against glass had him rushing towards the window, and this time when he yanked it open, he was more cross than curious. 'Can't you wait a minute? I'm trying to find my keys.'

He was about to shut it again, when the glimmer of light on metal caught his eye, and he realised what Hattie was holding. Or should he say, swinging smugly in her fist. She rattled the keys. *His* keys.

'Are you looking for these?' she sang, keeping her voice low.

'Where did you find them?' His heart sank. God knows where he'd left them. In the van probably. No wonder Hattie and Logan wanted him to come down for them. They could hardly post them through the letterbox. And if they'd have left it until the next time he'd seen one or the other of them, Sara would already have been aware that he'd lost them and she'd have been even more reluctant to allow him out by himself.

'Wait there,' he whispered, and headed back across the landing and down the stairs as quietly as his creaky old bones would allow. He decided to go out the back way, through the utility room which was just off the kitchen. If either Sara or David caught him, he could say he'd popped down for a drink.

He didn't get caught though, and he eased the door open before slipping outside into the night.

'Thanks,' he said when he reached Hattie and she handed his keys to him. 'Where did you find them?'

'In your pocket,' Hattie said. 'Come with us, we've got something to show you.'

'Now?' Alfred rubbed the back of his neck.

'Yes, now. It won't take long.'

'Can't it wait?' He saw Hattie and Logan exchange a look, and Logan shrugged. 'What's going on?'

Alfred demanded, thoroughly confused.

'Time is getting on a bit,' Logan said. 'Maybe it should wait until tomorrow?'

'Bah, it's not that late,' Hattie objected.

'I thought you said you wanted to be in bed by ten?' Logan reminded her.

'What I say and what I mean are two different things,' she replied loftily, and Logan muttered, 'You can say that again.'

'Will one of you please tell me what's going on?' Alfred could practically feel his blood pressure rising.

'You have to see it for yourself,' Hattie insisted.

For Pete's sake! 'Right, hurry up and show me, then I can go to bed before Sara notices I'm gone.'

'If she does, will you be sent to the naughty-step?' Hattie chuckled.

'It's not funny.'

She sobered and her expression held a fair amount of sympathy. 'No, I don't suppose it is. Come on; I know just the thing to cheer you up.'

Hattie took hold of his arm and led him down the drive. Alfred was reluctant to go with them, but he guessed the sooner he did, the sooner this mad pair would bugger off and leave him alone. That Hattie was here didn't surprise him too much, but that Logan had allowed himself to be roped into her madcap scheme, did. On the other hand, the publican had been more than happy to visit his house in Shorbrook with the express intention of loading his furniture onto a van and spiriting it away before Sara disposed of it, so he shouldn't be shocked at all. The pair of them were as batty as each other.

'Get in,' Logan said, opening the van door and jerking his head.

'Where are we going? Are you kidnapping me?' Alfred wasn't entirely sure he was joking.

'No point. We wouldn't get much for you,' Hattie stated as she clambered up to sit beside him. 'We're going to my house.'

'Why?' Alfred tried for firm and demanding, but what came out of his mouth was more of a petulant worried whine.

'You'll see.'

Hattie's excitement was back, but she still looked worn out, and a spike of worry pricked at him. She hadn't looked like this earlier, when they'd dropped him off at Sara's. Was she ill? Had she received some bad news?

The drive from Sara's to Hattie's was about three minutes. Hattie lived in the heart of Ticklemore and Sara's house was on a newish estate on the outskirts, but even so, Alfred was on edge; the longer he spent out of the house, the greater the risk of Sara realising he'd absconded. It was ridiculous to be fretting like this. Sara was hardly likely to knock on his bedroom door before she retired for the night – she hadn't as yet, so why should tonight be any different? – and he should be able to stick his head around the living room door and say he was popping out for a while. Mind you, if David had said the exact same thing to Sara at ten-thirty at night, she'd have given him the third degree, too, which made Alfred feel a little better.

When they pulled up outside Hattie's cottage, Alfred practically pushed Hattie out of the van in his haste to find out what was going on and get back to Sara's house. He vaguely took in the old stonework, the ivy growing around the quaint porch and the crazy-paved path leading from the gate to the front door.

He didn't take much notice of the inside, either, except to run his gaze around the hall and then the kitchen, as he tried to figure out why he'd been brought here. He was even more perplexed when Hattie led him out the back and into the garden, Logan bringing up the rear. The only thing out here apart from the plants was a shed and a garage, and to be honest, neither of them looked particularly inspiring.

They got to the end of the garden and stopped.

'Close your eyes,' Hattie said.

'I don't think so.'

'Please? Pretty please? It's nothing nasty, I promise.'

'I'll be the judge of that.'

'Can you just humour her, Alfred?' Logan asked. He sounded as weary as Hattie looked, despite her perky tone of voice. 'It's been a long day, and I've got to take you back home first before I can go to bed.'

'Hmph. OK, but be quick, and you'd better pray it *is* something nice, or else…' he warned.

'It had better be, after all the trouble we've gone to,' Logan muttered.

Alfred reluctantly closed his eyes. He wasn't in the least bit happy about it, but the sooner he complied, the sooner he'd be taken back to Sara's.

There was a scrape and a scuffle, then a light behind his eyelids, and he guessed they'd unlocked the shed and turned on the light.

'You can open them now,' Hattie said.

Alfred opened his eyes.

'Ta da!' she cried.

He was aware of Hattie doing the clapping, bouncing thing and he sensed the pair of them looking at him, but he was too shocked to do anything other than stare at the scene in front of him.

The shed was larger than he'd expected from the outside – not as large as the one he had at home, but not far off it – and it was dominated by a table that had seen better days, which was sitting in the middle of it. The table was wonky, scuffed and scratched, and had blobs of old paint or something similar daubed across its surface. A stool, looking suspiciously like the ones by the bar in the Ticklemore Tavern, had been drawn up to it, and a clamp was attached to the far end.

Was that his clamp? It certainly looked familiar…

An old sideboard, made of dark wood and ornately carved, sat on the wall underneath the window. The top of it held boxes of tools and paints. And those were definitely some of his toys stacked on a metal shelving unit. The rest were in boxes stacked from the floor to the ceiling. Rows and rows of boxes…

'What do you think?' Hattie asked finally.

Alfred wasn't sure. He was having difficulty taking it all in.

'We – Logan, actually, so blame him not me – thought this might be more useful to you than storing furniture that you'll probably never use again.'

Alfred tore his gaze away. 'I'll never use those again, either.' He swept an arm towards the tools on the sideboard.

'Why ever not?' Hattie demanded.

'I'm done making toys.'

'Are you sure?' Her shoulders drooped and she put

a hand on the doorframe to steady herself.

Alfred shook his head. Was he sure? He hadn't picked up a piece of wood since Dorothy had passed away. He'd not had the inclination, and he couldn't decide whether the thrill of making the toys in secret had been the driving factor, or whether grief had quenched his creative fire. The reason didn't matter — he was never going to make another toy again.

Having them safe though, that was a different thing entirely. He still wasn't sure what he was going to do with them, but at least they weren't going to a landfill site.

'Have you got any grandchildren?' he asked Hattie. Maybe she could take a couple of them off his hands, although he had no idea what he'd do with the rest of them. Over the years he must have made several hundred of the damned things, from large intricate dolls' houses to simple animal shapes.

'No.' There was regret in her voice.

'Logan?' Alfred asked.

'I'm too young to have grandchildren,' the man quipped.

Alfred rolled his eyes, then sobered. 'Thank you for rescuing them.' It must have taken the two of them from the minute they dropped him off at the end of Sara's road until when they threw gravel at his window, to shift all this. No wonder Hattie was so exhausted.

'You don't have to decide now,' Hattie said. 'Sleep on it. They'll still be here tomorrow. We thought… Never mind.' She took a deep breath. 'Logan, you'd better get him back home.'

Home? For a minute his heart leapt, until he realised she meant Sara's house. No matter how long he lived in the house in Castle Lane, he had a feeling it would never be anything other than "Sara's house" in his mind. His home was gone. There would soon be nothing left of it but an empty shell.

He didn't know which was worse – his home lying empty and unloved while prospective buyers tramped all over his wool carpets; or the house having a new family living in it, a family who would tear out the old bathroom suite and pull up those same carpets, or who'd knock the sitting room and dining room into one to create an "open plan living space"…

Alfred shuddered.

He was about to turn away, to leave the final remnant of his previous life behind when he paused, his heart filled with sharp and sudden gratitude.

Hattie and Logan, who hardly knew him from Adam, had done this lovely thing for him. Without being told, they'd known what was truly important to him when he hadn't even realised it himself. When he'd thought up his mad-cap plan of rescuing his and

Dorothy's heavy old furniture, he hadn't given much thought to the toys. Yet, these people, without being asked, had gone straight to the heart of the matter, and had saved what had mattered to him the most.

He sniffed loudly, tears smarting behind his eyes. His toy-making days might be over (even if he had the inclination, how could he escape Sara's eagle-eye for the serious amounts of time needed to make even a simple item?), but he'd like to think of them going to good homes. Toys needed to be played with – *he* needed them to be played with, otherwise all the love, time, and care he'd lavished on them would be for nothing.

He'd sleep on it, as Hattie had suggested, although he knew he wouldn't change his mind; but the fact that these people had done such a wonderfully thoughtful thing for him, deserved the due consideration they asked for.

Alfred felt Hattie's hand on his shoulder and he sniffed again. But despite the imminent tears and the heavy feeling in his chest, his heart felt lighter than it had done in a long time.

CHAPTER 13

HATTIE

Everything ached – more than it usually did, that is – and Hattie struggled to heave her body up the bed until she was sitting with her back propped against the pillows to survey the damage.

The worse bits were her back, her shoulders, her forearms, her wrists, her— Everything, really. There was hardly an inch of her which didn't hurt, and all her joints appeared to have welded themselves together overnight. It was going to take more than a cup of tea and a stern talking to, to sort this lot out.

Still, she didn't regret it for one second. The aches and pains had been worth it to see the look on Alfred's face. Stunned didn't begin to describe it, and at first she'd worried that they'd done the wrong thing in fetching Alfred's toys and associated equipment from his old house. Then she'd seen him trying to hold back tears, and she knew it had been worth it. Although she wasn't certain whether he'd ever wield a saw again, at least the opportunity was there if he wanted to take it and it wasn't as though having it sitting in her shed was inconveniencing her. It could stay there indefinitely.

It was a shame that the toys wouldn't be used, though. Items like the ones Alfred had made needed to be played with. At the very least they should be on display somewhere and not boxed up in her shed gathering dust.

Maybe she could ask Nell from the Ticklemore Treasure Trove to display a few pieces in her shop. Maybe… and here was a thought… Nell could sell some of them? On a commission basis, of course – Hattie wouldn't expect the woman to buy them, in case they were sitting there for years.

Struggling out of bed, her reluctant body out of synch with the enthusiasm coursing through her mind, Hattie did her ablutions, dressed as quickly as she could and made a cup of tea. There was nothing so important that it couldn't wait until she'd wet her whistle.

Tea drunk and cup washed, dried, and returned to its proper place, Puss fed, watered and let out for the day, Hattie was ready. She'd have to choose the pieces with care, not because some were better than others, but because she had to carry them from her shed to the Treasure Trove, and she was acutely aware that she wasn't as strong as she used to be. Yesterday evening had taught her that. A couple of the more intricate, smaller toys which showed off Alfred's craftsmanship to the full would be best, and if Nell was interested then Hattie would invite her round to take a look for herself.

After some deliberation, she chose a Noah's Ark, which was a carrycase all by itself and contained Noah, his wife, and a selection of animals, plus a little wooden frog on wheels, whose legs pistoned up and down when it was pushed along the floor.

Giggling, she wrapped them in an old pillowcase and popped them in her shopping bag. Then she drew her shoulders back, lifted her chin, and was on her way.

With there being only six full shopping weeks to Christmas, Nell's shop was already showing signs of the impending festive season. There were fairy lights strung around the picture rails, the shop looked fuller than it usually did, as though Nell was preparing for the rush, and there was a hint of cinnamon, spices, and pine needles in the air.

The Ticklemore Treasure Trove was exactly what it said on the tin – a trove of treasures from years gone by that you didn't know you wanted or needed in your life until you saw them. Nell only stocked items of good quality, and many of them were handmade or unusual, and all of them were beautiful in their own right. Collectively, they were fascinating and eye-catching, and Hattie felt she could spend the whole day in there and not see the same thing twice.

'Hattie! How nice to see you? Are you keeping well?' Nell was in the middle of decorating her Christmas tree and as the woman hurried around the counter to give her a hug, Hattie caught a glimpse of old glass baubles, the sort she remembered from her own childhood. She would have liked to have taken a moment to study them, but she was enveloped in Nell's arms. Nell was a hugger and everyone she knew tended to get the same treatment whether they wanted it or not.

When she was released, Hattie stood back and studied the woman, satisfied to see that she seemed to be on top form. There was a time, not long after Nell's husband had told her he was leaving her, that Nell had become thin and listless, all the joy of life sucked out of her. It hadn't helped that her twin boys had gone away to university the week before and she'd been suffering from empty-nest syndrome.

It had served the bastard right, Hattie had thought at the time, when, after announcing that their fabulous house on the outskirts of town would have to be sold, that Nell had fought back and had begun to sell off first the paintings, then the furniture, bit by expensive bit. And she'd enjoyed the process so much, that she'd gone into business, using her half of the proceeds from the house to buy a three-storey building in the heart of the village and set up her own shop.

'I've got something I hope you'll be interested in,' Hattie said, handing her the shopping bag.

Nell put it on the counter and unwrapped the contents. She didn't say anything for the moment; she simply looked at them, her face giving nothing away.

'Well?' Hattie demanded, desperate to hear the verdict.

'Where did you get them?'

'First, tell me what you think.'

'They're very well made, by hand I'd guess, and they're very desirable. There is a growing trend for parents to want more traditional toys, and not cheap plastic tat which will break after a couple of weeks. This,' she fondled the frog's smooth little head, 'is built to last.'

'Are they worth anything?'

'Yes, but I don't know how much. I'd have to do some research. I don't have a great deal of experience with toys.'

'Could you sell them on a commission basis?'

Hattie asked.

'I only sell antiques as you know, but these are such good quality that I might consider it, especially since it's toy-buying season. Of course, it does depend on how much you want for them in the first place.'

'Oh, I don't want anything for them – they're not mine.'

'How about you take a seat,' Nell gestured towards a plush high-backed chair covered in white velvet, 'and tell me about it?'

Hattie sat down gingerly, hoping her orange skirt (in honour of Bonfire Night, which had taken place a couple of weeks ago) didn't have any dirty marks on it, and she balanced on the edge and folded her hands in her lap. 'They belong to a friend of mine who makes them as a hobby,' she began.

'Does he have any more, or is this it?'

'There are more. Lots more.'

'What numbers are we talking about, and are they all the same, or is there a variety?'

Hattie hesitated. 'It's probably better if you see for yourself.'

Nell shot her a curious look, her eyes slightly narrowed. 'If you give me two minutes, I can come now. Adam is home for the weekend and he can earn his Sunday roast by keeping an eye on the shop for a few minutes. As long as we're not going far, that is?'

'Only to my house,' Hattie assured her.

Nell called her strapping son down from the flat above the shop, leaving him with strict instructions to behave himself, to be nice to customers, and to phone her if he was unsure about anything.

'I won't be long,' she added. 'And don't forget to phone me.'

'Mum, I've worked here before. I know what I'm doing,' he said, ushering her out the door.

Hattie gave him a conspiratorial wink. She'd known Adam and his twin, Ethan, since they were born.

Adam winked back.

They both knew Nell was a bit of a control freak.

'Anyone would think you don't trust him,' Hattie said as they walked along the pavement.

Nell laughed. 'I don't – how can you trust someone who eats cold Pot Noodle for breakfast?'

'Ew!'

'Exactly. He must get his bad habits from his father, because he certainly doesn't get them from me.'

'How is Simon?'

'Still breathing,' Nell replied sourly.

'Do the boys see much of him?'

'Enough to keep a relationship of sorts going, but nothing more.'

'Pity – he's missing out on such a lot. You've got two lovely boys.'

Nell grinned. 'I know – they are lush, aren't they?'

Lush? What kind of a word was that? These youngsters said some strange things… And Nell was a youngster in Hattie's eyes. Anyone who was less than seventy was, and Nell was only in her late forties, although she looked considerably younger than that.

'Through here,' Hattie said, showing Nell into the hall and from there through the kitchen and out into the garden. Her heart was fluttering and she was oddly nervous, but she didn't know why. She had a strange feeling again and she just knew that these next few minutes were going to lead to something…

'Oh, my word!' Nell exclaimed as Hattie pushed the door open and switched the light on.

Nell stepped into the shed and walked slowly to the table, then she stopped and did a gradual twirl, her eyes scanning the shelves, the boxes, the sideboard. And all the while, Hattie watched her, searching the woman's face for clues. Was she interested? Could she shift any of it? Would it even be worth Nell's while, or was Hattie on a hiding to nothing?

'I can't believe how much stock is here,' Nell cried, dipping in and out of the various boxes and running her fingers across the larger toys on the shelves.

Hattie empathised with Nell's need to touch everything – Alfred's creations were almost organic and so very tactile. She could imagine little hands being unable to resist them. 'What do you think?'

'I think these are wonderful. You said a friend makes them? Do I know him?'

'You might – he's not long moved to Ticklemore. An older gentleman, comes from Shorbrook and now lives on Castle Lane with his daughter and her husband, name of Alfred... something or other. Walks with a stick.' If Hattie was going to introduce him as her friend, she really should ask him his surname. 'Will you be able to sell them, do you think?' Hattie bit her lip.

'Definitely, but I won't be able to sell all of them before Christmas – there's enough stock here for him to open a shop of his own.'

Hattie froze.

She looked at Nell and Nell looked at her.

Then both women began to smile...

CHAPTER 14

ALFRED

Sunday was the day Alfred found the most difficult to get through. This was because David wasn't in work and, unlike Saturdays which tended to be busier and more out-and-about, Sunday was more of a stay-at-home and lounge about the house type of day. The house felt fuller because of it, with both Sara and David around for most of the day (although David did pop out at about ten o'clock for a couple of hours) and Alfred simply wasn't used to so much company. No matter where he went, someone was always nearby. He didn't even have a shed to retreat to, because the one in the garden was barely the size of a postage stamp and was stuffed full of lawnmowers and other assorted gardening equipment.

The only other place was the garage, and David guarded it in the same way Cerberus guarded the gates of hell. It was the only thing his son-in-law seemed to be passionate about, and at one point Alfred wondered whether David had his own secret workshop inside; until he spotted a pristine and almost empty space when the roller-door was open one day and understood that the garage was there purely to park the man's sports car in. The one he hardly drove, not even to go to work because he had a Mercedes for that. Sara owned an eminently practical Ford which reflected her personality perfectly.

At least he'd get to see his granddaughter today, so that was something to look forward to.

'What time will Shelley be here?' he asked. He was sitting in the kitchen, at a bit of a loss.

'I told you, Dad – she's coming for lunch.' Sara was slicing green beans and she paused to give him one of her looks. The look that made him feel as though she was judging him and finding him lacking.

'Yes, I know, but what *time*?' he insisted.

'About two-ish.'

'I know you think I'm going ga-ga,' he grumbled, 'but in my eyes lunchtime is twelve-thirty. One at a push. Two o'clock is almost the middle of the afternoon.'

'Does it matter? Did you have plans?'

Alfred knew his daughter was being sarcastic. Of

course he didn't have plans. 'I might have.'

'Like what?'

'I might have fancied taking a stroll.'

Sara rolled her eyes. 'You can go for a walk *before* lunch.'

'I can *now*,' he said. 'But if lunch had been at the proper hour, I wouldn't have had time to.'

Sara put the knife down on the counter and rubbed the back of her hand across her brow. 'Well, you *have* got the time, haven't you,' she said, then, when he failed to make a move, 'Are you going for a walk, or not?'

'I haven't made up my mind.'

'Give me strength,' she muttered. 'When you have decided, let me know.'

'Why?' He knew he was being awkward, but he couldn't help it – Sara brought out the worst in him since her mother had died. The girl had always been a bossy little so-and-so – she took after her mother in that regard. Dorothy had always wanted to know the ins and outs of a duck's backside (he loved that phrase – it was one of his mother's old sayings), and Sara had turned out the same. Sara going on to become a teacher hadn't helped, because the job had enabled her to take bossiness to a whole new level. It must stem from all those years of ordering little kids around.

'Because I like to know where you are,' Sara said, chopping the rest of the green beans with unwarranted aggression.

'Why?' He sounded like a petulant child, which wasn't helping his case any, but again, he couldn't prevent the word from slipping out.

Sara shook her head slightly, opened her mouth, then closed it again. Alfred could see her jaw clenching and guessed she was grinding her teeth. He'd thought she'd have grown out of the habit by now.

'You know why, Dad,' she said.

'I don't.' He genuinely didn't. He might get the day of the week wrong, or forget he'd been told something, and once or twice he'd forgotten to turn off a ring on the hob (shh, don't tell Sara) but it wasn't as though he had taken to wandering off and forgetting where he was, and had to be brought home by the police.

'I worry about you,' she said. 'Indulge me, please.'

'And you suffocate me.' The words were out before he'd thought about them. Oh, dear…

Sara's reply was stiff. 'I'm sorry you feel like that. 'I'm just trying to look out for you.'

He flopped back into his seat, all the defiance suddenly gone. 'I know you are, love, and I appreciate it.'

'It doesn't seem like it.'

'I do,' he protested. And he did. He just wasn't used to his daughter's level of concern. Dorothy used to let him get on with things, let him potter. He'd done the same with her. And since her passing, he'd become even more used to doing his own thing. It was hard when he suddenly had someone to answer to. 'I'm just not used to it,' he said.

'Aw, Dad, that makes me feel awful. I have tried to look out for you since Mum died, but it's not been easy with you living so far away. It wasn't as though I could pop in on the way home from work every evening.'

He couldn't win. He'd upset her again, and now she was grim-faced and pursed-mouthed. How the hell was he supposed to carry on living like this? He didn't know what David thought about him moving in, but it wasn't working out. He and Sara kept rubbing each other up the wrong way; he had to shoulder most of the blame (take the last few minutes of him being childish, for instance), but dear God she deserved it sometimes.

Why was he surrounded by annoying, bossy, do-good women? Sara was bad enough, but now he had Hattie Jenkins to contend with, too.

Despite him not wanting anything more to do with toys or toymaking, what Hattie and Logan had done for him yesterday touched his heart. The fact that a pair of complete strangers had gone to so much trouble made him tear up. That his own daughter hadn't even asked what he'd wanted to do with all the stuff in his shed and had immediately relegated it to the skip, made him feel like crying even more.

Despondent and miserable, Alfred retreated to his bedroom, trying to stay out of Sara's way, and listened to Radio 2 until he heard Shelley and her boyfriend arrive.

Shelley was nothing like her mother. She was bubbly and outgoing, and full of life and happiness. It was a joy to have her around, and Alfred often wondered if she'd been swapped at birth in the hospital, because she didn't follow Sara or David, although she did remind him a little of his Dorothy when he first met her, before life became serious and grown up.

Shelley might have a responsible job, and she might have a mortgage and a live-in boyfriend (Shelley called Callum her "partner", which to Alfred made him sound more like a business proposition than a love interest), but his granddaughter was still like a bottle of champagne with the cork out – all fizz and effervescence.

She was a breath of fresh air. But what Alfred loved about her the most, was that she didn't treat him like an old person.

With a smile on his face, he hurried downstairs.

'Grandad! Yay!' Shelley cried, pushing past her mother and throwing herself into his arms.

'Oof!' Alfred staggered back, glad that the wall was directly behind him. He hugged her back.

'I've got some news,' she whispered in his ear at the same time as her mother said, 'Shelley, be careful, you almost knocked your grandad over.'

Shelley pulled back in concern and Alfred winked at her. 'No, you didn't.' He waited until Sara turned away before he whispered back, 'What's the news?'

'Later, after lunch. Try to be pleased for me, Grandad? Because I don't think Mum will be.'

Alfred nodded and caught Callum's eye. Callum smiled, but he also looked nervous, and Alfred made an educated guess as to what the news might consist of.

His guess was correct, he discovered as, with lunch over, Sara rose from her seat to clear the table and Shelley said, 'Um, sit down, Mum, I've…' She smiled at Callum. '*We've* got something to tell you.' She paused for the briefest of seconds before announcing, 'We're pregnant.'

There was a small silence, and Alfred jumped in to fill it. 'That's wonderful news. I'm going to be a great grandad!'

'Yes, wonderful, darling,' Sara said, looking less than pleased, but trying to pretend she was. 'Gosh, I'll be a grandma. Not granny, or nanny; *grandma*.' She put a hand to her chest. 'I feel so old.'

Try being *my* age, Alfred nearly said.

'Age is just a number, Mum, and you're as old as you feel,' Shelley said.

Ah, the confidence and ignorance of youth, Alfred thought. A twenty-six-year-old Alfred wouldn't have been able to imagine being old, either. You had to live it, to fully appreciate it he thought – if *appreciate* was the correct word to use. In a way, Shelley was right though, because if you didn't know Hattie was eighty, you'd put her age at ten or fifteen years younger. She was as full of beans as Shelley was, so Sara couldn't use her own age as an excuse for being a miserable sod.

Alfred had a feeling that Hattie and Shelley would get on like a house on fire. They had similar outlooks on life and a similar enthusiasm for it.

Tuning back into the conversation, he saw that Sara's initial shock had worn off and she had her organising head on and was discussing the practicalities of childcare and living arrangements.

'I might have retired,' his daughter was saying, 'but I'm not sure how much help I'll be able to give once the baby arrives.' She sent a meaningful look in his direction, and Alfred immediately felt guilty for being a burden to her.

Not that he'd asked for her help – she'd insisted on providing it – but he still felt bad that Sara thought he needed looking after to the extent that she wouldn't be able to mind the baby a couple of days a week, like Callum's mother had offered to do.

'I'm not sure how you're going to manage,' Sara said to Shelley, but David jumped in with, 'I'm sure they'll cope. They know what they're doing,' and Alfred saw the grateful smile Shelley gave him.

'It'll work itself out,' Shelley breezed. 'These things always do, and it's not as though we haven't thought it through.'

Sara blinked, and Alfred realised that his daughter had assumed the pregnancy had been unplanned. Before she could wade in and spoil what should be a wonderful moment for Shelley, Alfred said, 'I know it's a bit soon, but I've got some lovely wooden toys the baby could have.' He'd pop over to Hattie's shed and set aside a few pieces before Hattie got rid of them.

'I don't think so, Dad,' Sara interjected. 'They're hardly baby-friendly, and it'll be ages before the baby is old enough to be able to play with them. We simply haven't got the room to store them. Besides, I bet they don't meet today's stringent manufacturing standards.'

'Grandad?' Shelley was staring at him, her head tilted at an angle as she studied him. 'Are you talking about toys from when you were a child?'

'No, I—' Alfred began.

'Everything is being cleared on Friday, Dad. I thought we'd agreed?' Sara rose again, and began to stack the dishes, her face determined, and he knew the subject was closed.

His daughter was probably right – who'd want tatty cobbled-together, hand-made toys for their child, when they could pop down to one of the big shopping centres and buy some colourful character-driven stuff that was all the rage. He had thought his toys weren't half bad, but he was probably wrong. He guessed he always knew that, which was why he'd never told anyone of their existence, not even Dorothy.

It looked like Sara was right, and that he wouldn't be able to give them away. Oh, well, it was Hattie's problem now; he was in no position to dispose of them.

While lunch was being cleared away, Alfred made his excuses and took himself back upstairs, for once not in the mood to listen to his granddaughter's excited chatter.

He dropped down on the foot of the bed and

stared morosely out of the window. In five days his house would no longer look like his house. Stripped of everything which had made it his and Dorothy's home, it would be an empty box, and the thought made him incredibly sad.

Laughter drifted up the stairs, and he knew he should join the others, if only to stop Sara from saying something she'd regret. Plus, he didn't want her to think that having Shelley and Callum here was too much for him to cope with.

He clambered heavily to his feet, his heart a dead weight inside, and he was about to leave the room when he spotted his bunch of keys on top of the chest of drawers. Most of them were of no use to him now, so he picked them up and, with a bit of a struggle (his fingers weren't quite as dexterous as they once were) he removed the keys to his old house from his key ring. He'd never need them again. It was a wonder Sara hadn't asked for them to give to the estate agent when it went on the market, but he supposed it was only a matter of time.

All he was left with was the front door key to Sara's house and one other which he didn't recognise. It was long and silver-coloured and for the life of him he couldn't think which lock it fitted. In fact, he couldn't remember it at all, and the blood froze in his veins. Was this confirmation of Sara's suspicion that he was in the early stages of dementia?

He brought it closer to his face and squinted at it. There was a tiny sticky label and he struggled to read the small spidery handwriting. It said "Shed", and he knew without being told that the lock it was meant for was on Hattie's shed door.

He should tell her how grateful he was for what she and Logan did – and also tell her that he'd made his decision and that she should get rid of the lot of it. Maybe they could take it back to his house and shove it all back in his shed? Let someone else dispose of it.

He'd take his walk now, and pop in to see her and tell her his decision. It wasn't far into the village and the fresh air would do him good.

'We're just leaving, Grandad,' Shelley said when he went downstairs, and once more she gathered him into a hug. 'Thanks for being so understanding. I think it was a bit of a shock for Mum.'

'It certainly was, but a good shock.'

'Hmm.' Shelley didn't sound so sure.

'Whatever your mum thinks, it's your life and you've got to live it your way,' he told her.

'Back at ya, Grandad,' Shelley countered, kissing him on the cheek. 'Don't let her boss you around.'

'Easier said than done.'

Shelley looked him in the eye. 'Is it?'

He was about to say that it was, when a thought

struck him. If he did decide to put his foot down a little more, what was the worst that could happen? Sara was hardly likely to throw him out, but even if she did, he'd still have the money from the sale of his house to fall back on.

He hadn't thought of that before, and he filed the knowledge away to examine later.

He'd be quite well off...

'I was about to give you a shout and let you know that Shelley and Callum were just off,' Sara said, appearing in the hall, and he waited for his granddaughter and her partner to leave before he announced he was going for a walk.

'It's four o'clock. It'll be dark in half an hour,' Sara pointed out.

'I'm not scared of the dark.'

Sara rolled her eyes and huffed. 'Where were you thinking of going?'

'Just around the village. I like to have my daily constitutional.'

'You should have gone earlier.'

'I didn't want to go then. I want to go now.'

'I'll come with you.' She sighed as she said it, so he could tell she didn't fancy the idea one little bit.

'I'll go,' David offered. 'I could do with some fresh air, myself. And I need to walk off that fantastic lunch.'

'You don't have to,' Alfred protested. 'I'll be fine on my own.'

'I know you will, but with me working all week I don't get to spend much time with you,' his son-in-law said.

No, he didn't, Alfred agreed, but why did the bloke have to pick this afternoon to spend time with him? He wanted to let Hattie know about his decision so she could get on with shifting the toys out of her shed. It must be an inconvenience for her to have it chock-full of his old rubbish.

'I went to your house this morning, Alfie,' David said to him, once they were clear of the drive.

'Oh, yes?' Alfred tried not to let his sorrow show. 'Would you mind awfully, if you called me Alfred, not Alfie?'

David said mildly, 'Of course not. It is your name, after all.'

'Thank you.'

'Just out of curiosity, what's wrong with Alfie?'

'Nothing, I suppose. Except I never felt like an Alfie. It's too…' He tried to find the right word.

'Childlike?'

'Yes!'

'Alfred it is. As I was saying, I popped along to your house today. I've been checking on it every few days to make sure there's not been a leak, or a break in, or anything...' He trailed off and Alfred was conscious of the man's stare.

'Was everything OK?' It was bound to be – Alfred had only been there yesterday.

'Fine, although one of the neighbours said something strange. You remember Mrs Snelby...?'

'Why wouldn't I? I lived next door to the woman for twenty-odd years.'

'She said she thought she'd seen you there yesterday, along with a woman and man, neither of whom she recognised.'

'Did she? How strange.'

'That's what I thought. She also said someone had been in your shed last night. She was going to call the police, but she saw it was the same couple who'd been there earlier with you.'

Alfred gave David a blank look, all the while trying frantically to think of a reasonable explanation.

'I took a look in the shed,' David said. 'It was empty.'

'Really?'

'Yes, really.'

'I suppose that saves the house clearance company from having to dispose of it.' Alfred's thoughts churned along with his stomach. 'Was anything else missing?'

'Nothing. It looks like they were only interested in

the contents of the shed.'

'Blimey.'

'Yes, blimey. Any ideas of what might have happened to it?'

Alfred shrugged.

'Let's hope it's gone to a good home, eh?' David said. 'I bet you're pleased that Sara talked you out of giving any of the toys to Shelley for the baby. There's nothing left in the shed to give her. Not even a stick of wood.'

Alfred looked straight ahead and kept on walking. For a while the only sound was their footsteps and the tap, tap, tap of his walking stick as it hit the pavement.

'I must say, whoever has taken them was very thorough,' David added. 'And the timing is good, too. If they'd left it until next weekend, then the place would have been empty.'

'Shame,' Alfred muttered, glad it was too dark for David to see the heat in his cheeks. He was certain he must be blushing.

A few more steps brought them to the bridge over the river. It wasn't much of a river. Hardly more than a stream, Alfred thought, even after all the rain they'd had. But it was pretty enough, and visitors to the village seemed to like it. It was strung with lanterns, their light reflected in the dark water below. It made the bridge look festive and cheerful, and when he looked at the streets which lay to either side, he noticed the street decorations were lit.

Christmas wasn't the same any more, not without Dorothy to enjoy it with him.

'Shall we turn back?' he suggested, feeling suddenly tired.

'If you like. I'm glad we had this little chat.'

Alfred wasn't.

'Sara has got your best interest at heart, you know,' David added. 'She's just got a funny way of showing it, that's all.'

'I know.'

'We want you to be happy living with us. Please tell me if there's anything we can do…?'

Alfred breathed deeply, the scent of the river filling his nose, the cold air sharp and refreshing after the warmth of the house. He shrugged again. Sara was Sara, and she wasn't about to change. For her, backing off and leaving him to it wasn't in her nature. Especially when she thought she was doing the right thing.

Dear God, was this what his life was going to be like until he pushed up the daisies?

He bloody hoped not. He didn't think he could bear it. He wasn't sure what was worse – living on his own, lonely and depressed, or living with Sara where it was like being in prison, and he was still depressed and still lonely, despite the other occupants in the house. If this was what it was going to be like for however many years he had left, then they might as well shoot him now and put him out of his misery.

'There is one thing that baffles me,' David said, as they started to stroll back, their breath pluming in the air. 'There was no sign of a break-in; absolutely no damage whatsoever. If I didn't know better, I'd say they'd had a key.'

The look his son-in-law gave him was loaded with meaning, and Alfred's heart sank.

Then David winked, and suddenly life didn't seem quite so dreary after all.

CHAPTER 15

HATTIE

There were less than six weeks to Christmas. If they were going to do this, they would have to do it soon, Hattie mused. And they hadn't got any money to spend, so it would all have to be done on a shoestring. Plus, there was nothing available in terms of shop space to rent anywhere in the village.

After having a long hard think for most of the day yesterday and a great deal of last night, she had come to the conclusion that it was a fab idea to open a temporary shop in the run-up to Christmas to get rid of all Alfred's toys, but unfortunately it was dead in the water.

With her mind still churning and getting nowhere, Hattie went into work. As the festive season began to ramp up, she knew she'd be asked to do a few more hours – but this also meant that even if the idea of opening a toy shop was a goer, Hattie's ability to help make it a reality would be seriously curtailed. Ticklemore wasn't a large place, but its wonderful selection of little specialist stores and artisan shops attracted people from miles around who were hoping to find that extra-special or unusual gift. Then there were places like the butcher and the baker, even a candlestick maker (stockist actually, since the Soapbox, who sold handmade soaps and all things bath related, also sold candles) where people could pick up their food supplies. All that shopping invariably led to the need for coffee and cake in one of the three cafés in the village, and Bookylicious received its fair share of patronage, especially since books were also a great idea for Christmas presents.

Instead of a shop (which was rather ambitious, she conceded) maybe they could hold a sale in the church hall? That might work. The vicar had loads of trestle tables because regular jumble sales and sales of bric-a-brac were often held there. Of course, there was the danger of it actually looking like a jumble sale. What Hattie had in mind was more in keeping with the Ticklemore Treasure Trove – upmarket and tasteful. To do them justice, the toys needed a proper shop.

But that was where the idea she and Nell had yesterday, had fallen apart.

Hattie didn't want to do this half-heartedly. In fact,

she wasn't sure she wanted to do this at all.

It was a silly idea – she'd been swept along by Nell's enthusiasm. But then, Nell was a businesswoman, who'd reinvented herself after she'd discovered her husband had cheated on her. She was strong and determined, a bit of a go-getter. She wasn't old and past-it and totally out of her depth, like Hattie was. Despite Nell's offer of help, Hattie knew it would be mostly down to her if she wanted to get a toy shop up and running, and she wasn't sure whether she had the time or the energy, despite having enough enthusiasm to open twenty shops.

There was another problem, too – Alfred.

For any of this to work, Hattie would have to present the idea to him fully formed. Not the half-arsed vague idea that it currently was.

Forget it, she told herself. She'd pop in and see Nell later and ask her if she could stick with the original plan of the Treasure Trove stocking a few bits and pieces. If they sold, great. If they didn't, no one had lost anything.

'Morning,' Maddison chirped. 'You look like you've got the weight of the world on your shoulders. You look tired, too. Are you feeling OK?' She walked past with a slice of chocolate and pear cake on a plate. It looked delicious.

'I am a bit tired,' she said, when Maddison walked

past her the other way, having delivered the cake to a customer. Hattie followed her out to the kitchen at the rear, where she divested herself of her coat.

'What's up?' Maddison rubbed Hattie's arm and gave her a look of concern.

'A man by the name of Alfred, that's what.'

'What's he done? If he's upset you, I'll sort him out. Is he here now?' Maddison peered through the door with narrowed, suspicious eyes and scanned the café.

'He's not done anything. Well, he has, but not the sort of thing you're thinking, and no, he's not here now. He was in on Thursday – I asked if you knew him. Espresso and red velvet cake? I had a feeling in my water about him?'

'I remember the conversation, but I thought you said he was elderly?'

'He's about my age,' Hattie said, pulling a face. 'He was in on Saturday, too, but he was looking for a copy of the Yellow Pages.'

Maddison frowned. 'I've never heard of it. Do we stock it?'

'No – it's a telephone directory that BT used to deliver to every property which had a phone.'

Maddison raised her eyebrows.

'It's true! It wasn't too long ago that the internet didn't exist, you know. Anyway, Alfred wanted me to look up the number of one of those places you can rent to put stuff in that you want to store, and he also wanted the number of a man with a van.' She took a deep breath and forged on. 'The long and the short of it is that his daughter has made him move out of the house he's lived in for donkey's years because she says he's a danger to himself, and she made him move in with her.'

'You make it sound like he's had his arm twisted.'

'He did, I reckon. Anyway, the daughter has arranged for one of those clearance companies to empty the house, and he decided to put everything in storage instead because he couldn't bear to part with it.'

'It's a compromise, I suppose,' Maddison said, checking that no customers wanted to be served.

'Hardly. He didn't intend to tell his daughter, but when we got there—'

'You went with him? That was kind of you.'

'Me and Logan. I said Alfred could put everything in my shed and Logan offered the use of his van and his muscles.' Seeing Maddison's bemused expression, Hattie added, 'Don't ask. Anyway, when we got there, Alfred had so much stuff and most of it was old and hideous, that there was no way all of it was going to fit in my shed. Me and Logan made him see sense, though – when was he ever going to use any of it again? I mean, even if he got himself one of those OAP flats, only a fraction of his stuff would fit in. Maybe his bed, but even that was a great big sleigh bed made of dark brown wood.'

'That sort of furniture is coming back into fashion,' Maddison pointed out.

'That's as may be, but Alfred decided that hanging onto his furniture wasn't such a good idea after all, so we came away empty-handed.'

'The poor man. I bet he was upset.'

'He was, but I think what upset him the most was that he had to leave behind what was in his shed.'

'Oh?' Maddison began to look alarmed. 'And what was in his shed?' A hand flew to her mouth and her eyes widened. 'Don't tell me it was a huge chest freezer with a body in it?'

Hattie screwed up her face. 'Don't be silly! You've been watching too much crap on TV. There was no body, nor a chest freezer for that matter.' She paused dramatically. 'His shed was full of toys.'

Her boss froze as she thought about it. 'I'm not sure that's much of an improvement on the body. An old man hoarding loads of toys is slightly creepy, isn't it?'

'Not when he's made them all himself. You should see them – they're bloody marvellous. All of them are made out of bits of old wood, and they're the traditional kind, like dolls' houses and pull-along dogs, and a Noah's Ark. Not a bit of plastic in sight.' She took another deep breath. 'And that daughter of his wants to bin the lot. It's criminal, I tell you. So that's why me and Logan heisted Alfred's keys and went back on Saturday night and took them to my shed.'

'Okaaay…' Maddison blew out her cheeks. 'You're telling me that you broke into some old guy's house and stole the contents of his shed.'

'We didn't break in; we had a key.'

'Which you also stole. I can't believe you roped Logan in – I thought he was more sensible. Does anyone else know about this?'

'Nell.'

'From the Treasure Trove?'

'Yep. Me and her came up with the idea of opening a shop. I went to ask her if she'd sell a couple of bits in the Treasure Trove but when she saw just how many toys there were…'

'Does she know they're stolen?'

'Not stolen. Alfred had agreed that his daughter should dispose of them. Anyway, he knows we rescued them because he saw them on Saturday night.'

Maddison sighed with relief. 'That's OK then. For a minute, I thought I might be harbouring a criminal. Tell me more about the shop.'

Hattie waved a hand dismissively. 'It was a great idea, but it's simply not feasible, I'm afraid. For one thing, there isn't anywhere suitable in Ticklemore, and for another the stuff mightn't sell. And think of the money it would cost to get it up-and-running.'

'It was Nell's idea, you said?' Maddison was tapping her lip with her fingers and frowning.

'We both thought of it.'

'But Nell did mention it?'

'She more than mentioned it – we talked about it in depth.'

'If Nell thinks a shop would work, then it probably would. She's one astute lady and has good business acumen. And if this were to work, now is the best time of year to open a toy shop,' Maddison pointed out. 'Hang on, I'm just popping out for a couple of minutes. Will you and Teresa be OK on your own for a while?'

'We should be, although I'd better get out there and give her a hand. We've got a few more customers in. Who is manning the bookshop?'

'Rhea – her mother is looking after the baby on Mondays, Wednesdays, and Fridays. I won't be long. I've got my mobile if you need me.'

Hattie made shooing motions with her hands. 'We'll be fine.'

And they were, although there was a rush at about

eleven-thirty, with mince pies and hot chocolate selling like billy-oh because there was an offer on.

Hattie was just giving a new order to Teresa who was on coffee-machine duty, when Maddison returned.

She was grinning like the Cheshire Cat as she bounced in through the door and hurried straight over to Hattie.

'I think I might have an answer to your shop problem,' she said in a low voice. 'The Soapbox has closed down.' She opened her hand to reveal a small bunch of keys.

'Are you sure? I walked past it this morning, and it didn't look closed to me – there's stuff in the window.'

'Dusty stuff, and the sign on the door says closed. There wouldn't have been any lights on, either.'

'Now you come to mention it…'

'I'd heard on the grapevine that Prue and Cheryl had handed the keys back to the letting agent and the shop was available to rent again, so when you mentioned suitable premises in Ticklemore, I immediately thought of it.'

'Why are they giving up the shop?' Hattie was immediately suspicious. She'd been under the impression that the Soapbox had been doing OK. So why cease trading just before the busiest time in most shop-keepers calendar?

'Personal reasons,' Maddison said. 'Nothing to do with the business or sales.' She shook the keys at her.

'I don't know…'

'Talk it over with Alfred and see what he thinks. In the meantime there's nothing to stop you from taking a look at the place. You can pop along now, if you want.'

Hattie thought furiously. It seemed like the answer to the problem – one of them, anyway, and there wasn't any harm in taking a look, was there? She snatched the keys from a smug-faced Maddison, and folded them into her hand.

But as for talking it over with Alfred… hmm.

CHAPTER 16

ALFRED

Is Hattie in today?' Alfred gazed around Bookylicious expectantly, hoping to spot her. He didn't see her serving in the café, but she could well be in the bookshop part. He didn't think Hattie worked every day, although he didn't know for sure. He'd have to pop along to her cottage instead, and see if she was in.

'Sorry, she's not. Are you Alfred, by any chance?' a young lady wearing a pinny with the name of the shop emblazoned on it asked.

'Yes, that's me.'

'I've heard a great deal about you,' the woman said, and Alfred shot her a sharp look.

'Nothing bad, I hope?' What *had* Hattie been saying about him?

'All good, I assure you,' she said, and he turned to

leave. 'She's taking a look at your new premises, if you want to join her. It's called the Soapbox and it's only three doors down.'

He gave her a blank look.

'Of course!' the woman exclaimed. 'She probably hasn't had a chance to tell you yet, and I expect she wanted to check it out first in case it isn't suitable.' A movement caught her attention. 'Sorry, I've got to go – customers.'

Bemused, Alfred watched her hurry over to a lady hovering by the counter, then he left the café and stood uncertainly on the pavement. Should he wait here for Hattie to come back, or should he wait outside the Soapbox?

He opted for the Soapbox, in case she came out and went in the opposite direction. He didn't want to miss her – the sooner he told her, the sooner she could get rid of everything in her shed. He hated to be a nuisance since she'd gone to all that trouble.

The Soapbox showed a remarkable lack of soap. Or much of anything else. The window display was intact, but if one made the effort to look past it, the inside was practically bare. There was a blind pulled down over the glass in the door and a sign which said closed.

He couldn't see any movement and he hoped he hadn't missed her. He was too old to go chasing all over the village looking for her, so he pushed the handle down and gave the door a nudge in the vague hope that Hattie was still there and out the back somewhere.

It opened and he stepped inside, his walking stick making a dull noise on the wooden floor. 'Hello? Anyone there?' he called.

The silence deafened him.

Great. Now he'd have to go back to Bookylicious and tell the nice young lady who owned it that Hattie had left the door to the Soapbox unlocked, which meant more running around and his poor old legs simply weren't up to it today. Neither was the rest of him, if he was honest.

He was about to leave, wondering if there was a latch he could engage, when he heard a noise behind him.

'Alfred?' Hattie had emerged from a door at the rear of the shop and was looking rather surprised. 'How did you know I was here?'

'The nice young lady at Bookylicious told me.' Now that he was standing in front of her, he wasn't sure how to break it to her, and he found himself doing a slow turn and scanning the space, then saying instead, 'What do you think then?'

'About the shop?'

'Yes, the shop,' he replied.

'It'll need a good clean and some bright paint, but everything you need is here – shelves, counter, till. There's a storeroom out the back, a loo, and a tiny kitchen area. Are you any good with windows?'

Alfred squinted at her. 'I've cleaned a few in my time.'

'Yes, they'll need that too, but I meant decorating them.'

'For Christmas?'

'Well, yes. That's the whole point, isn't it? Unless…?' Hattie's eyes lit up. 'Ooh, that's wonderful news!' Then she immediately sobered. 'Oh dear, you won't be able to do both, not at the same time anyway. Why don't you see how the shop pans out first? I mean, I understand that making the toys is what you enjoy doing, but—'

'What are you talking about?' Alfred interrupted. She was blathering on and he didn't have a clue what she saying. What did making toys have to do with any of this?

'Alfred, you need to be sensible. You can't be in two places at once. If you intended to keep the shop on after Christmas – and I think that's a wonderful idea, by the way – then you'll have to employ someone to run the place. And that's a whole heap of work. Have you thought of a name for it?'

She was seriously cuckoo. It was a wonder the nice

young lady in Bookylicious let Hattie work there – the woman was a menace. Look at how she'd scared him off the first time he'd met her. If she spoke to all the customers the way she'd spoken to him, it was a miracle any of them came back. He had to take his hat off to the owner though – not many people would employ someone like Hattie. Maybe the girl felt sorry for her. Or maybe they were related and she felt obliged to give Hattie a job. Or, and this was the more likely explanation – they were related and giving Hattie a job meant that the girl would keep an eye on the old biddy for most of the day. And maybe Hattie had good days and bad ones, and this was one of her bad ones. She'd seemed quite with-it on Saturday when she'd looked up those storage facility details that he'd asked for, so this must be one of her not-so-good days.

Poor sod. He sometimes got confused, but he was nowhere near as bad as this old lady was today. He couldn't make head nor tail of what she was saying.

'You need something catchy, like Bookylicious, only nothing to do with books, obviously,' Hattie continued.

'I've come to tell you to get rid of all the stuff in your shed,' he said, trying to make her understand.

'I thought that's what we were doing.' Hattie gestured around the shop, and Alfred shook his head.

It must be awful to be OK one day, then not have a clue what was going on the next. It made his own occasional forgetfulness pale into insignificance.

Actually, for the past week or so, he'd been feeling tonnes better. More on the ball, so to speak. He was still as miserable as sin (he'd turned into a right grumpy git since Dorothy had passed on) but his mind felt sharper than it had for a long time. It might have something to do with having to use his brain to try to circumvent his daughter. They do say the brain is like any other muscle, and if you don't use it, you lose it.

'I don't care what you do with them,' he said. 'Give them away, put them in the skip – just get shot of the lot. Let's face it, that part of my life died when—' The words caught in his throat and he stopped speaking. Every so often a wave of grief rolled over him, usually when he least expected it.

'But I thought…? What did Maddison tell you I was doing here?' Hattie was studying him intently, as if she knew he was close to tears.

Maddison! That was her name. 'She told me you were taking a look at her new premises.' He frowned, wondering what was going on, because something most definitely was.

'She said that? Those were her exact words?'

'Er… I'm not sure.' Please don't let me be having

one of my episodes, he prayed. 'Um… she said…' He snapped his fingers and pointed, as he suddenly remembered. 'She said, "she's taking a look at your new premises, if you want to join her". I think. No, I'm sure that's what she said.'

'What else did she say?'

'That was it, apart from saying it's called the Soapbox and it's three doors down from Bookylicious.'

Hattie heaved in a deep breath and rolled her eyes. 'No wonder you look so confused. When you said Maddison had told you where to find me, I assumed she'd told you everything.'

Alfred pursed his lips. 'You mean there's more?'

'Oh, yes, much more,' Hattie chirped happily. 'This is *your* shop, not hers or mine. I can see how you got the wrong end of the stick, though.'

'Mine.' His voice sounded as blank as his mind currently was.

'Don't you think it's a wonderful idea? I didn't come up with it all on my own, of course; it took two of us. Nell from the Treasure Trove had the same idea at exactly the same time. What do you think of that?'

Alfred wasn't thinking much of anything apart from "what the hell?"

Hattie stared at him expectantly, but he had no

idea what to say to her. In fact, he wasn't sure he had heard her correctly. Maybe he should make an appointment for another hearing test. It had been a while since he'd had one.

Hattie took another deep breath and dived back in. He could almost see her squaring her shoulders and rolling up her sleeves as she said, 'We think it's a marvellous idea. The shop is empty, the rent and business rates have been paid up to the end of January, and all it needs is a clean and a lick of paint. You'll have to sort out some insurance, but Nell or Maddison will help you with that, and you'll need to get the electric and telephone put into your name, but that's only a ten-minute job.' She stopped. 'What?'

'Are you listening to yourself?'

'What do you mean?'

'You're spouting all this rubbish about a shop and painting and insurance, and I still don't know what you're on about, woman.'

'You, opening a shop. Selling your toys.' She appeared to be perplexed by his lack of understanding.

Alfred looked around for a chair. Not seeing one, he perched on the edge of the window, the dusty and careworn display of soaps and candles at his back. He felt a bit wobbly and out of sorts, and totally and utterly perplexed. How had he gone from saying goodbye to the toys in his shed, to this nutter of a woman (*women* – there now appeared to be more than one of them) talking about him opening his own shop.

For God's sake, had the whole world gone mad?

'Think about it.' Hattie walked over to him, plonked her backside on the window ledge next to his, and sidled along until they were almost touching. Alfred shuffled away, a small cloud of dust rising up around them. He coughed and waved a hand in front of his face.

'You must be joking,' he said.

'I'm not. You don't want your toys to end up in a skip, do you?'

His fingers curled around the top of his walking stick. 'No.' He didn't, despite what he'd just said.

'Well, then. This way they won't have to.'

'Give them away,' he instructed.

'To whom?' Hattie had lifted her chin and was looking down her nose at him. 'I'm sure charity shops would take them, but they'd only sell them for a couple of pounds, and the people who buy them won't value them as much as if they'd paid what they're truly worth.'

'And how much is that?' he demanded, his tone sarcastic. 'Four pounds, five? Ten?'

'Nell reckons she could sell the pull-along dog for

over twenty-pounds. The Noah's Ark, fifty. And do you want to know how much she said the rocking horse is worth?'

Despite his reluctance to even entertain the idea, Alfred was curious. That particular toy had taken him months and months to make, and he'd poured his heart and soul into it, making sure he found just the right colour hair for the mane and tail, and putting layer after layer of varnish on the dappled paintwork of the body.

'Four hundred and fifty pounds!' Hattie declared triumphantly.

Alfred shook his head. No way was that possible. It simply wasn't.

'It should take pride of place in the window,' Hattie carried on, while he sat there, his mouth hanging open and his heart beating wildly. 'A beautiful thing like that is bound to draw people in. You must be so proud of it.'

He *was* proud; the rocking horse was one of the best things he'd made. He was also shocked, and he squeezed his eyes shut and lifted a trembling hand to his face. This couldn't be real. Could it? Hattie must be mistaken. This Nell woman, whoever she was, must have got it wrong.

Alfred could feel his blood pressure rising. These toys would be the death of him, he feared. If he'd known what he was letting himself in for by asking Hattie for help, he never would have spoken to her. Hell, he would never have made the damned things in the first place if he had known the trouble they would cause.

'What have you got to lose?' Hattie continued. 'I've got some spare paint, and I'm sure other people have, too. We can rope in some bodies to help with the cleaning. Nell will advise you on what to charge for each item. You only need to stay open until Christmas Eve, and what you don't sell you can give away.'

'It doesn't seem right.'

'What doesn't?'

'Selling them. Not when I'd already made up my mind to give them away or throw them in the bin.'

'Then don't.'

Tension drained out of him, and he slumped forward. Thank God Hattie was seeing sense. The sooner the toys were out of her shed and out of his life, the sooner she'd forget about this ridiculous idea. Maybe she'd also forget about him and find some other poor sod to annoy.

'Can I leave it up to you?' he asked. He didn't want to have to look at them again – he didn't think he could face another goodbye.

'If you want, but haven't you got a favourite

charity or two?'

He shook his head. 'A children's charity would be the most appropriate, don't you think?'

'An excellent idea. We need a name, though. How about the Ticklemore Christmas Toy Shop? After all, it *is* a toy shop and it *will* only be around for the festive season.'

Alfred tugged on his ear. He had a feeling that things were spiralling out of his control again. 'I don't follow.'

We can get some signs printed that says all proceeds to go to charity. But we need to decide on what those proceeds are because, as I said, we'll have to have insurance, and then there's the electricity.' She laughed and waved a hand in the air. 'Listen to me saying "we" all the time. It's your shop, your toys. I'm happy to be involved as much as you want me to be and as much as I'm able, of course.' She paused, gazing at him expectantly.

'I thought we agreed you were going to get rid of them,' Alfred said, finally, after a silence that went on for far too long. During that time, he'd watched Hattie's face transform from hopeful to glum.

'And I thought you'd decided to sell them and give the money to charity,' she retorted. 'Never mind.' Hattie got slowly to her feet and retied her scarf. 'I'll make sure they go to a good home.'

Alfred put out a hand and gripped her coat sleeve. 'How much did you say your friend could get for the rocking horse?' He watched the light creep slowly back into Hattie's eyes.

'Four hundred and fifty pounds,' she said.

'How much do you think a charity shop would sell it for?'

'Around here? A hundred, give or take. More if it was in London, I expect.'

'You promise that every penny of profit will go to charity?'

'It's your shop, your toys, your money.'

'And it only stays open until Christmas Eve?'

'Yes, but the lease—'

'Let's do it!'

'Are you sure?'

'You seem to be,' he replied, dourly.

'I don't want you changing your mind again.'

'I wouldn't have had to change it at all if you hadn't stolen the toys out of my shed.'

'That's harsh,' Hattie said. 'We thought we were doing you a favour. It's not too late to put them back.'

Oh, it *was* too late, David's visit to his old home had seen to that. And now Hattie had put the idea in his head, he knew that opening the shop and selling the toys was the right thing to do. So was giving the profits to charity.

There was a problem though – apart from the time and effort of getting the place ready – and that was, how was he going to keep this from Sara? It was all well and good David having a suspicion that Alfred had spirited the toys and all the equipment away, and his son-in-law possibly thought that he might take up toy making again, but it would be a different matter when he started selling the damned things for profit. Sara really would think he was suffering from dementia.

And on that note, when Hattie offered to show him around his new empire, Alfred muttered sotto voce, 'Challenge accepted.'

He just hoped he didn't live to regret this madness.

CHAPTER 17

HATTIE

'Order, order!' Hattie banged her fist on the table, then winced. She rubbed it ruefully and shot a quick look at the rest of the people in the Ticklemore Tavern to check they hadn't noticed.

They hadn't, she realised, when everyone kept on talking.

'Oi!' she yelled, and six pairs of eyes swivelled in her direction. She cleared her throat. 'Alfred can't be with us this evening because his daughter won't let him out to play. Besides, it's got to be kept a secret from her otherwise she'll put a stop to it, and we simply can't let that happen, for Alfred's sake.'

'I don't get it,' Silas Long said. 'Why bother?'

She wasn't sure she "got it" herself. All she knew was that Alfred needed this. Giving his toys away, or even holding a charity auction, wouldn't be the same.

It would be too easy, over too soon, and then he'd be back to being miserable again.

She understood why he was (God knows she'd been miserable enough when her Ted had passed away) but with help from her friends, she'd picked herself up and got on living the rest of her life as best she could. Hattie knew she was lucky – she'd been younger than Alfred when she was bereaved and with Maddison offering her a job at Bookylicious despite her age, she'd had plenty to interest her and keep her going.

Alfred didn't. She guessed that he felt he'd lost everything. It was down to her to make him realise he hadn't.

'Alfred is one of us now, a Ticklemore, and we look after our own,' she said. 'He needs our help and we're going to give it to him. After all, it's for a good cause, and I'm sure once people know you've donated your time – and other things – they'll be most appreciative. You know what they say about publicity, and this is good publicity.'

'What I don't get is, why won't Alfred's daughter let him come to the pub?' Silas asked.

'Because she thinks he's got dementia,' Hattie stated.

'Has he? Poor man.' Juliette from the Ticklemore Tattler shook her head. 'It's a terrible disease.'

Juliette should know, Hattie thought – her gran had suffered from it for years. She was dead now, bless her. Hattie remembered her well – she'd been in school with her, although Juliette's gran had been a couple of years above her. Gloria her name was and—

'I can't see it myself; can you, Hattie?' Logan said, breaking into her thoughts.

'See what? Oh, yes, we were talking about Alfred and dementia. No, I can't see it, either. Although he does have a bit of trouble following conversations, so there may be some truth in it. I suspect the problem is that he's not kept the old grey matter ticking over – which is why we need to help him get this shop up and running. Now then, Nell, can you sort out the lease thing and the rent? I know it's covered until the New Year, but we need to get something in writing.'

Nell nodded and made a note on the pad she was holding.

'Juliette, can you approach a couple of children's charities to see if they're happy for us to use their names? They might like to come to the official opening, too.'

'We're having an official opening?' Logan asked.

'I don't see why not.'

There were nods of agreement around the table.

'Juliette, might I talk to you about the charity thing

later?' Silas asked and Hattie sent him a curious look, but his expression was closed.

'Of course. Any suggestions would be welcome.' Juliette smiled at him, and Hattie was relieved to see that Silas managed a small one in return.

'How about another pint?' Benny asked.

'In a minute. Let's get this sorted first, then I'll treat everyone to another drink,' Hattie said.

'Oh, no you won't. You're a pensioner, you can't afford it. This one is on the house,' Logan said.

Hattie reached across the table and patted Logan on the cheek. 'You're a good boy. If I was twenty years younger...' She cackled loudly.

Nell said, 'It might be an idea to sort out some flyers and posters and put an advert in the Tattler. And I can ask the mayor if she'd like to support the event. I can also let you have some tissue paper for wrapping but not bags, I'm afraid, because they've got the Treasure Trove emblazoned all over them, but I can source some plain ones for you, if you like?'

'Brilliant. Juliette, if you could arrange for a piece to go in the paper? Benny and Logan, if you'd help with the cleaning and the painting, that would be great.'

'I've got a stack of paint down at the allotment,' Benny said. 'You're welcome to use as much of it as you like. I must warn you, the colours are rather boring.'

'Boring is good,' Hattie said. 'We want people looking at the toys, not the walls.' She also hoped the founding member of the Allotment Association would be up to stringing some lights and other assorted festive decorations around the shop – but she'd ask him for the next favour after he'd done the cleaning.

'What about me?' Silas asked. 'What can I do to help?'

'Can you design the flyers? I'm thinking of something old-fashioned, like a Victorian shop, in keeping with the type of toys being sold. And…?'

'Go on.' Silas shot the others a resigned look.

'Paint the sign above the shop?' Hattie sent him an ingratiating smile. 'Pretty please. You are Ticklemore's resident artist, after all.'

Hattie knew it was a big ask, and outside Silas' comfort zone. His work tended to be more watercolour than enamel, and more landscape than words. Meh, he'd manage.

'No problem,' he said, 'but I seriously don't like ladders.'

'Can we take the signage off and paint it on the ground?' Hattie asked.

'Possibly,' Father Todd, the final member of the Toy Shop Team, said. 'I'll fetch some ladders from the vicarage tomorrow and take a look.'

Hattie thought for a moment, while everyone who hadn't already finished their drinks, upended their glasses. 'I think we're done for this evening,' she said. 'If we can make a start on the cleaning tomorrow, Benny, assuming you haven't got anything on?'

'I'm all yours,' he said. 'I'll see if Marge can come, too.'

Benny's wife was a whirling dervish in the Women's Institute and was always busy, so Hattie wasn't hopeful, but if the woman could help out, Hattie would be very grateful. The more hands there were, the lighter the work would be.

Hattie banged the table again, though not so hard this time. 'One last thing – I propose an opening date for 30th November, which means the shop can trade for four whole weeks, and can also take advantage of the Christmas Fayre. I'm sure none of you have forgotten that it will take place the weekend after the opening date, so the shop needs to be up and running and all the wrinkles ironed out before then. What do you think?'

'That gives us less than two weeks to get everything ready,' Nell pointed out, a frown creasing her forehead.

Hattie thrust out her chest and gazed slowly around the table. 'We'd better pull our fingers out then, hadn't we? How about we meet again on Friday, same time, same place? And no excuses. This is for charity remember?'

She ignored the subsequent grumbles and helped Logan bring a fresh round of drinks to the table.

Once everyone was settled again, Hattie noticed that the grumbling had been replaced by curiosity about the toys themselves.

'Are they honestly good enough to sell?' Juliette asked.

Logan nodded, and put his pint down. 'Definitely. I'm no toy expert, but they looked very well made and bang on trend, too.'

Benny and Hattie, being the oldest of the group exchanged glances. 'I've never been quite sure what that phrase means,' Benny said.

Nell took up the reins. 'It means it's the "in" thing, that everyone wants.'

'Everyone wants wooden toys?' Benny looked mystified.

'Not toys, per se. Hand-made, good quality things. Original pieces. It helps that these toys hark back to customers' childhoods – or what they would have wanted their childhoods to be like. Personally, I had a hideous plastic doll called a Chatty Cathy. You pulled a cord in her middle and this scary mechanical voice came out.' Nell shuddered. 'But nostalgia is all the rage, as is the drive to use less plastic. It helps that toys like the ones Alfred has made, don't go out of fashion and they don't fall apart if you so much as look at them. Parents and grandparents will love them.'

'What about the kids themselves?' Silas asked.

'I don't know of one little girl who could fail to fall in love with a traditional dolls' house, or that gorgeous rocking horse.'

'Not just little girls! I always wanted a rocking horse,' Logan protested. 'And little boys like dolls' houses, too.'

'OK, Mr Politically Correct, you can get down off your high horse.' Hattie chortled and elbowed Logan in the ribs. 'High horse? Eh?'

Logan rolled his eyes and Nell tutted. 'Please tell me she's not always like this,' she said to the room in general and everyone laughed, including Hattie. If this lot didn't know her by now, then there was no hope for them. Take me as you find me, that was her motto.

She climbed unsteadily to her feet, clutching the table for support. 'I'd better be off home,' she declared, feeling suddenly weary.

All this thinking and planning had worn her out, not to mention the unaccustomed excitement. These days she wasn't used to anything more thrilling than listening to Mrs Hamilton's latest tale about her piles. The woman took a blow-up rubber ring with her everywhere she went, which she stuffed into her drag-along shopping trolley.

'I'll walk you back,' Silas offered, taking her by the elbow.

Hattie shook him off. 'I'm perfectly capable of making my own way home,' she snapped, then her attitude softened when he put his mouth to her ear and said, 'I want to see the toys.'

He waggled his eyebrows at her.

'Now?' she demanded.

'Yes, please.'

'Why—? Oh…' She hissed back, 'For the flyers?'

He nodded.

'Why didn't you say?' she asked in a more normal tone.

His breath tickled her ear as he said, 'Because I didn't think you'd want everyone else to come.'

He was right about that. Silas on his own she could just about cope with. He was a gruff character and tended to keep himself to himself and wasn't prone to chatter. She'd been surprised when Nell had managed to persuade him to get involved. He'd lived in the village for about five years, but so far he'd eluded Hattie's efforts to discover more about him. She knew where he lived, how old he was, that he liked a drop of Scotch and could eat a hotdog in one mouthful (village fete two years ago – she was still impressed), but that was it.

Despite her tiredness, she was more than happy for him to accompany her – if she was honest, it was *because* of her tiredness; she'd be able to hang onto his arm – as she would also use the opportunity to quiz him on his private life.

After saying their goodbyes and Hattie stringently reminding everyone of the necessity of them attending the next meeting, she slipped her arm through his and allowed him to steady her as they walked slowly towards her cottage.

'Can I ask you a personal question?' she said, and she felt Silas stiffen.

His reply was mild enough, as he said, 'It depends. I might not answer.'

'Have you got someone special in your life?'

'No.'

'Do you want to?'

'No.'

'Why not?'

'I just don't. What about you?'

'I can see what you're trying to do, young man. You're changing the subject.' She craned her neck and peered up at him. He was smiling. 'You're not going to tell me, are you?'

'Nope.'

'Spoil sport.'

'Nosey.'

'If you don't tell me, I won't let you see the toys,' she wheedled.

He snorted. 'I'm not ten, and I need to see them to get some ideas for the flyers.'

Hattie drew to a halt. She'd taken him down the alley at the rear of her cottage, rather than go through the house. She hadn't washed up the dishes from her evening meal, and she didn't want him to think she was slovenly. To be honest, she'd spent the time when she should have been clearing up her dinner things, resting in her armchair and psyching herself to go back out again. At this time of year, once she was indoors, she tended to want to stay there.

'Knock yourself out,' she said, flipping the latch on the garden gate and unlocking the shed door. She turned the light on and waited for Silas's reaction.

For a moment, there was none. He was as motionless as a block of ice, and she began to wonder if she, Logan, and Nell were deluding themselves into thinking Alfred's toys were better than they were. Silas was an artist – surely he should know quality when he saw it, and she had the awful feeling that he did and this wasn't it.

Biting her lip, she watched him take one step

deeper into the depths of the shed, then another, his eyes darting everywhere, from one object to the next, pausing briefly now and again, before moving on.

He picked up the nearest item, a stacking toy in the shape of a teddy bear, and ran his hands over it, scrutinising it closely as he did so. Putting it back, he picked the next thing off the shelf, this time a wicker basket filled with an assortment of brightly coloured fruit and vegetables.

But Hattie noticed that his attention kept returning to the rocking horse and the smaller hobby horses stacked next to it.

Unable to wait any longer, she cried, 'Well?'

'There are plenty of things I can work with,' he said. 'I especially like the hobby horses. They are such old-fashioned toys.'

'I mean, do you think they're as good as Nell says they are?'

'Oh, definitely. Without a doubt. It's rare to see this kind of quality and attention to detail these days.'

Hattie's breath whooshed out of her. 'Thank the Lord, for that! For a minute there, I thought you were going to say it was all rubbish.'

He plucked a little pink rabbit on wheels out of a box and cradled it, a faraway look in his eyes. 'It's remarkable. All of it.' He turned to her. 'I'm honoured to be involved. And you can tell your

Alfred that he's just made his very first sale.'

'But you don't know how much it is.'

Silas smiled. 'At the moment, neither do you. Whatever the amount, I'll pay it. Just let me know.' And with that, he turned smartly on his heel and was out of the door and down the lane before she could gather her thoughts.

Hattie remained where she was. Silas Long had a story inside him, and stories were meant to be told. She'd winkle it out of him one way or another, but for now she had more pressing things to attend to.

Slowly and with much huffing, she lifted one of the boxes of smaller toys off the shelf and carried it indoors. It was too cold to stay in the shed, and she fancied a bit of comfort, too. And a cup of cocoa and some hot buttered toast.

Once it was made and demolished, Hattie, all thoughts of bed gone, settled down to clean every single item in the box until it gleamed.

By the time her tired old bones sank into her mattress, the image of wooden toys floating behind her eyes, she was more exhausted than she could ever remember being. But what was really making her smile was the final image in her head before sleep claimed her – Alfred's dear grumpy face.

CHAPTER 18

ALFRED

Alfred waited for Sara to leave the house before he hastily donned his coat, hat and gloves and shuffled out of the door. Now that Hattie had talked him into a shop, he was desperate to find out what had been discussed yesterday evening at the pub.

He felt incredibly bad that he'd not been able to attend, and a part of him had been inclined to let David in on his secret. After all, the fella thought that he was responsible for the shed being emptied (when he hadn't been) so what harm would there be in confiding in him about the shop?

Then common sense kicked in and he realised it would be unfair of him to expect David to keep such a secret from Sara. It was one thing David *thinking* he knew something and Alfred not admitting to it, but if his son-in-law knew the full facts then he'd feel morally obligated to inform his wife; and that was as it should be. It wouldn't be right of Alfred to draw David into this batty scheme of Hattie's, and it would be even less right to expect the man not to tell the woman he loved. Alfred didn't want to put him in that position, no matter how much he needed David's help in escaping from the house on Castle Lane, because Sara wouldn't bat an eyelid if David suggested he took Alfred to the pub. But if Alfred tried to go there on his own at night? God help him, but he wouldn't hear the end of it, and if he insisted then the odds were that she'd do her own insisting and demand to accompany him.

It didn't take him long to make his way into the village and along the pretty high street, and as he walked, he paid more attention than usual to the shops he passed. All of them were looking very festive and jolly, and there was a definite feel of Christmas in the air. He could hear carols and other Christmas songs pouring out into the street every time a shop door opened – it seemed as though every shopkeeper in the village was getting in on the act. And it was something he should consider, too.

Although… and here was the strange thing… he felt the toy shop was far more Hattie's than his. Hell, everyone who turned up to the meeting last night had more claim on it than he did. He didn't even know the names of all those involved – but he intended to rectify that as soon as he spoke to Hattie. It would also help if he could phone her, so he'd ask for her number. Surely Sara couldn't object to him making friends? And neither could she object to him speaking to those friends on her telephone. He'd even pay for any calls he made; not that Sara and David were short of money (because they weren't) but he was hardly destitute himself, so it was only fair he paid his way.

As he walked past Bookylicious, the aroma of coffee wafted over him and he would have loved to have popped in for an espresso and a slice of Christmas cake or an iced ginger biscuit, but he didn't have the time, not if he wanted to do his bit at the toy shop. He did crane his neck to see if he could spot Hattie though, but it was no use. There were quite a lot of customers in the café side of the shop, and it didn't help that the windows were steamed up. He hesitated for a second, wondering if he should go inside, but decided against it. He'd try to catch her later. Anyway, she mightn't be working today.

Lights were on in the Soapbox – now renamed the Ticklemore Christmas Toy Shop – which was a good sign, and he could see a couple of figures moving around inside, so he opened the door and stepped over the threshold. As he did so, the smell of bleach and disinfectant, together with a lingering scent of the soaps and various bath products which used to inhabit the place, assaulted his nose, and he sneezed loudly.

'Bloomin' heck, mate you nearly gave me a heart attack,' a man's voice said, and Alfred dabbed at his watering eyes, just making out the figure of a middle-aged man who was sporting a snazzy pair of bright yellow Marigold gloves and clutching a large pink sponge. A bucket of water steamed at his feet, and a woman was standing next to him and gazing at Alfred curiously.

'I'm Alfred,' he said, and let out another almighty sneeze.

'Nice to finally meet you, isn't it, Marge?' the man said. 'I'm Barney, and this is my wife, Marge. We're part of the Toy Shop Team,' he added with some importance.

'Oh, well, thanks. I appreciate it.' Alfred wasn't entirely sure what the Toy Shop Team was, but if it meant that people were helping to get the place ready, then he was grateful. He was out of his depth, though – he could make toys in his sleep, but all this opening a shop malarkey was disturbing and worrisome. At least these strangers seemed to know what they were doing, and they appeared to be doing a good job of it.

The shop was already looking considerably more loved and cared for than it had when he'd last seen it, and that was only two days ago. It was easy to tell which bits had been cleaned and which were still to do, so he took off his coat and draped it over the counter. He eyed the electronic till which had been left behind by the previous owners with distaste. It obviously did the job it was intended to do, but it was an ugly monstrosity, not at all in keeping with his image of what the interior of the shop should look like, and he made a note to himself to replace it with the wooden one he'd made. It didn't work, obviously, but he could use a calculator to add up any purchases, and an old-fashioned duplicate book and pen for the receipts.

Suddenly, the thought of standing here, surrounded by all his toys and having to cope with people who wanted to buy them filled him with dread. What did he know about selling stuff? What did he know about running a shop?

Why, oh why had he let Hattie's enthusiasm run away with him?

It wasn't too late to back out. He hadn't signed anything, and all that had been done so far was some cleaning. He'd go to Hattie right now and let her know he'd changed his mind – that the idea would never work, and that they should knock the whole thing on the head. What had he been thinking of, agreeing to such a ridiculous notion? Maybe they could compromise and have a one-day sale in a community centre or church hall, or something?

'May I just say how wonderful we think you are,' Marge announced, and Alfred whirled around to find the woman standing right behind him. She looked incredibly formidable with her apron and rubber gloves. She had a bottle of disinfectant in one hand and a wire-wool soap pad in the other, and she looked as though she meant business.

'There aren't many people who'd be as generous, and the shop idea is simply genius,' she continued. 'Nell explained it all to me, about the amount of money which might be realised by doing it this way. Of course, we haven't seen the toys ourselves, have we, Benny? But Nell assures us that they're going to fetch a tidy sum.' She peered at him hopefully.

Alfred took the hint, but he didn't feel comfortable with yet more sets of eyes on his creations (how the hell he was going to cope with half of Ticklemore traipsing in and out of the shop was beyond him), so he said, 'They're locked away for now, but I'll see what I can do.'

Marge appeared satisfied with that because she nodded and returned to the shelf she was scrubbing, setting to with enthusiasm. Benny was going ahead of her and cleaning the walls, Marge following behind. Maybe Alfred could tackle the floor?

He was wondering whether there was a sweeping brush or a vacuum cleaner hidden away somewhere, when the door opened and Hattie breezed in.

'Hello, my lovelies! Oh, aren't you doing an excellent job?' she exclaimed taking in the progress. 'We'll be ready for painting by tomorrow at this rate. Well done! I knew we could rely on you, didn't we, Alfred?'

Alfred nodded, vaguely.

Hattie strode over to him and grasped his elbow. 'I want to show you something in the stockroom,' she said to him, and he allowed her to guide him through the door to the rear of the shop and out the back.

When they were safely out of earshot of the others, Hattie said, 'That's Benny Everson, and his wife, Marge. He used to work for the council but he's retired now, but is a big noise in the AA.'

Alfred's eyebrows rose.

'The Allotment Association,' Hattie explained. 'Marge is in the Women's Institute – if you want anything practical done, ask Marge. Everyone in the WI is terrified of her.'

She went to the door and peered through the crack, then came back to stand next to Alfred.

'We all met last night in the Ticklemore Tavern – it's a pity you couldn't have been there, but never mind. There was me, Logan, and Nell, of course, along with Benny who's going to help with the cleaning and painting, Juliette from the Ticklemoor Tattler, who's going to print some flyers, put a notification in the paper and organise the grand opening. Oh, and Silas Long, our resident artist – watercolours, you know – who's going to paint the sign for the shop and design the flyers I mentioned. And I mustn't forget Father Todd – but I'm not entirely sure what part he's playing.'

She paused for breath and Alfred blinked at her. Goodness, things certainly were moving at a bit of a pace.

'Nell is sorting out the lease with the property company and other stuff.' Hattie glanced at the ceiling. 'It looks like she's got the electricity switched on already – good for her! And she's arranging to have the phone line reconnected.' She paused. 'I think that's it; for now, unless you can think of anything else?'

Alfred shrugged. He wouldn't have thought of half of what had already been arranged. 'Can I stay and do some cleaning? I feel as though I should.'

'You do what you want,' Hattie told him. 'It's your shop.'

Was it? He didn't think so. It certainly didn't feel like it. Marge was more in control of it than he was. Bloody hell, the spiders had more ownership rights than he did. Not that any of the little creatures would dare show their faces in the shop after Marge had been through it. He could hear the rasp of soap pads on wood even from this distance.

Hattie must have seen the scepticism in his face, because she patted his arm. 'It *is* your shop. It's your idea and your toys. We're just helping you get it off the ground, that's all.'

His idea? Hmm. As far as he recalled, he'd had to be talked into it. However, it was for a good cause, and he knew that without the help of all these people (half of whom he had yet to meet) the shop would be dead in the water.

After Hattie returned to Bookylicious, Alfred helped in the toy shop for as long as he dared, then he made his way back to Sara's in plenty of time for dinner.

'Where've you been?' Sara asked as he propped his walking stick up against the wall in the porch. For once she sounded interested and not accusatory.

'Into the village. I popped into a shop or two, had a look around. I like to take a walk most days.'

'I know, and I'm glad to see you having some exercise. Did you buy anything?'

'Not today, but Christmas is coming, and I wanted to get a couple of ideas.'

'Don't spend too much, Dad.'

'I can afford it, especially now my house is being sold.'

'Don't start.'

'I'm not starting anything. I'm just saying that I'll soon have more money than I know what to do with. Fancy a cup of tea? I'm going to make a sandwich to go with it.'

'I'll make it, but dinner will only be an hour.'

'Sara, love, you've got to stop treating me like an invalid. I'm old, not incapable.'

'But—'

'No buts.'

Sara stepped closer and put her arms around him. Awkwardly, he patted her on the back. Since when had giving his only child a hug become so uncomfortable? It was like cuddling a stranger.

'I know, Dad, and I'm sorry. It's just that I worry about you. Ever since Mum died, I've worried about you – are you looking after yourself, are you lonely, are you coping on your own, are you eating properly?'

Alfred pulled away to look examine her face. 'I know you're only trying to do your best, but look at it from my point of view; I might have forgotten to eat a meal once in a while, I might not have cleaned the house to your mum's standard, and I mightn't be as steady on my feet as I once was, but to go from being completely independent to being treated like a naughty child hasn't been easy. Or pleasant.'

Sara's expression was horrified, but as much as she didn't want to hear it, it needed to be said. If he was to remain under her roof, then she had to loosen the reins.

'Dad, I—' Her voice broke and her eyes swam with tears. 'I care about you, that's all. I couldn't bear it if I lost you, too.'

'It is going to happen, love. Sooner or later.' Some days, especially during those immediately after Dorothy left him, he'd prayed it was sooner. 'So let's make the most of the time we do have, eh?' She didn't need to know how deep his despair had been – how deep it still was on occasion, although not so much these past few days.

Trying to lighten the mood, he hugged her to him then released her. 'So, what would you like for Christmas, eh? Any ideas? And what can I get David?'

'You sound as though you're looking forward to it this year,' Sara said and he knew she was thinking about last year and the year before that, when all he'd wanted to do was to forget the festive season existed and lock himself away until it was all over and sanity had returned to the world. This year he felt different, and the reason was clear. To him, at least.

'I am looking forward to it.' He still might not want much to do with carols and holly, baubles and fairy lights, but what he *was* looking forward to was seeing people's faces as they entered the shop and were transported back to a simpler era. He continued to have doubts that his little toys were as good as Hattie, Logan, and Nell said they were, but he brushed them aside.

The sound of the front door opening made both Alfred and Sara jump, and David strode in, halting when he saw the two of them.

'What's up?' he asked, his gaze going from one to the other.

'Nothing, my boy, just talking about Christmas,' Alfred said.

'Dad has been prowling around the village looking for ideas for presents,' Sara added, as David indicated they should move to the kitchen.

It was getting rather crowded in the hall and Alfred could murder a cuppa, so he hurried on ahead. All that emotional stuff had made him thirsty.

'Presents, eh? I've got one here that your dad might find useful,' David said, and Alfred turned around in time to witness his daughter and son-in-law exchanging the kind of look that made him realise the pair of them were in on it (whatever "it" was) together.

David handed Alfred a box. The picture on the lid depicted a mobile phone. Alfred took it warily, eyeing it as though it might contain an explosive device.

'Go on, open it,' Sara urged.

'It's one of those simple ones, where you can make phone calls or send texts but nothing else,' David explained as Alfred gingerly drew the phone out of the box and turned it over in his hands.

It had a flip top (Captain Kirk, anyone?) and buttons with numbers. It looked nothing like the flat, blank screens that were seen nowadays, but he remembered seeing mobiles like these years ago.

Experimentally, he flipped the top up and put it to his ear.

'You've actually got to phone someone first, Alfred,' David pointed out.

'I know that – I'm not totally past it.' He did wonder how that was done, though, as he scrutinised the buttons.

'I've pre-programmed it with the house phone number, my mobile, and Sara's mobile,' David said. He moved closer until he was standing shoulder-to-shoulder with him. 'Press number one and then this button, and…' He held up a finger and cocked his head to the side, listening.

A ringing noise emanated from the mobile, swiftly followed by the sound of the landline in the living room.

'When you want to end the call, you simply press

this button here,' David continued.

The ringing ceased.

'What do I do if I want to call someone else?' Alfred asked.

'Like who?' Sara tilted her head to the side.

Alfred gave her a look.

'Sorry, I'm doing it again, aren't I?' she said.

'Yep,' he agreed; she was, but at least she now realised when she was doing it. Taking pity on her and knowing that curiosity would be driving her mad, he added, 'Hattie, from Bookylicious. I might want to call her.'

Sara's eyebrows rose so far up her forehead that they nearly became airborne. She quickly glanced at David, before turning her attention back to Alfred, who was trying not to chuckle at the incredulous expression on her face.

'Got yourself a lady friend, have you?' David teased. 'Good for you.'

'Not at all. Not in the way you mean. She's a lady and she's a friend, but that's all.'

'It's OK to have a girlfriend.' David winked at him.

Alfred stuck his nose in the air. 'Are you going to show me how to make a call to someone I might actually want to speak to?' he asked, and his son-in-law barked out a laugh.

He showed Alfred what to do, then left him to it. Alfred examined the phone thoughtfully. It was easy enough, just a smaller, pocket version of the landline phone in the living room, so he soon got the hang of it. Wondering what Hattie's number was, he vowed to ask her tomorrow – he hated feeling out of the loop, but at least they could keep in touch. He'd ask her for the number of the Ticklemore Tavern, too. But he'd wait until he knew the others slightly better before he started ringing them, and he hadn't met half of them yet.

Maybe, now that he was contactable, Sara wouldn't get so uptight if he went out, which might mean more freedom for him. He didn't think she'd be at all happy about him opening a shop, though, so he needed to continue to keep schtum about it. God knows what he would do when the place was open and he had to be there all day, but he'd cross that bridge when he came to it – one step at a time, he told himself.

He took the phone upstairs for safekeeping and decided to put it on the chest of drawers next to his keys. There was one thing he wanted to do though, before he switched it off to save the battery, and he sat on the side of his bed and rang a telephone number that he'd carry in his heart to the end of his days.

It wasn't a surprise when he heard the tone which

signified that the phone number in his own house was no longer in service.

Of course, it wasn't, but why did he feel as though it was another nail in the coffin of his old life?

CHAPTER 19

HATTIE

Benny and Marge had gone by the time Hattie popped back into the shop after work. That the electricity was on was a bonus because it was already dark outside and she could see that the pair of them had worked fast. The place was spotlessly clean, even the overhead lights had been dusted, and she guessed that was down to Marge, who undoubtedly had sent Benny up the ladder as per her instructions (she must remember to buy her a bunch of flowers as a thank you). Now for the painting.

The shop looked good but not quite good enough; there were scuff marks that no amount of scrubbing would remove and some chips in the woodwork that only a dab of paint would hide. Hattie noticed a couple of tins of paint stacked neatly in one corner, along with several brushes, some rollers and a folded stack of dustsheets, which appeared to have once been duvet covers and curtains.

She bent down to take a good look at the colours on the outside of the tins before she prised the lids open to see how much of each was left. A soft rose colour, magnolia (of course – who didn't have a stash of left-over magnolia paint somewhere?) a drop of sage green and a deeper beige were the paints on offer.

Then she straightened up and looked around the shop. Those were old-fashioned colours, but they'd work perfectly well in an old-fashioned shop such as this was going to be. The walls with the floor-to-ceiling shelves would benefit from the magnolia because they'd be mostly hidden, but the wall behind the till would look lovely in that old rose colour, and she was sure she could make use of the rest of the paint. Once all the toys were in situ, no one would be taking any notice of the walls anyway, although she hoped they'd notice the decorations because she intended for there to be a Christmas tree, and appropriately coloured bunting strung around, along with any other Christmas decorations she might be able to beg, steal, or borrow. They would have to be tasteful, of course; she didn't intend the shop to look like an explosion in a tinsel factory. What she was aiming for was Santa Claus's workshop, where the elves made their toys. She'd spent some time that afternoon pulling up images on the internet to get an idea of exactly what it was she was after.

Her musing and planning was interrupted by the door opening behind her and she turned to see Father Todd step inside.

'I was hoping I'd catch you at Bookylicious, but you'd already left, then I saw the light on in here,' he said. 'So, this is it, is it?'

He stared around and walked slowly about the room, nodding. 'Looks OK. I've only been in here a couple of times when it was still the Soapbox and it looked good when it was full. There's something a bit sad about an empty shop, isn't there?'

'It won't be empty for long. By this time next week, I hope to have all the stock in place.' Hattie couldn't wait. It was going to look wonderful.

Father Todd sucked on his teeth. 'I've been thinking; who is going to man it? I haven't met your Alfred yet, but from what you've told us it doesn't sound as though he'll be able to manage this place on his own.'

Hattie froze, thinking fast. 'I can do the days I'm not in work, but both Nell and Logan have their own businesses to run. Juliette might be able to do some hours...' Shit, she hadn't thought of that. She'd been so busy trying to persuade Alfred it was a good idea to have a shop in the first place, then dealing with the practicalities of getting the thing ready to open, that she hadn't once considered the sixty-hour weeks it would take to sell the toys themselves. Maybe seven or so hours could be shaved off that figure if the shop didn't open on Sundays – but nearly every other retailer would be open every Sunday right up until the big day, so it would be a shame to lose out on all the trade.

She was going to struggle if she had to work seven days a week, what with this and Bookylicious, and she was much more robust than Alfred, who needed a stick to get about. There was no way he'd be able to cope with even half that amount of hours.

Damn it! And she was so sure she'd thought of everything, too.

'I might be able to manage a couple of mornings,' Father Todd said, 'but it's coming up to one of my busiest times of the year, so I'm not sure how much help I can be. You could try asking Marge if any of the WI ladies would be up for it – they love a good cause. Oh, and you could try Juliette. She only works part-time and most of that is done from home these days, although I think the Ticklemore Tattler does still have an office above the butchers. OK, best be off – I need to have my dinner before the choir arrives for practice this evening. It's all go, you know!

You can say that again, Hattie thought. She watched him leave, then took a steadying breath. It would be all right. It *would*.

Hating to admit that she might have bitten off more than she could chew, she vowed to phone Benny when she got home. For now though, there was a pot of paint and a roller with her name on it. She wouldn't risk getting up a ladder, but she could do a fair amount of one of the walls before she called it a day.

She walked out to the loo at the back of the premises and changed out of her work clothes and into the elasticated trousers and old top she used for doing the gardening. She wished she'd thought to bring a different pair of shoes, because her bunions were playing up a bit, but she hadn't so she'd have to put up with wearing the ones she had on. She supposed she could try taking them off and walk about in her pop socks, but the floor was wooden and she was worried she might slip. Besides, it wasn't the weather to not be wearing shoes or slippers. Winter had taken a firm grip and the long-range forecast promised snow before Christmas, which she was ambivalent about. On the one hand a dusting of the white stuff would be very atmospheric, but on the other it could be treacherous underfoot, especially for oldies like her. And if too much of it fell, it would impinge on the number of visitors who came to the village; and if a significant amount fell on the weekend of the Christmas Fayre, then it would be disastrous.

It took some fiddling about to get the lid off the tin of magnolia emulsion, but she eventually managed it, cursing under her breath. Not all that long ago she'd have had the little blighter off in a tic – today it had taken her nearly fifteen minutes. Why did manufacturers make things so hard to get into these days, she wondered? Take those blasted shrink-wrapped plastic containers that the supermarkets had taken to selling their lamb chops and other cuts of meat in. She'd done herself some serious damage with a pair of scissors once when trying to get into one. These days she bought her meat from the butchers, where it was wrapped properly. It tasted better, too, and she much preferred supporting local businesses whenever she possibly could.

Carefully, she poured a hefty amount of paint into one of the paint trays and dipped a brush in. Kneeling down (with a bit of effort and some grunting) she dabbed the brush along the wall just above the skirting board, shuffling along until she'd done a fair length, then she swapped the brush for the roller and swiped it up and down the wall. It was probably going to take two coats she decided, after checking the coverage, although it would be difficult to tell until it was dry and seeing it in daylight would be of benefit, too.

After a while (and a much shorter amount of time than she'd hoped) she found she was struggling – her arms were aching, her back was in half from all the bending, her feet hurt, and she was knackered.

Hattie put the roller down. She wanted to go home and have a good cry, but as she was the one who'd started this, it was up to her to see it through, and she couldn't expect everyone else to do it, not when they had jobs and other commitments.

She'd just do this bit here then she'd stop, she vowed. It would take her a while to clean the roller, the tray, and the brush and she didn't want to get to the point where she didn't feel able to do it.

Trying to ignore her various aches and pains, she attempted to distract herself by wondering how Silas was getting on with the design for the signage. He was a talented landscape artist, but she wasn't sure writing bloody great big signs was his forte. Still, he must—

A loud banging on the window almost made her drop the roller and she put a hand to her heart without thinking, the paint making a streak across her already spattered chest.

'Bloody hell!' she shouted as the banging came

again, this time on the door, and it swung open.

A girl's voice called, 'Bit old for that, aren't you?'

'Cheeky bugger,' Hattie grunted. The girl was right though, she *was* too old for this. 'Are you volunteering?'

'Nope, not me. What's it going to be?' The girl, possibly in her late teens (it was so hard to tell, these days, and they all tended to look alike with their ripped jeans, hoodies, trainers and too much makeup), stepped over the threshold and walked inside. 'Is it going to be one of those places that sell hearing aids and wheelchairs and stuff?'

She was a cheeky little madam, and Hattie resented being stereotyped. 'A toy shop,' she replied sharply.

The youngster nodded and made a face. 'Wish we'd had one of those in Ticklemore when I was a kid.'

She was still a kid, as far as Hattie was concerned. 'What's your name?'

'Why do you want to know?'

'No reason. I don't care; I was just making conversation.'

'Zoe Arnold. What's yours?'

'Hattie Jenkins. How old are you?'

'How old are *you*?'

'Eighty.' It wasn't far from the truth and a couple of months didn't matter.

'I'm seventeen.'

'Where do you live?'

Zoe narrowed her eyes. 'Ticklemore. What about you?'

'Same. Are you still in school?'

'I'm planning on going to college.'

'What do you want to study?'

'Carpentry.' She sounded defensive. 'I'm applying for an apprenticeship.'

'Any chance of getting one?'

Zoe shrugged. 'Might. It depends.'

'On what?'

'On who's offering to take me on. Are you always this nosey?'

'Are *you*? You started it,' Hattie retorted.

Zoe smiled and it lit up her face. She was rather pretty when she wasn't scowling, Hattie thought. 'I did, didn't I?' the girl said. She glanced at the stepladder that Benny had brought with him and had left propped up in the corner. 'You're not going to stand on that, are you?'

'Might do.' Hattie shrugged, as if she often scurried up and down ladders.

'You'll break something. Here, give me that.' Zoe held out her hand for the roller and Hattie passed it over. 'I can get one wall done for you.'

'Thank you. Wanna go to the pub after you've

finished?' It was only polite that Hattie repaid the girl's kindness.

Zoe had been about to dip the roller into the paint tray when she paused and narrowed her eyes at her.

Hattie added, 'I haven't had my tea yet, so if you're hungry you can join me. My treat. No worries if you haven't got the time.'

The girl continued to stare at her, as if debating the pros and cons of her offer. Zoe was right to be wary, because Hattie had a proposition in mind. For now though, Hattie was content to watch the girl work, even holding the ladder for her when she climbed up it to reach the top of the wall.

Hattie felt quite put out at the speed with which the girl worked. In no time at all most of the wall was done, except for cutting in with the brush at the very top where the wall met the ceiling. This was duly done under Hattie's strict supervision, with her issuing instructions.

'You're good with your hands,' Hattie stated as she watched Zoe wash the brush and roller under running water, not letting her stop until she was satisfied that the items were suitably clean. 'You can prop them up on the draining board. I doubt they'll dry overnight though, so it's lucky there are more brushes and another roller.'

'I enjoy stuff like this,' Zoe said. 'I always have. It's

better than gaming or playing about on the net. You ought to see my bedroom at home. My mum let me decorate it myself, and I even built some shelves out of an old pallet.'

'Impressive.' Hattie examined the sink and decided it was tidy enough. 'Ready for that meal I promised you?'

Zoe thought for a second, then nodded. 'I was supposed to meet my friends, but they won't mind if I'm late. I'll give them a call.' She winkled her phone out of the pocket of her tight jeans and turned away.

Hattie didn't even pretend not to listen.

'Yeah, it's me. I'll be a bit late.' Pause. 'Yeah, no, it's fine. I'll sort myself out. All the more for you and Aiden.' Pause. 'Helping an old lady with some painting.' Another pause, then a laugh followed by, 'I know I'm wonderful. I won't be late, OK? Bye.' Zoe turned back to find Hattie watching her. 'They don't mind. I'll see them later.'

Hattie kept her smirk to herself; she guessed who it was Zoe had been speaking to and it didn't sound like it was a friend. Bless her – she'd had to tell her mum she'd be late. At least the girl was being responsible, even if she was trying to save face.

'I can help you again tomorrow, if you want?' Zoe offered as they strolled along the road. Hattie was going as fast as she could – Zoe was positively dawdling.

'That would be nice. Thank you,' she said as Zoe pushed the door open and held it for Hattie to walk through. The girl had manners and Hattie appreciated that. And Zoe wasn't being condescending or patronising with it, either.

'What would you like to drink?' Hattie asked, taking her purse out of her handbag and heading to the bar.

'A pint of cider, please.' Zoe was close on her heels.

'Over my dead body. Try again.'

'A glass of lemonade?'

'That's better. Two lemonades, please, Logan, and can we have a couple of menus?'

'Certainly. Here are the menus. If you sit down, I'll bring your drinks over to you.'

Hattie and Zoe sat, then spent the next few minutes deciding what they wanted to eat. After shouting their order over to Logan, Hattie got down to business.

She knew she was making an executive decision and that she should be involving Alfred, at the very least, but she couldn't go on the way she was.

'There's a chap called Alfred Miller,' Hattie began, 'and he's made all the toys that are going to be sold in the shop. It's his shop – I'm just helping out, along with Logan there,' Hattie jerked her head at the publican, 'and a couple of others, like Nell who owns the Treasure Trove and Silas Long, who owns the Studio.' She mentioned those two because Zoe was more likely to recognise those, rather than Marge from the WI or Benny from the allotment. 'There are a few others, as well. Anyway,' Hattie looked up as Logan popped their drinks down on the table. 'Logan, I was just telling my friend Zoe about Alfred and the shop.'

Logan's face lit up. 'You ought to see the toys he's made. They're absolutely brilliant. He's made them from off-cuts of wood, and they're the old-fashioned sort, like in the Victorian era. I reckon they'll sell like hot cakes.' He pulled up a chair and perched on it. 'How is it going at the shop?'

'That's why I brought Zoe here with me this evening. She helped me paint the main wall, so I'm treating her to some supper.'

Logan was about to say something but he was called back to the bar. 'We'll talk later,' he promised. 'Duty calls.'

Hattie waited for him to leave, then she said to Zoe, 'Do you want a job? It will only be until Christmas and it's not carpentry, but you would still be working with wood. Sort of.'

Zoe sent her a long look. 'How do you know you

can trust me?'

'I know your mother. Any nonsense from you and I'll be sure to pay her a visit.'

The girl's eyes widened. 'You know my mum?'

'This is Ticklemore we're talking about. There are very few people in the village I don't know. I thought I recognised you when you came in, but I wasn't certain until you told me your name. Kids grow up so fast – I think the last time I saw you, you were about eleven. Your mum brought you into Bookylicious to get some books to help you with your reading before you went up to big school. How did you get on with those?'

Zoe screwed up her face. 'How do I know? That was years ago.'

As far as Hattie was concerned six years was a mere blink of an eye. 'About this job,' she carried on. 'I've got a good feeling about you. Don't let me down.'

'I won't, I promise. What will I be doing? And...' She paused and bit her lip nervously. 'How much will I be paid?'

It was a valid question. 'I'll have to look into your wages, but I can guarantee it won't be below the minimum rate. As for what you'll be doing? For the rest of this week you'll be helping to finish the painting and get the shop ready to open a week on

Saturday. After it's open, you'll be serving customers, replenishing the stock, and tidying up. It's not exciting, but all the proceeds from the sale of the toys are going to charity, so not only will you be off the streets for a few weeks, you'll be helping a good cause, and it'll be something to put on your CV. You can start tomorrow, and I'll open the shop on the way to work, so be there at nine-thirty sharp.'

Nine-thirty? Zoe looked horrified, then quickly assumed a blank expression. 'OK. Um, where do you work?'

'Bookylicious.'

'Eff— I mean, are you still there?'

'Why wouldn't I be?'

'You're old— Oops.'

Hattie glared at her. 'Did you or did you not, see me painting earlier?'

Zoe grimaced, shrugged, and then nodded.

'Age is just a number, my girl, and you'd do well to remember that.' Zoe clearly thought she was past it; Hattie could tell by the look on her face. In a way, the youngster was right, because Hattie was aching so much she didn't know what to do with herself, and she was so tired she was worried she'd fall asleep in the middle of her steak and ale pie.

After she'd eaten she intended to go home, have a long soak in a hot bath, then go to bed. And if Alfred didn't like the new addition to the team, then tough, because she couldn't carry on the way she was and it wasn't fair on the others to expect them to do everything, not when they had jobs and families which took priority. If she had to pay Zoe's wages out of her own pocket, then so be it.

Either way, Hattie was determined that the girl would help, and that the shop would be ready for its grand opening in ten days' time.

After all, it was for a good cause, and she wasn't necessarily referring to charity, either.

CHAPTER 20

ALFRED

'And who might you be?' Alfred asked as he stepped into the toy shop and spied a girl wearing a pair of scruffy dungarees which had one of the shoulder ties dangling loose, and a long-sleeved T-shirt underneath. She was wielding a paint roller and she looked as though she knew how to use it, even though she was nothing but a slip of thing; she was barely five feet tall and as skinny as a lathe. Honey-coloured hair was piled on top of her head, she had freckles across her nose, and a splodge of paint above one eyebrow.

Rapidly revising her age down from his original guestimate of early twenties, Alfred decided she was probably in her mid to late teens – although it was so difficult to tell these days.

The girl straightened up from where she'd been bending over to paint underneath some shelves on the back wall and said, 'I'm Zoe; I work here.'

Alfred nodded – the more helpers the better. He felt incredibly guilty that he wasn't being much use. Even a schoolgirl was making more inroads into preparing the shop for business than he was, and it was supposed to be his damned shop! However, he still hadn't addressed the issue of running it, and he had yet to address the even bigger issue of Sara. She'd do her nut when she found out, but at least she wouldn't be able to blame it on him losing his marbles because that would mean a substantial contingent of Ticklemore's finest citizens would also have to be given the same accolade, including the vicar.

'Shouldn't you be in school?' he asked. 'Don't get me wrong, I'm grateful for your help but does your mother know you're here?'

'I'm seventeen. I left school last summer, and my mum knows exactly where I am. Are all old people this nosey?' She muttered the last as she bent down again.

After a few swipes she called over her shoulder, 'If you're here to find out what's going on, it's going to be a toy shop.'

I know. It's *my* toy shop. Apparently.' It was his turn to mutter as he said the last word.

Zoe hurriedly straightened up. 'You're Alfred?

211

Hattie's been banging on about you.'

'Yes, I'm Alfred.'

'But you're *old*!'

'And you're cheeky.'

Zoe had the grace to look contrite. 'Sorry. I was expecting someone… erm… My bad.' She put the roller down in the tray and walked towards him, holding her hand out. 'I suppose I'd better be nice to you seeing as you're my boss, 'n' that.'

Alfred shook the girl's hand, bemused. She was a funny little thing. 'Hattie roped you in, eh? Or was it one of the others?'

'Hattie. She was in here yesterday evening, and we got chatting and she offered me the job. Thanks for that. It'll give me some spends for Christmas, but maybe if you like me, you'll keep me on for a bit afterwards? Until I get an apprenticeship, yeah?'

'Hang on, young lady. I don't know what you mean when you say "job", and the shop is a Christmas shop, ergo it'll only be open until Christmas.'

Zoe was frowning. 'What does "ergo" mean?'

'Therefore,' Alfred explained impatiently.

'Ah, that's a bummer. Never mind.' She brightened up. 'This time yesterday I didn't have a job at all, so things are deffo looking up.'

'I still don't understand what you mean when you

say you've got a job. Do you mean here?'

'Yep.' She grinned at him.

'A paid job? You're not just lending a hand?'

'Yeah, a paid job.' Her eyes narrowed. 'Why? What's wrong?'

'Bloody Hattie! What the hell does she think she'd playing at, going around offering people jobs willy-nilly?'

'I don't get it. Don't you want me working here?' The girl's cheeks reddened and there was a suspicious glint in her eyes which made Alfred think she was close to tears.

Aw, hell, now he'd gone and upset her.

Bugger and damnation. Bloody Hattie.

'What exactly did she say?' he asked.

Zoe frowned, her brow furrowing. 'She said it would only be until Christmas, and I'd be selling stuff, and filling the shelves, and that. Oh, and she said I was to help get the shop ready.' She jerked her head at the pot of paint. 'That's what I'm doing now. Didn't she tell you she was taking me on?'

'I'm afraid not.'

'Do you want me to go? I mean, I don't want paying for the work I've already done, or anything. I can just wash the brushes and go.' She looked upset, despite her offer, and Alfred didn't blame her.

He thought for a moment, then stepped nearer to

the rear wall. It was a bit of a struggle to bend far enough down to see underneath the shelves, but he saw what he needed to.

'How much am I paying you?' he asked.

'I don't know. Hattie didn't say, except that it'll be above the minimum wage.'

'I see.' And he did see, that with the best will in the world, there was no way he could manage this shop on his own. Even with help from Hattie (she had her own job), Logan (he had a pub to run), Nell… All those people had their own lives to lead.

Alfred supposed they could maybe manage some kind of a rota or shift system, but ultimately it would be down to him and Hattie, two old-age pensioners neither of whom could devote more than a couple of hours to the place, if he was being truthful. Even if Sara knew all about it (and she would have to at some point – he was lucky to have kept it from her so far), he knew he would struggle to be on his feet all day every day for the four weeks the shop would be open.

'You can stay,' he told the girl.

'I can?' Her face lit up and she did a little jig. 'I thought you were going to fire me on my first day!'

'Hattie should have consulted me, but it's done now, so…' He waved a hand in the air. 'You can carry on. And I'll have a word with Hattie about your wages. If you do a good job, you should get decent pay.'

'Like a commission thing? The more I sell, the more I earn?'

'No, you'll get a flat wage, regardless of whether the shop does well or not.' He was very conscious that it mightn't, and if that was the case, then he'd pay the poor girl's wages out of his own pocket. And he didn't believe in the nonsense of paying someone less because they were young, either. Work was work, and this shop wasn't going to be easy.

'OK.' She beamed at him and Alfred smiled back. 'I'd better crack on,' she said. 'You seem like a cool guy, but Hattie is a bit of a dragon.'

He chuckled; he wasn't sure dragon was an accurate description, however steam roller was, because the elderly woman didn't let anything stand in her way and she simply flattened anyone who tried to. Look at how she'd made him go from letting those house-clearance people dispose of everything, to opening a shop and selling his toys – and all this in less than a week. The woman was a menace.

'I don't want her showing up and telling me off,' Zoe was saying. 'And if she decides to do the painting herself like she did yesterday, I'd be well embarrassed.'

'She did what?'

'Painting. I saw her from outside, so I came in to

ask what she was doing.'

'Hattie was in here last night, by herself, painting?'

'Yep.'

'What time was this?'

'Seven-ish?'

'The silly bugger. She's going to make herself ill if she carries on.'

'She did look tired. I came in because I was being nosey,' Zoe said, running the roller up and down the wall with broad, efficient strokes. 'But when I saw the state of her, I offered to help.' She turned to face him with panicked eyes. 'I wasn't expecting anything for it, or nothing. I just thought she could do with a hand, see?'

'I think I'll be having words with our Hattie. She might think she's still a spring chicken, but she's more like an old broiler.'

'Eh?'

'Hattie's an old bird, like me. She shouldn't be doing stuff like painting. She needs to take things a bit easier at her age.'

'Yeah, that's what I was thinking. She looks good for eighty, though – my gran is sixty-five and I thought Hattie was the same age, but with more wrinkles.'

Alfred was about to reply when loud tinny music filled the air, making him almost jump out of his skin.

'What the hell?' He patted his pockets, wondering where the noise was coming from.

'It's yours, not mine,' Zoe said. 'Mine don't make a noise like *that*.' She wrinkled her nose in disgust.

'Your what?' he asked.

'My phone. Aren't you going to answer it?'

Once he understood that the noise was his ringtone, he seriously thought about doing exactly that for a moment, then he realised that Sara would keep on calling. So he wrestled it out of his pocket, put a finger to his lips and flipped up the lid, feeling like Captain Kirk with his communicator. He was tempted to say "beam me up, Scottie" but he wasn't sure Sara would appreciate it.

'Hello, Sara,' he said, mouthing, 'Shhh' at Zoe.

'Where are you, Dad?'

'In Bookylicious. Why?'

'I hope you're not drinking coffee. You know it's bad for you.'

Yes, so is life, he thought. 'Decaf tea,' he replied, not giving a hoot that he was telling his daughter an out and out lie. 'I'm reading the paper,' he added purely on the grounds of authenticity.

'I might join you. I'm about to have an eye test, but I should be done in half an hour. Will you still be there?'

Hmm. If he said he wasn't going to be, she'd only

expect him to be at home when she got back, and he wasn't in the mood for daytime TV.

'I'll still be here,' he said, stifling a sigh of resignation, before hanging up.

Zoe was smirking. 'Your wife?'

'No, she died a couple of years ago. That was my daughter. She treats me worse than she does a kid.'

Zoe shuffled her feet and looked at the floor. 'Sorry about your wife.'

'It is what it is. At least I've got this place to take my mind off it. I'd better go. You're doing a good job,' he said, meaning it. 'I'll swing by as soon as I can.'

'Do you want my phone number?' Zoe asked. 'Just in case.'

In case of what he had no idea, but he asked her to write it down for him anyway.

'Give us your phone and I'll put it in for you,' she offered.

Marvelling at the wonders of modern technology, Alfred handed it over, smiling to himself as Zoe muttered about not having seen a dinosaur like his gadget before. He didn't like to tell her it was brand new and appeared to be manufactured purely for oldies like him.

Phone numbers exchanged, Alfred took himself off to Bookylicious, hoping he'd find a free table, and when he did, he looked around for someone with whom to place his order. Ten minutes had already gone by, and he didn't want to risk Sara wondering why there was no pot of tea in front of him. He was probably being paranoid and she wouldn't notice, but he didn't want to take the chance.

Hattie was in the café today. Her back was to him and he waited for her to turn around, hoping to catch her eye.

When he saw her face though, he was shocked at how sallow she looked and how exhausted. Her usual bustling walk had been replaced by a shuffle, and there were dark circles under her eyes which hadn't been there previously. Not only that, but the lines on her face were deeper and her shoulders were hunched. He had to do more to help, no matter how awkward it became for him. The shop might have been her idea and she might be the driving force behind it, but ultimately it was his business, his responsibility, his toys.

'Hattie,' he called, beckoning her over. 'I've just been into the shop. You didn't tell me you'd taken someone on.'

'I was going to speak to you about it as soon as I saw you.'

'Tell me about it after it was a done deal, you mean?'

Hattie pursed her lips and huffed. 'I'll have you know that without me, there wouldn't be a shop.' She glared at him and Alfred realised he'd offended her.

'You're right. Please accept my apologies. It was just a bit unexpected, that's all. She seems like a nice girl.'

'She is. I know her mother and if there's any nonsense she'll come down on Zoe like a tonne of bricks. She's a bit green and she's a bit younger than I would have liked, but she's keen and she likes working with wood – she wants to do an apprenticeship in carpentry – and I realise that she won't exactly be working with wood as such…' Hattie trailed off.

'I know I should have checked with you first,' she admitted, 'but she was there, and the idea came to me, and we can't do all this by ourselves. Look, if you keep Zoe on to do all the heavy work until the shop is ready to open – she's a dab hand with a paintbrush – you don't need to keep her on to help run it.' She took a breath and carried on talking, not letting him get a word in edgeways. 'Um, if it's her wages you're worried about, then don't be; I'll pay her myself for all the painting and stuff.'

'You will not. We've already agreed that there will be some overheads like the electricity, which will need to be taken out of any profits first. Zoe's wages are just such an overhead, and I've already told her that her job is safe. I just wish I could do more to help— Oh, hello love.'

He spotted Sara behind Hattie and smiled brightly at her. Damn it. He hadn't ordered yet, and there he was sitting at an empty table without even a glass of water in front of him, and his daughter *did* notice, much to his annoyance. Crikey, it was like living with MI5.

'I thought you were already having tea? Or did you wait for me?' his daughter asked.

'I waited—' he said, at the same moment as Hattie, who'd caught on pretty quickly, said. 'I've just cleared the table—'

Hattie gave her an innocent smile. 'What would you like?' she asked Sara.

'A cappuccino, please.'

'Alfred? Coffee?

'No thanks. I'll have that pot of decaf tea I was talking about. Coffee is bad for you.'

'So are daughters,' he heard Hattie mumble as she walked away.

Sara took her coat off and draped it over the back of her chair before taking a seat and gazing around. 'This is nice. I haven't been in here before. Very Christmassy. Those mince pies look good. Now that I've retired, I can do more of my shopping in

Ticklemore. Of course, I'll still have to go to the supermarket to do a main shop, but the meat in the butcher's shop looks fresh and good quality, and I ordered the turkey from there, as well as a ham. I can pick them up on Christmas Eve. Oh, and I got us some nice apples from the greengrocer. You like apples, don't you?'

Alfred never touched them. As far as he was concerned apples were only good for making cider, otherwise they didn't taste of much – just water and crunch. He was partial to peaches, though, and plums.

Hattie arrived with their drinks and as she was decanting them off her tray and onto the table, Sara said. 'Do you make the cakes you sell?'

Hattie put a little jug of milk next to the teapot and scowled at her. 'No, and I don't write the books we sell, either.'

Trying not to chuckle, Alfred watched her walk away in a huff, with her head held high and her shoulders back. He had to admire her – as worn-out as she was, she could still take Sara on.

His daughter was unimpressed. 'Gosh, she's rude. I'm not sure I want to visit here again.'

Hattie wasn't rude, Alfred decided. She was thoughtful and considerate, and a little eccentric, but not rude. OK, maybe a little, but that was only to Sara. Hattie was sweetness and light to the other customers, and he smirked at the way his friend had taken an instant dislike to his daughter. Although, he realised it wasn't Sara Hattie had an issue with, it was the way she treated him.

It might have taken a while, but Alfred had come to understand that Sara's attitude stemmed from worry about him, and he was ashamed to admit that it had been his despair and emptiness after Dorothy had died, which was responsible for Sara's concern. He'd let things slip; had retreated so far into himself and his misery that he hadn't been able to find a way out.

No wonder his daughter had acted the way she had (and was still acting); it was going to take her a while to trust that he was as OK as he insisted he was. Or as near to OK as he was going to get.

He still had days when he wasn't quite himself, and it had crossed his mind that he'd never be the same as he had been, but he was slowly reconciling himself to his new living arrangements. And he might not be enamoured of living with his bossy daughter, but coming to Ticklemore had given him a whole new lease of life, and had made him think about something other than his own problems.

Although, what he'd do and how he'd feel once Christmas was over and done with was something he didn't want to think about too closely.

For now, it was enough that he felt he had a place

in the world again.

And it was all thanks to Hattie.

CHAPTER 21

HATTIE

Hattie watched proprietarily as Alfred shook hands with those members of the Toy Shop Team he had yet to meet. She'd kind of come to think of him as hers, which was ridiculous, but she felt like a football manager who'd discovered a potential top goal scorer, and she was inordinately proud of him. Which was also ridiculous.

'It's nice to finally meet the man behind the toys,' Juliette said, getting to her feet and reaching over to shake his hand. 'I'm Juliette.'

Hattie noticed that Juliette was as immaculately dressed as usual, and was brimming with her typical confidence. It was so like her to be the first to introduce herself, but Hattie didn't hold that against her. The woman might appear brisk and forthright, but she had a heart of gold. Hattie recalled that

Juliette had been the same when she was a child, and hadn't changed in the slightest as she'd matured into a fifty-something woman.

'And I'm Silas – love your work, by the way.' Silas also half-rose and shook Alfred's hand.

Poor Alfred looked a little taken aback at the number of people around the table, although he shouldn't be because he'd met most of them before. It was only Juliette, Silas, and Father Todd who were new to him. Everyone was gazing at him expectantly, though, so Hattie supposed it was only natural that he was a tad discomforted. Especially since she'd got the impression that he hadn't socialised much in the past couple of years.

All that was about to change – it was impossible to keep oneself to oneself if you had to chat to customers all day – and Hattie felt vaguely alarmed as she wondered how he was going to cope.

'Last but not least is Father Todd,' Hattie said, and the man in question nodded and smiled.

'I won't get up,' the Father said, indicating the distance he'd have to stretch across the table and the fact that he was well and truly wedged in between Benny and his wife on one side and Nell on the other. 'But I will buy you a drink, if Logan would be kind enough to fetch it for me. What are you having?'

'A pint of ale, please.'

Logan got up to fetch it, and Hattie patted the seat of the chair next to her, which she'd purposefully kept free for him. Alfred sat and Hattie beamed at him.

'You've escaped then,' she said. 'How did you manage that?'

'Sara and David have gone to his Christmas office party. I thought it was a bit soon to be having one of those – it's not even December yet – but she says it's better to have it now, rather than nearer to Christmas when everyone has so many other commitments. Thank God they did, otherwise I'd be stuck at home again, and missing the meeting.'

'We're mighty delighted that you're here,' Father Todd said, with another beaming smile and Hattie wondered if he'd been nipping at the communion wine, despite the fact that he was Anglican and not Catholic.

'Shall we get down to business?' Hattie suggested, taking charge; she didn't think Alfred was up to it right now, despite the shop being his. 'Firstly, many of you know Zoe, and she's with us this evening because Alfred and I felt that he would need some help in the shop once it's open. It's unrealistic to expect him to run the place singlehandedly, as Nell will be aware.' Nell nodded and Hattie carried on. 'Her wages will be taken out before any money is sent to charity, along with any other expenses such as the electricity and so on. Agreed?'

There were nods all around the table, and Zoe's grin stretched from ear to ear.

'Welcome to the Toy Shop Team,' Juliette said and raised her glass to her before taking a deep swallow.

Hattie frowned. Here was another team member who seemed to be on more than their first drink of the evening.

'If we go around the table, we can all give updates before we decide what needs to be done next. Silas, how far have you got with the flyers?'

Silas bent down and rummaged around under the table, bringing forth a folder which he opened. 'I've made a copy for everyone,' he said, handing out sheets of A4 paper.

There was a brief silence whilst they examined the design. Hattie, for one, was extremely pleased with it. 'I think it captures the feel of the shop beautifully,' she said, running a finger over the exquisitely painted rocking horse. The colours were Christmassy and the lettering was Victorian in style. It was perfect.

'Is everyone happy for me to put this in the paper?' Juliette asked. 'I can also run off a few hundred copies and we can do a letterbox drop. I'm happy to stand on the high street tomorrow and hand out a few, too.'

'Count me in for that,' Marge said, and Benny chimed in, 'I'll shove some in a few people's letterboxes. The exercise will do me good.'

'If you let me have some, I'll give them out in church on Sunday. They'll probably elicit a better response than my sermon,' Father Todd added good naturedly.

'How about the signage?' Hattie asked Silas.

'Take a look at this and tell me what you think.' Silas drew out a length of paper and unfolded it to reveal a template with the same colours and the same lettering as the posters.

'You've missed off the word "Christmas",' Marge pointed out.

'When I tried to fit it all in, the letters became too small. I can put it back in, if that's what everyone wants?'

Hattie was happy with it just the way it was. 'What do you think, Alfred?' she asked, conscious that he wasn't saying much.

'I like it,' he said, studying it. 'I don't think it matters whether the word "Christmas" is on there or not.'

After it was agreed that Silas could go ahead with painting over the current sign, and Benny, along with Father Todd, had volunteered to help take it down and also source the enamel paint needed for the job, the discussion moved on to the condition of the shop. Every single member of the Toy Shop Team had made a point of popping into the shop in the past day or so, so all of them knew that only a bit of painting still needed to be done before the fun things like stocking the place could begin.

'I've spoken to the mayor, Councillor Taylor, and she's agreed to officially open the shop on Saturday. She can only do ten o'clock, because she has other commitments. Is that OK?'

'I'm sure it's fine? Is there any objection?' Hattie asked and was relieved to see there wasn't.

'I've put some feelers out with a couple of contacts in the trade,' Juliette said, 'and I think we can get some coverage, or a mention at the very least, on the local radio, and maybe the regional news. I'm afraid it does depend on whether anything more exciting happens that day.' She shot an apologetic glance around the table. 'The charity angle should help enormously, though, and the two we have approached are happy to send representatives to the opening.'

'Before we adjourn the meeting,' Hattie said, quite enjoying the role of chairperson, 'we need to discuss the opening itself. Should we provide drinks and snacks? I'm not sure what the done thing is. And do we need a ribbon and a pair of scissors?'

Everyone began talking at once and Hattie was about to call for order when Alfred said, 'I think we should serve milk and cookies,' and the table fell silent for a moment until Zoe clapped her hands.

'That's ace, that is!' she cried, and suddenly everyone was grinning and nodding their heads in agreement.

'Can we also provide hot chocolate, too?' Nell asked. 'It'll be cold outside and a hot drink might be welcome.'

'Good plan, and for the cookies I can ask if Maddison will make some of her reindeer and Santa Clause shaped ones. What a lovely idea. Alfred, you're a genius!'

Alfred was looking at the table and was embarrassed, but she could also tell he was as pleased as Punch.

'Leave the refreshments to me,' she said. 'That's kind of my area of expertise, even though I only serve them, not make them. Apart from pots of tea – I'm pretty good at making those.'

'You've only got to pour boiling water in the pot and throw in a couple of teabags,' Logan teased. 'You can't possibly go wrong.'

'Ah, now, that's where I beg to differ,' Benny began, but his wife intervened.

'Time for us to go,' she said. 'I've got chutney to

make.'

'At this time of night?' Benny looked appalled. 'I thought we could watch a nice film.'

'It's only eight-thirty. You can watch the film; I'll be crying over some onions.' And with that, Marge pulled her husband to his feet and they said their goodbyes.

It was a signal for the rest of them to head off, too. Nell said she was going out with friends. Father Todd had to lock up the church hall after the choir had finished rehearsing. Juliette murmured something about having things to do, and Silas was out of the door with barely a word to anyone, Zoe following on his heels and calling over her shoulder that she'd be in the shop in the morning. Logan disappeared behind the bar, leaving Hattie and Alfred sitting alone at the table.

'I suppose I'd better make a move,' Hattie said, hauling herself to her feet with a grunt.

Alfred stood up, too, and reached for his stick. 'I'll walk you home,' he offered. 'It's dark and I don't like the idea of you wandering about in it.'

Making straight for her cottage was hardly wandering, but she appreciated the offer. Alfred was quite sweet when you got to know him, she thought, having almost forgotten his grumpiness when she'd first met him.

Outside the Tavern, the air was chill and damp, their breath pluming around their heads in the light from the streetlamps and the glow spilling through the pub's windows.

'Brr.' Hattie shivered. 'I think it's time I got my thermal vest out.' She sniffed the air. 'They say we're going to have snow before Christmas.'

'I hope not,' Alfred grumbled. 'It's bad enough getting about when there isn't any snow and ice, and I bet Sara will do her best to stop me leaving the house if there's even the slightest hint of a snowflake.'

To her surprise, Hattie found herself slipping an arm through his, and she huddled closer to him for warmth and to steady her aching legs. It had been a long day, but in a short while she'd be able to put her feet up and snooze in her chair.

'Have you settled in, do you think?' she asked Alfred after a few steps. 'Ticklemore, I mean.'

'It's a lovely village with some nice people in it. I can't believe how welcome they've made me, and how they're willing to help a complete stranger.'

'They're a good bunch. I've known most of them for years. Take Zoe's mum, for instance, I remember her when she was a babe in arms.'

'I take it you've lived here all your life?'

'I most certainly have. Never wanted to live anywhere else. My Ted, God rest his soul, made a few noises about emigrating to Australia, but when he read about the snakes, and spiders, and whatnot, he soon changed his mind. He didn't much like the heat, either, so living over there wouldn't have done him any good whatsoever. The daft man.'

'Has he been dead long?'

'Fifteen years.'

'Does it get any easier?'

'Yes, it does. But you have to keep busy and not let yourself dwell on things.'

'Like I've been doing?'

'I suppose.' She meant "yes" but didn't want to be too blunt. He was well aware that he'd spent the previous two years brooding, so he didn't need her to point it out.

'Is that why you're still working?'

'At my age, you mean?' She chuckled. 'You've got to do something with your time, haven't you, else you'll go doolally.'

'Like me,' he said, his tone morose.

'You're not doolally,' she scoffed. 'You're bereaved. There's a whopping great big difference.'

'I miss Dorothy so much…'

'Of course you do. And I miss Ted. But life does go on.'

'She'd have loved all this shop business. I wish I'd told her about my little hobby. I reckon she'd have been proud of me.'

'I expect she was proud of you anyway.'

Alfred gave a tiny nod, a barely perceptible move of his head that Hattie only noticed out of the corner of her eye. 'I suppose you're right. It's just that with the move to Sara's, and the shop, and now the new baby, I'm missing her more than ever.'

'What new baby?'

Hattie heard the smile in his voice as he said, 'Shelley, my granddaughter, is expecting.'

'That's wonderful! You must be thrilled.'

'I am. Dorothy would have been, too. Fancy me being a great-grandad? Have you got any grandchildren?'

Hattie sagged. 'No, and no children, either. We tried, but it never happened.'

'I'm sorry, Hattie. Here I am, chattering on about Shelley and the baby…' He trailed off.

'Don't be afraid to talk about your family. They are a part of you; you can't not talk about them for fear of upsetting me. I made my peace with it years ago. When is it due?'

'Do you know, I never thought to ask.'

'Men! You're all the bleedin' same – useless when it comes to the important stuff.'

She felt his shrug travel down his arm where it was linked with hers. 'It'll arrive when it arrives. She hasn't got so much as a bump yet, so she must have a way to go.'

Hattie gave an exaggerated sigh. 'Useless,' she repeated. She halted outside her front door. 'Here we are; thank you for seeing me home safely.' She giggled softly. 'It's a long time since a fella has walked me home.'

'I'm not… I wasn't—'

'Hush, I was only teasing. Now, you get off home yourself, before that daughter of yours discovers you've been out without permission.'

'I'm surprised she hasn't called me,' he said. 'If she'd have rung the house phone and I didn't answer, then she would have rung me on this.' He patted a pocket. Then he patted another one. Eyes wide, he patted himself down with the thoroughness of a copper searching a suspect. 'Bugger, damn and blast! I've only gone and left the damned thing at home.'

Hattie's eyebrows were raised as she watched his antics. 'Don't tell me you've got a mobile phone?'

'I didn't buy it, David did. And I've forgotten to bring it with me. I'd best be off, before Sara calls the police and declares me a missing person.'

'Before you go, you'd better give me your number, just in case I decide to employ someone else without asking you,' Hattie said, and grinned when she saw Alfred's alarmed expression.

He fished around in his pocket, drew out a crumpled piece of paper, and read the number out to her.

Hattie put it straight into her phone, then reached into her handbag for a pen; snatching the piece of paper out of his hands, she scribbled her own number on it and shoved it back at him. 'There you go. If you need me, you call me.'

Alfred took it, looked at it and nodded, before folding it carefully and putting it back in his pocket. He took one step, then he halted and turned back to her, and before Hattie realised what was happening, he'd stepped towards her again and leant in to peck her on the cheek.

'Thank you, Hattie, for everything,' he said. Then he was off, his stick tapping along the pavement.

Hattie watched him walk away, bemused, one hand to her face where his lips had touched her skin, and she wondered what all that had been about.

She was still musing about it a little while later as she sat at her dressing table unpinning her hair and preparing for bed. It was long, almost down to her waist and as thick as it always had been. Once, many moons ago, it had been glossy and brown, but now it looked like she'd spent a fortune on expensive grey, silver, and white highlights, when the colour was purely natural. Ted had loved her long hair and she'd toyed with having it all cut off after he'd died, but she simply hadn't been able to bring herself to do it.

One hundred strokes of the brush was her nightly ritual, just like her granny had taught her, and Hattie was a little over halfway, Puss purring contentedly on her lap, when her phone rang, making her almost jump out of her skin. The cat leapt off her and shot out of the bedroom, his tail all fluffed up, and she cursed whoever it was for disturbing her.

'Who is it?' she demanded crossly, as she answered it.

'It's me, Alfred. I just wanted to say goodnight. Goodnight, Hattie.'

The phone went dead, and Hattie was left with a bewildered smile on her face and an unaccustomed warmth in her chest.

CHAPTER 22

ALFRED

As he'd walked back from Hattie's house last night, Alfred's thoughts had been churning like socks in a washing machine. In one week, Ticklemore's Christmas Toy Shop would be open, and he felt guilty that he hadn't been able to help much. He had also been worried about what Dorothy would have made of all this if she'd been alive, and he'd fretted about kissing Hattie.

It had only been on the cheek, and he hadn't meant anything by it, but he was worried she would take it the wrong way, and read more into it than he'd intended. Friends often kissed each other, didn't they? It was the done thing these days. The fact that he'd never kissed any other women on the cheek (Sara and Shelley didn't count) was neither here nor there.

Now, though, he felt awkward about it, as if he'd

crossed some invisible line.

Logically, he knew Hattie wouldn't give it a second thought, so neither should he.

But he did, and he gave it a third thought, and a fourth for good measure. It had felt nice kissing her, and the softness of her cheek on his lips had surprised him. He'd caught the scent of rose in her hair, and briefly he'd wondered just how long it was, because she always wore it coiled in a bun at the nape of her neck. And why was he thinking about her at all? That was the question which was giving him the most grief.

To top it all off, when he'd arrived home, he'd discovered several messages on his mobile, and the light on the answering machine had been flashing. Shit, he'd thought; he'd better come up with an excuse as to why he'd not answered his new mobile or the landline.

After some frantic thinking, he'd called Sara back. The conversation hadn't been wonderful. She'd demanded to know why he hadn't answered either phone and had claimed that she'd just been about to cut their evening short and come home. He'd informed her that he'd been in the bath.

'For an hour and ten minutes?' The incredulity and disbelief in his daughter's voice had been very apparent.

'Yes. I was listening to the radio. They had a play on,' he'd told her.

He hoped she'd bought his story, only remembering at the last minute to splash water around the bathroom and to dampen a towel. Afterwards, he'd changed into his pyjamas and went to bed, sniggering to himself.

This morning he was certain she believed him because she had gone to the supermarket to do the weekly shop, which she probably wouldn't have done if she'd thought he'd gone walkabout last night, therefore giving him the opportunity to escape for another couple of hours. David was playing golf and would be gone all day, so Alfred waited until Sara's car disappeared down the road, then he fetched his coat, flat cap, scarf, and gloves, making sure he wrapped up warm against the increasingly chilly weather.

Oops, he thought as he reached the front door and realised he'd nearly forgotten his stick. He hated having to use it, but he felt steadier on his feet if he had it. Although the last fall he'd had (which had ultimately led to him moving in with Sara) had been *inside* the house – and who uses a stick in the house? – it gave him a small amount of reassurance whenever he went outside.

As fast as he could, he toddled into the village,

nodding at people he recognised and, on occasion, at those he didn't. He was beginning to feel part of this community, and the streets, houses, and shops were becoming increasingly more familiar every day.

Unsurprisingly, the main street was busy, what with it being a Saturday, and only a few weeks away from Christmas, and he took his time conscious of the prevalence of ankle-catching pushchairs and people stopping suddenly in front of him as something in a shop window caught their eye.

There was a definite atmosphere in the village, one of subdued anticipation, with the odd spike of premature excitement from the youngest members as the children worked themselves up into a frenzy at the thought of a visit from the man in red. Their elders mostly wore looks of resignation, as they traipsed from shop to shop.

Alfred noticed that the usual suspects like the butcher and the grocer were doing a roaring trade, and he also saw that Nell's Treasure Trove was busy, too. Bookylicious and the other cafés along the street were bustling with customers, and he realised that this all boded well for the toy shop's grand opening next weekend.

He drew up in front of his shop (*his shop?* how had that happened?) and stood near the edge of the pavement, in order to take a good look at it.

The old window display was gone, and had been replaced with poster-sized versions of the flyers. Silas had been right to call it the Ticklemore Toy Shop, and not to mention Christmas and not just because it didn't look good on the sign. Alfred supposed it might put people off if they knew the shop would shut on Christmas Eve – some people were funny like that and others might assume everything was discounted then get annoyed when they found out it wasn't.

He couldn't see much of the inside, but what he could see looked bright and airy. The largest wall was a soft cream colour, which reminded him of Cornish vanilla ice cream, and, eager to see how far the painting had progressed, he pushed the door open and went inside.

The radio was on, blaring out goddamn awful music with no real words and no tune, and the smell of fresh paint made him sneeze.

Zoe, who was halfway up the ladder, turned around, smiling when she saw him. 'What do you think?'

'It's looking good, but I'm finding it hard to imagine what it'll look like with all the toys in here.'

'Hattie said you made them all yourself.'

'That's right.'

'She says there are loads of them; enough to fill

this place and more.'

Alfred absently fingered the new key on his keyring. The girl looked so eager, he made a decision. 'Would you like to see them?'

'Now?'

Alfred nodded, and Zoe let out a squeal, sliding down the ladder as though she was made of rubber and would bounce if she fell, and making him wince on both counts. Oh to be young again and to think you were invincible and immortal...

'They're at Hattie's place,' he informed his young friend, as he led her down the high street. 'She's keeping them in her shed for me, but the sooner they're out of there and in the shop, the better. You can hardly move in there.'

'You're right about that,' Zoe agreed a short time later when Alfred opened the shed and stood to the side to let her enter ahead of him.

A movement at his feet made him look down to see a large ginger cat, weaving around his legs. The cat rubbed against him, purring loudly, then darted into the shed. Alfred followed it at a slower and more sedate pace.

Zoe's mouth was open and she was gazing around her with huge eyes. 'Wow!' She looked at him. 'You made these?'

'Yes.'

'All of them?'

'Yes.'

'There must be hundreds. Thousands, even.'

'Thousands may be an exaggeration, but there are definitely a good few hundred pieces.'

'Have you seen this?' Zoe demanded, lifting a protective sheet of clear plastic over the rocking horse's head.

'I might have seen it once or twice,' was his slightly sarcastic reply.

Zoe shot him a sideways look. It was a fleeting glance as her attention immediately reverted to the myriad of toys in front of her.

Slowly, she wandered from shelf to shelf, and box to box, peering at the contents, occasionally moving an item for a better look at what was behind or underneath it, and all the while her fingers trailed across surfaces and her hands stroked the clean lines and the inviting curves of the smooth wood.

Then Zoe did something that Alfred hadn't been expecting – she manoeuvred her way through the stacked boxes and over to the dresser. She delved into one of the boxes of offcuts (he'd never thrown any piece of wood away, no matter how small), and she brought out a length of sweet chestnut. Zoe held it in her hands for a moment, turning it over and over, studying it intently, then she lifted it to her face and inhaled.

'Mmm, I love the smell of raw wood,' she murmured, and Alfred had to agree with her.

He continued to watch her, realising that he'd found a fellow carpenter, despite her youth and her inexperience, and he sincerely hoped she didn't allow herself to be pulled into a direction she didn't want to go in. If anyone deserved an apprenticeship, it was Zoe.

When the pair of them returned to the shop, Alfred removed his gloves, scarf, and hat, and shucked off his coat, making sure he put them out of the way to avoid getting any paint on them. He was wearing old clothes that Sara wouldn't notice if he splashed paint on (he'd throw them in the bin when he got the chance), and he picked up a brush and began to work.

To his surprise, they'd finished what they'd set out to do long before the time Alfred had set himself to return to Sara's house – and neither had his daughter phoned him, which he took as a step in the right direction.

Feeling more contented than he'd done in a long time (it was amazing how a bit of manual work can lift one's mood) he decided to pop into Bookylicious on the way home.

'I've got news,' he announced as soon as he

spotted Hattie, who was in the book side of things today. By the way she was engrossed in a paperback, Alfred gathered she preferred working with books rather than cakes.

'Hmm?' Her eyes had a glazed faraway look to them when she glanced up at the sound of his voice. As she closed the cover, he saw she was reading a courtroom drama.

'Good book?'

'Brilliant. I'm going to have to buy this one – I can't put it down. You said you had news?'

'We've finished the painting.'

'That's fantastic, but when you say "we", are you talking about the Toy Shop Team in general, or you and Zoe.'

'Um, me and Zoe.'

'Didn't you tell me off for painting?'

'That's different.'

'Hmph.' She glared at him, and Alfred smiled at her. Hattie's version of concern was very different from his daughter's and, far from feeling stifled by it, he was comforted to think she cared enough.

Which was why he picked up the book she'd been reading, along with a recently published horror for himself and, when he'd paid for his purchases, he presented her with it.

And all the way home, the only thing he saw was

the look of astonishment and pleasure on her face, and he felt enormously pleased that he was the one who'd put it there.

CHAPTER 23

HATTIE

The fact that she had a job made days off extra-special for Hattie, and today was no exception. She valued her free time precisely because it was limited to a certain extent, and although she didn't normally work a full week, on the run-up to Christmas her hours increased, so having a day off was to be revelled in.

The type of revelling she intended to do on this particular Sunday was to fetch the Christmas decorations down from the attic. Hattie had some old ones, quite a lot of them, Most of them of the glass bauble variety that she'd seen Nell decorating the tree in the Treasure Trove with. Hattie loved Christmas, but she didn't usually bother with a tree, only putting up a few bits and pieces, mainly because all her stuff was up the attic and she was too proud to ask for help getting them down and putting them back up again.

The shop was a different cause. She wasn't too proud to ask for help where that was concerned, and for exactly the same reason neither did she mind someone rooting around in her attic.

Hattie instinctively knew that a traditional shop such as the one they were about to open, needed something special to set it off. And she had just the thing in her attic. Baubles; loads and loads of them.

'Zoe?' Hattie shouted down the phone at the very reasonable time of eight-thirty. She'd been up for an hour and she was worried that if she didn't call Zoe while she thought about it, she might forget. Such a thing was rare, but it had been known to happen, and she had other things to occupy her mind and her time today, like doing some laundry, for instance.

'Mmnnah?' came the mumbled reply.

'Zoe? Is that you? You need to speak up.'

'Yeah, iss me.'

'Are you OK? You sound a bit offish.'

'Jusss woke up.'

'Did you? That's good. I called at the right time, then.'

'You woke me.' Zoe sounded a bit more with it and also slightly cross.

'Can you come around and help with getting some decorations out of the attic? It's for the shop. You were planning on going in today, weren't you?'

'No. The painting is done.'

'There's a lot more to getting the shop ready than painting, my girl.'

'Like what?' Zoe was perkier and she sounded genuinely interested.

'There's the stock, for a start, and the window display, and that floor needs a good wax and polish. You don't see old wooden floors like that anymore. And there are the Christmas decorations to put up.'

'Have we got any?'

Hattie loved that Zoe was taking ownership and including herself. 'We have,' she said. 'Or rather, I have, but they're more useful in the shop than in my attic. Which is why I need you to come round and help me get them down.'

Zoe sighed. 'What time do you want me to be there?'

'Ten? That'll give me time to do a few chores.'

It was only after she'd ended the call, that Hattie realised what she didn't have – and that was a tree.

Tapping her fingers on her chin, she had a think. Logan was the obvious choice, because he had a van and the pub didn't open until twelve. But she didn't trust him to pick a nice one. He was too blokey to think of the aesthetics. He'd most likely grab the biggest and be done with it. Silas, on the other hand, was arty-farty. He had an eye for what looked right.

'Silas? It's Hattie,' she said. 'I need you to get a tree. Now. This morning.'

'Good morning, Hattie, and how are you?' Silas sounded a tad sarcastic.

'I'm fine. But I won't be if I don't have something to hang my baubles on. Now, are you going to fetch me a tree? The garden centre on the Hereford road usually sells them. I want a nice one, mind, one with plenty of branches, and not a half-dead one, neither. If you don't think you can fit it in your car, ask Logan to take you in his van. But don't let him have any say in which one you buy. I'll be in the shop at midday, so you can drop it off then. Thanks, Silas.'

Hattie ended the call without giving him a chance to object. She found that tack often worked, although she could imagine Silas swearing to himself right now, and she grinned.

Right on the stroke of ten, Hattie heard her doorbell chime and she went to answer it, delighted that Zoe was punctual. Her instincts about the girl had been correct, and it was with a certain degree of self-satisfaction that she showed her upstairs and pointed to the hatch in the ceiling.

'God knows what's up there all together,' Hattie warned. 'I haven't been up the attic for years – can't get the ladder down, and even if I could, I'm not sure

I could get through the hole.'

Zoe looked her up and down. 'You should be able to squeeze through.'

'I wasn't talking about my size.' The cheeky little thing. Try getting to my age and not having some middle-age spread, Hattie was tempted to say, but the look of contrition on the girl's face as she realised what she'd said, stopped her. Instead, she showed her how to lift the hatch and pull the ladder down. It was so stiff it took both of them, but eventually it was fully extended and Zoe scuttled up it with all the speed of a rat going up a drainpipe, as the saying goes. Hattie watched her nimbleness with a certain amount of envy, and an equal amount of nostalgia. It didn't seem all that long ago she was able to do the same thing. These days, her mind might still be willing but her body had a different opinion on the matter.

'I think they're towards the back, near the chimney breast,' Hattie shouted up.

'Flippin' heck. There's loads of stuff up here. Argh!!'

'What? What?' Hattie was frantic. Zoe had sounded frightened.

A weak laugh trickled down the ladder. 'It's OK. It's just one of them mannequin things, but the head, arms, and legs are missing. You should think about throwing it out.'

'That, my lovely, is a dressmaker's dummy.'

'A what?'

'Never mind.' Kids these days didn't know the first thing about dressmaking. And why would they, with all the cheap clothes piled up in the shops. When Hattie was a girl, her mother had taught her how to sew, and she was fairly sure that the dummy in the attic was the very same her mum had used. 'Stop messing about, and find the Christmas decorations,' Hattie urged.

'You come up here and try to find them – you could open another shop with all the— Ah ha! Got 'em!'

'Bring them down, then.'

'Hang on a sec, I'm trying aren't I, but I'm having trouble getting at them,' Zoe grumbled.

Eventually, though, three boxes of decorations and one large plastic bag were sitting on the floor of Hattie's kitchen.

Zoe made to open one of the boxes, but Hattie shooed her away. 'Let's get them over to the shop first, then we can have a look to see what's what. I'll grab this bag, you bring a box.' Hattie pointed to the largest of the three and Zoe bent down to pick it up.

It took them two trips, but they did it – with a considerable amount of huffing and puffing from Hattie, and an equal amount of complaining from

Zoe.

By the time they'd transferred everything, the pair of them were ready for a hot drink and a slice of cake, so Hattie gave Zoe a tenner and sent her out for supplies from Bookylicious.

When the girl returned, with a delicious smell of rich coffee emanating from the reusable cups, Hattie was ankle-deep in baubles and memories.

'Look at this,' she said, holding up a delicate glass star in red and gold, with the middle cut out to reveal another smaller star inside.

Zoe bent down and squinted at it. 'That's cute. I've never seen one like that before.'

'I'm not surprised. It's over seventy years old.' She pulled aside the newspaper which the baubles were wrapped in. 'Every single one is different.'

Reaching out a hand, Zoe carefully picked one up. 'They're so delicate.'

'Yes, and that's a worry because I'd hate for any of them to be broken, but it's a shame not for anyone to see them, and they're perfect for the shop.'

'They are,' Zoe agreed. She had a thoughtful look on her face. 'I've got an idea. Why don't we put the tree in the window, and we can arrange the toys around it like they'd just been delivered by Father Christmas. But without the wrapping, obvs.'

'Obvs,' Hattie repeated, wryly. 'I'd better give Silas

a call and ask them to get one about four foot high. What do you think?'

'How big is four foot?'

Hattie held a hand up.

'I only do metres, but I think it needs to be bigger than that.' Zoe jumped up onto the deep windowsill which doubled as the shop's window display area. There was about a foot to spare above her head. 'You'll need it as tall as me if you want to make an impact. You don't want no piddling little thing; you want people to notice it.'

'You're right,' Hattie agreed, and called Silas. Luckily he and Logan had arrived five minutes ago, and they had yet to choose a tree, so after she'd issued the new instructions, Hattie and Zoe carried on with unpacking the decorations and preparing the display area.

'I need some toys,' Zoe said, scratching her head.

Hattie handed her a set of keys. 'Go and fetch some, then. This is the key to the shed. You can go down the back lane. Bring whatever you need.'

While she was gone, Hattie busied herself with what was inside the large plastic bag.

It was an ornate garland of fabric holly, ivy, and mistletoe and she knew it would look simply fabulous strung across the top shelf behind the counter.

It didn't take her long to drag the ladder across

and set it up, and with the utmost care and a great deal of huffing, she clambered up a couple of rungs until she could reach the shelf in question. Yep, she was right – it did look good, providing a backdrop to the area where customers would stand to make a payment.

She was about to climb back down when she became aware of a face peering around one of the posters. Half a face, because the posters took up most of the available window area.

She didn't need to see the whole of it to know who it was. Sara, Alfred's daughter, was frowning at her, and all Hattie could think was "oh, shit" as the pair of them made eye contact.

Neither of them moved for a moment, then Sara shook her head and walked away, leaving Hattie to breathe a sigh of relief.

Then she wondered why she should be feeling relieved at all. It wasn't as though the woman knew Alfred was involved. As far as Sara was aware, Hattie might have swapped her job in Bookylicious for one in the Toy Shop.

And not only that, it was none of the woman's business anyway.

But it didn't prevent Hattie from experiencing a little twinge of unease; her water had a lot to answer for.

CHAPTER 24

ALFRED

The smell of roasting chicken filled the kitchen and Alfred licked his lips, his mouth watering. One thing he didn't miss about living on his own was having to cook for himself. He hadn't cooked at all if he was honest, having existed on a supply of microwaveable meals and tinned food. And he must say, Sara was a fine cook.

At least he didn't feel as guilty today, not after his stint in the shop yesterday, and the fact that today was a Sunday and no one would be in the toy shop, made him feel better still. All that needed to be done now was to move the toys across and arrange them. He couldn't believe how much they had achieved in just one week.

The smell of food gave him an idea – maybe he'd treat everyone to a meal to say thank you. It was the least he could do, and he was thinking about the best place to go (he didn't want to take them to the Tavern, because it wouldn't be fair on Logan) when Sara said something that halted him in his tracks.

'There's a new shop opening in the village,' she said, as she popped a pile of steaming potatoes into a tureen. 'Take this into the dining room for me, will you? I'll bring the chicken, and then I think we're ready to eat.'

Alfred took the tureen from her, careful to wrap a tea towel around it because it was hot, and took it into the dining room. Obediently, he sat down, but his (hopefully) outwardly calm exterior was belied by his churning thoughts.

David entered the room and took a seat. 'Mmm, this looks wonderful. If Christmas lunch is going to be anything like this, we're in for a treat.'

Sara began dishing vegetables onto Alfred's plate and he breathed an inward sigh of relief that the subject had moved on from the new shop in the village.

'It's next year that I'm looking forward to,' David added. 'Our grandchild's first Christmas.'

'We'll have a brand new baby to spoil,' Alfred said, unexpected joy bubbling deep inside him. He never thought he'd live to see a great-grandchild, and his only regret was that Dorothy wasn't here to share the joy with him.

'Talking about spoiling babies, there's a toy shop opening up in Ticklemore,' Sara told David, and Alfred's heart sank as she carried on, 'It looks like they're selling those old-fashioned wooden toys. It's so nice to see a new business opening up, no one likes to see boarded up shops.'

Sara chattered on, but Alfred tuned her out and tried to keep his expression neutral. How naïve of him to think she wouldn't notice a new business on the high street now that she had taken to shopping in the village.

For some reason he'd assumed (actually, he hadn't thought about it at all) that Sara would continue to shop elsewhere, as she always had done in the past. Although she and David had lived in the village for several years, they never shopped there – both of them left early in the morning and didn't get home until late – which wasn't conducive to normal shop hours. He knew that in the past Sara tended to pop to Hereford and the large out of town supermarket to do her shopping – usually on the way home from work on a Friday. But now that she'd retired and had discovered the delights of Ticklemore, it was only to be expected that she'd take more of an interest in the village and its goings-on.

David didn't take his eyes of Alfred as he asked

her, 'Similar to the ones in your dad's shed, you mean?'

'I suppose so, but from the posters on the outside of the shop windows they look like the ones they'll be selling are properly made. Of course, the shop isn't open yet, and they're in the middle of doing it up so there aren't any toys to see.' She shrugged, and cocked her head to one side, a forkful of chicken poised between her plate and her mouth. 'You'll never guess who I saw working in there, Alfred – it was that horrid old woman from the café-cum-bookshop you spend so much time in. She was halfway up a ladder, the daft old thing. She needs to be careful at her age – if she fell she'd break a hip or worse. She's got to be seventy-odd.'

'Nearly eighty,' Alfred replied numbly.

'You're getting to know Hattie quite well,' David observed. 'Is this new toy shop hers?'

Alfred stared blankly at his son-in-law wondering how he should answer that, but Sara saved him.

'Oh, by the way, speaking of toys has reminded me, your old house has now been cleared, Dad, so we can go ahead and put it on the market. There's no point in waiting, and as long as we don't ask silly money for it, it'll soon go. David and I were discussing whether we should bite the bullet and do it up – you'd get more for it that way, Dad – but to be honest, David hasn't got the time and with the new baby on the way I don't think I'm up to project managing a complete refurb on your old house. Anyway,' she finally paused to take a breath. 'I've arranged for an estate agent to view it and give us – you – a valuation.'

Dear God, she'd been watching Grand Designs or Homes Under the Hammer, Alfred thought. Although, now that it had been emptied and he'd resigned himself to the fact that he'd never live there again, he was as keen to get shot of it as his daughter was. And so what if it could be sold for a few grand more if it had a new kitchen (although he didn't see anything wrong with the old one) – Sara would spend nearly that much on getting the work done.

'Did they take everything?' David wanted to know. Alfred heard the sub-text below the apparently innocent question.

Sara frowned. 'I assume so. I mean, I didn't hang about. I let them in and then popped to the supermarket – I didn't like that one nearest to you, Dad; I couldn't find half of what I wanted the last time I was in there – then I went back just as they were finishing loading up the van. I did a quick check to make sure they hadn't damaged anything, but to be honest, it wasn't easy to tell. Dad, did you know there are marks on the inside of the pantry door from when

I was growing up? I can't believe they are still there.'

Alfred could. He remembered Dorothy telling Sara to stand against the door and asking her to stand up straight while she drew a line to show how tall their daughter had grown, and then add a date next to it. Dorothy had done it religiously every six months or so until Sara was eighteen and had point-blank refused to be measured, anymore.

'What about the shed?' David asked. He was watching Alfred carefully, but Alfred kept his attention on his lunch and prayed futilely that David would shut up.

'Obviously I didn't look in there. Why would I?' Sara demanded. 'But if you want to pop over to Dad's house to make sure they emptied that too…?'

'No, it's OK. I'm sure there's nothing left in it.'

Alfred's appetite had disappeared completely, and he placed his cutlery down on his plate and pushed it away.

'You've not eaten much; are you feeling OK?' Sara asked him.

'I'm fine. I'll, um, just go for a lie down.'

He was conscious of his son-in-law's eyes on him as he left the dining room, and he was tempted to try to dash up the stairs to escape him. However, his dashing days were done, and if he hurried too much he'd risk falling and doing himself some damage.

Thinking about falls brought him to thinking about Hattie. What the hell was she doing in the toy shop today? It was her day off and she needed to spend it resting. She also had no business going up a ladder.

Crossly, he dialled her number.

'Hattie, what the hell are you playing at?' he hissed as soon as she answered.

'I know, I know… I almost died when I saw your Sara nosing through the window. She spotted me, too, and I swear she pulled a face at me.'

'She was probably pulling a face because you were up a ladder. You could have fallen.'

'But I didn't though, did I?'

'I don't know, you tell me.'

'I *am* telling you. I didn't fall.'

'But you might have done, and then where would you be?'

'In hospital probably,' she replied cheerfully and he was so enraged at her lack of concern and care for herself that he was sorely tempted to push her off a ladder himself.

'I wouldn't visit you,' he warned.

'Yes, you would. You wouldn't want to miss an opportunity to lecture me on my stupidity.'

'True.' He paused. 'What were you doing up there, anyway?'

'Putting decorations up. I've got a lovely garland that me and Zoe hung on the wall behind the counter. I've also got a couple of old tablecloths that had seen better days, so Zoe and I cut them into triangles, and stapled them to some ribbon to make bunting. Even if I say so myself, they look amazing – cream, green and red. Very Christmassy, and traditional colours, too.

'Did you say Zoe helped?'

'Yes, why? That's what she's there for, isn't she?'

Alfred was getting crosser and crosser. 'I can't believe Zoe stood by and let you climb a bloody ladder,' he yelled, before hastily lowering his voice.

'Dad? Are you all right?' Sara called.

He put his hand over the phone. 'I'm fine.'

'What was all the shouting about?' she wanted to know.

'I was, er, talking to Hattie. Telling her off about being up a ladder.'

'Hmm,' Sara called. 'Don't go upsetting yourself. It's bad for your blood pressure.'

There were a lot of things that were bad for his blood pressure, and Hattie was only one of them. 'OK,' he called back.

'Is she bossing you about again?' Hattie asked. 'If I were you, I'd—'

'Stop trying to change the subject,' Alfred

interrupted. 'I said, I can't believe—'

'I heard what you said, and she didn't. I'd sent her out to fetch some toys for the shed to go in the window.'

'Let me get this straight – you deliberately waited until Zoe was out and then went up a ladder?'

'Not exactly. It wasn't deliberate; it just so happened that I saw the garland and wondered what it would look like.'

'It would have served you right if you'd fallen.'

'But I didn't, did I?'

Alfred rolled his eyes as the conversation was about to go around in circles again. The woman was insufferable. And very annoying. He couldn't fault her work ethic, though, or the way she seemed able to make things happen. She never appeared to take no for an answer, or to be daunted by obstacles. She just ploughed on and expected everyone to fall in with her plans.

Just like he had.

Looking back, he realised he hadn't had any choice, and he fully suspected that if he had insisted on disposing of his toys, that she would have opened the shop with or without his blessing.

That woman was going to be the death of him.

But, if he was honest, he wouldn't want her any other way.

CHAPTER 25

HATTIE

Hattie did a slow twirl in the middle of the toy shop, to make sure nothing was out of place. It was looking fantastic, and was ready to go. She was tempted to open the place in the morning and she might very well have suggested to Zoe that they did precisely that, but the grand opening was scheduled for Saturday, and opening a whole day early would be exceedingly bad manners.

But she was itching to see the public's reaction to all those gorgeously tactile toys displayed around the store. To create a sense of exclusivity, Zoe, who had an old head on her young shoulders and had shown a flair for marketing and display, had suggested that the shelves weren't stuffed full, that some of the items were held back to replenish what was being sold. Besides, the girl had rightly pointed out, if they'd put everything out then no one would be able to see any of it. Hattie knew Alfred had a shed-load of stuff (literally – and she'd almost done herself in when she'd helped shift all of it on that night two weeks ago), but she hadn't realised just how much until a goodly portion of it was on display.

The couple of shelves behind the counter (on which sat a beautiful old till – purely for display purposes, mind you, and they had to be careful with it because Nell had lent it to them), held an assortment of small, inexpensive, impulse-buy toys, such as simple little cars on wheels that spun around, and a spider with jointed legs. There were also stacking dolls, Russian-style, and rattles for the younger kids.

Along the wall next to the till were some larger toys like a train set, wooden crates filled with an assortment of pretend food – the strawberries looked particularly convincing – and pull-along cats, cars, dogs, and a rabbit.

But what Hattie adored were the tables set out with a fort, complete with wooden horses and knights, a garage, and a doll's house. Next to them on the floor, because it was too big to go anywhere else, was a kitchen. Zoe had been canny, and had arranged a toaster (Hattie just adored the little pieces of toast which came with it), some pots and pans, and cooking utensils around it, in the hope that they would be add-on purchases, and a large barrel, courtesy of Logan, stood near the door and contained assorted hobby horses.

The pièce de résistance, however, was the window.

Zoe had decorated it single-handedly, spending a whole day on it to ensure it was perfect.

The main attraction (as well as the tree) was the magnificent rocking horse which had centre stage; and it had a hefty price tag to go with it – Zoe insisting that it could always be discounted nearer Christmas if it failed to sell at the amount they were asking for it.

It was show-stopper all right, and they were keeping it and the rest of the shop under wraps, until the mayor did her bit and declared it well and truly open. Zoe had rigged up some black material on the window and the blind on the door was pulled down, so no one could see in, and Hattie thoroughly enjoyed listening to the speculation which abounded throughout the village. In Bookylicious she was perfectly situated to hear all the talk and the fact that no one had caught a glimpse of even so much as a toy soldier was adding fuel to the fire of excitement.

Maddison had very kindly let Hattie swap her day off so she could be in the toy shop on Saturday instead of in the café, and between Hattie, Zoe, and Alfred, they should be able to manage. Anyway, they'd be hard pushed to get any other staff in the space, not if they wanted the number of customers they were hoping for to fit in, too.

Satisfied that everything which could be done had been done, including the sign having been hung (thanks, Silas) Hattie took a final look around before she locked up. She'd buy some festive scented diffusers tomorrow, just to make the place smell Christmassy, and she'd make the non-alcoholic mulled wine in the morning before work, to go with the milk and hot chocolate they intended to serve.

Maddison had also kindly offered to make some festive biscuits for the occasion for free, and Hattie thought the slices of carrot cake in the shape of a carrot were inspired (the orange frosting was to die for), along with the truffles which looked like miniature Christmas puds. It might take business away from Bookylicious for a short time, but Hattie was paying her employer back by slipping leaflets into every bag, advertising each of the businesses who had helped to transform the toy shop from a vague idea into a reality – which meant that the Treasure Trove, the Ticklemore Tavern, the Studio (which was Silas's gallery) and Bookylicious should all benefit too, and the church and the WI were also mentioned.

Hattie's thinking cap was still firmly on her head when she strolled into the Tavern a few minutes later and headed for the private function room upstairs. It wasn't very big but it suited her purpose perfectly, which was to host a meal for everyone who'd helped get the project off the ground.

As she walked into the room, she was concerned to see that the lights were off. Had she got the wrong day – were they all meeting tomorrow instead?

'Surprise!'

Hattie squeaked at the chorus of voices, then the lights came on and she saw everyone gathered around the table, all of them on their feet.

When they all started to clap, she felt a right idiot.

'You daft lot,' she cried. 'You've got the wrong person.' The bunch of muppets thought it was Alfred coming up the stairs, but they'd got her instead. Now they'd have to turn the lights back off and try to be quiet, because he was bound to be not far behind her.

'No, we haven't,' a familiar voice said, and she noticed Alfred was standing just off to the side, and out of her direct line of sight. 'Without you, the toy shop wouldn't exist. And without you, my toys would all be on the scrap heap.'

Hattie felt tears prick at the back of her eyes and she sniffed loudly. 'You made those toys, not me, You're the one who should have all the credit.'

'Nonsense.' He stepped forwards and took her elbow. 'Come and sit down, and have a glass of gin.

You deserve it.'

Hattie sat, choked up with emotion, and gazed at all the faces beaming back at her. Logan (who had been in it from the beginning), Nell (who had shared her vision), Juliette (who tirelessly went from door to door stuffing leaflets in letterboxes), Silas (for his creative talent), Father Todd, Benny and Marge for their help with the mucky stuff, and Zoe (who'd proved to be a little Godsend) all were there. And of course, Alfred himself, who had more talent than he was aware of.

'Hey, Alfred, what excuse did you give your daughter?' Zoe shouted irreverently and everyone dissolved into laughter.

'I told her it was an OAP Christmas night out,' he said. 'She's coming to pick me up at ten-thirty, so I'd best get my dinner eaten a bit quick, in case she's early!'

There was more laughter and Alfred was grinning from ear to ear, but Hattie could see that he was hiding something from the others, although he'd previously let her in on what was bothering him – he intended to tell Sara all about the toy shop tomorrow and he wasn't looking forward to her reaction one little bit.

Hattie didn't blame him. But one thing she did know, if Sara didn't like it then Sara could lump it, because setting up the toy shop had been the best thing that had happened to Alfred in a long time. Alfred was a different man to the one who she'd seen in Bookylicious barely two weeks ago, and she was determined she wouldn't let him slip back into the despondency and depression she'd sensed in him.

And if his daughter was going to make life difficult for him, then she'd have Hattie Jenkins to contend with!

CHAPTER 26

ALFRED

Alfred hadn't felt this apprehensive since the day he'd asked Dorothy to marry him. Thank God she'd said yes, although he didn't think Sara would be as accommodating when he told her his news.

He'd thought long and hard about how he would break it to her and had come to the conclusion that it would be best to show her. If she saw for herself how much had been achieved in such a short space of time, and how wonderful the shop looked, then she could hardly pooh-pooh it. He briefly wondered if he should organise some back-up in the form of Nell, who was as savvy a businesswoman as anyone he'd ever met (and he'd met a few in his day), and maybe Juliette, who also had her head screwed on the right way. But he decided against it. He knew that if Sara felt she was being ganged up on, she'd probably dig her heels in and hate the idea on principle.

He'd leave Hattie out of it for the time being, conscious that his daughter and his friend hadn't hit it off.

'Where are we going?' Sara asked as they walked past Bookylicious and carried on.

'I've got something I want you to see,' he told her, his mouth dry. Although why he should feel so apprehensive, he didn't know. He was a grown man, and she was his child. If she didn't like what he was doing, then tough. He didn't have to seek her permission. Hell, he didn't even have to tell her, if he didn't want to; but he realised that attitude would be a little silly.

'I thought we were going to have a coffee in that café you like so much?'

'We'll have one afterwards,' he said, but not in Bookylicious. He didn't think it would be prudent.

Alfred came to a halt outside the toy shop and reached into his pocket for his keys.

'Look, Dad, that's the new shop I was telling you about last night.' She looked over his shoulder. 'It says there's a grand opening tomorrow, with refreshments. Perhaps we should go along to it? There might be something for the baby.' She saw his expression and pulled a face. 'I know it's too early to be buying things, but they might have a snuggly bunny or a teddy bear.'

Alfred doubted it very much indeed. There was nothing snuggly about his toys, although teddy bears and rag dolls would have been a marvellous addition. His Dorothy had been a whizz with a needle and thread, and if he'd had confided in her, she might have wanted to make some toys, too.

Meh, who was he kidding? She'd had plenty of hobbies of her own to keep her occupied; she hadn't needed to join in with his.

'What are you doing?' Sara's face was a picture as he inserted the key in the lock and turned it.

He pushed the door open.

'Are we allowed? I mean, is this, you know,' she lowered her voice, 'legal?'

'Yes is the answer to both questions. After you.' He held out his arm and gestured for her to go inside.

Warily, as though she might have been asked to enter a lion's cage, his daughter took one step and then another, and all the while her eyes were darting everywhere.

'It's like Santa's grotto,' she said. 'Wow. It's gorgeous. Look at that!' She pointed at the kitchen. 'It's even got pots and pans to go with it.'

'They're sold separately,' Alfred informed her, and a long silence descended. An uncomfortable silence. His daughter was an intelligent woman, and he could see the cogs whirring as she joined the dots and made a full picture out of the scraps of information she had available to her.

'You'd better tell me what's going on,' she said, eventually.

'Would you like to sit down?'

'Just tell me.' Her tone was cold and commanding – she was using her head teacher voice and he could imagine how scary it must have been for a small child to hear it. Sara might not want to sit, but he did. His knees were trembling to such an extent he was sure he could hear them knocking.

'This is my shop. These are my toys,' he said, and waited for her reaction.

'Your toys? The ones out of your shed? The same toys which were taken away by the removal company?'

'Yes, yes, and no. They didn't take them, because they weren't there.'

'How—? What—?' For once, words seemed to fail her, and Alfred felt a twinge of satisfaction that he'd managed to shock her. No longer was he the predictable old git she thought him to be. And neither was he as incompetent and incapable.

In a matter-of-fact voice (because there was too much emotion hanging in the air already) he said, 'When you told me you'd arranged for people to come into my home and take everything away, I was devastated. It was like you were taking what was left of your mother away.'

'Aw, Dad.'

'Let me finish. I didn't like it, so I thought about putting everything into storage. I decided against it, but some friends of mine saw the toys, persuaded me they were good, and this is the result.' He waved his hand in the air.

'You should have told me how you felt about your things. I'd have understood. And I'm sure there's more to this little story than your telling me,' she added, her face tight.

'*Would* you have understood?' he asked.

'Yes.' Her nod was emphatic, but he could see doubt behind her eyes.

'Even if you understood, you would have gone ahead anyway,' he pointed out, and he knew he'd hit home when she dropped her gaze to the floor.

She soon brought it back up again, and it came to rest on him. 'I can't say I'm happy about this, Dad. Neither your involvement nor that you kept it from me. How long has this been going on? It can't have been long, because the toys were still in the shed two or so weeks ago.'

'Some of them are still in a shed – just not in mine,' he said wryly. 'If I'd told you, you'd have done

278

your best to talk me out of it.'

'Damned right, I would have. Look at this place.'

'I'm looking, and I'm very proud of what we've achieved.'

'When you say "we", I assume you're referring to that awful woman who works in Bookylicious?' A lightbulb flashed behind Sara's eyes. 'She was in here the other day. I saw her.'

Alfred's response was mild. 'That's right.'

'The stupid woman was up a ladder. At her age! And that's exactly what I'm talking about – I don't want her to be a bad influence on you.'

'I'm not seven years old, so don't speak to me like I'm a child.' He was starting to become cross now. He'd known telling Sara wasn't going to be easy, and that she'd object to what he was doing, but honestly, she was being obnoxious.

'Then don't behave like one,' she countered sharply. 'Can't you see that by sneaking around behind my back, you're not doing yourself any favours.'

'I suppose by that, you mean that you think I'm going gaga?'

'You said it.'

There was a hideous silence as both of them realised what they'd just said.

Alfred was the first to speak. 'Sara, my darling,

we've had this discussion before – I love you with all my heart, but I can't take any more of your controlling and bossy behaviour.'

'And I love you too, and that's why I'm so worried. I really am concerned for your health.'

'Physical maybe, what about my mental health?'

'That's part of it.'

'You'll have to explain. Surely all this should show that I'm not suffering from dementia?' He stared pointedly around the shop.

Sara's tone softened as she said, 'You're not yourself, Dad. Mrs Shelby next door told me she was worried about you long before you had your last fall. And I could see with my own eyes that you weren't taking care of yourself. Whenever I visited, the house was a mess.'

His daughter had a point. 'Yes, well, the house was always Dorothy's domain; she hated it when I interfered.'

'But Mum had gone, Dad. It was up to you to keep it clean and tidy, and that's not all – most of the time there was hardly anything in the fridge or the cupboards, you'd lost weight, and you had no interest in anything anymore…' Sara trailed off. Tears brimmed in her eyes and threatened to spill over. 'All you did was mope around. I felt I was losing you, too.'

'We've talked about this, Sara. I explained what was wrong.'

'I was worried you might have dementia – sometimes I don't think you knew who I was.'

'I knew,' he replied, bleakly. 'To my shame, I didn't much care. You weren't Dorothy, you see. And whenever I looked at you, all I saw was your mother, and it hurt more than words can say.'

'Oh, Dad.'

'Come here.' Alfred got unsteadily to his feet, tears trickling down his face as he watched his daughter begin to cry. He walked towards her and opened his arms, and when she stepped into his embrace, he held her to him fiercely. Gone was the awkwardness of their previous hug – she was his daughter and although they might have their differences, he loved her more than words could say.

Sniffling, she pulled back to look at him. 'I can tell you're better,' she said. 'You're putting on weight and you've got more of a spring in your step. But…' The worry returned to her face. 'I've been doing a lot of reading about dementia, and it doesn't happen all at once. It comes and goes, and it's so insidious at first that no one believes they have it. and…' She bit her lip and he could tell she was trying not to bawl.

'Is that truly what you think? That I have dementia?'

'Dad, the other day you left your phone in the fridge. What am I supposed to think?'

'That sort of forgetfulness is part and parcel of growing old. I'm forever going upstairs then forgetting what I went up there for. But the way I was before I came to live with you, wasn't dementia. At least, I hope it wasn't.' He shrugged helplessly. 'I simply believed I didn't have anything left to live for. What was the point of going on without your Mum? '

'There was me, Dad, there was me…'

'I know that, Sara-kins, but I was so lost in grief, I didn't know how to get myself out of it.'

The use of his old nickname for her brought fresh tears to her already waterlogged eyes, and she blew her nose into a tissue. 'Are you out of it now?' she asked, her voice muffled.

'It'll always be with me, but the blackness has lifted and I can see some colour in my life. Most of that is down to you. I'd still be stuck in that house on my own, if you hadn't insisted I come live with you.'

'What about this shop?'

'This has been my salvation. It has given me a purpose, something else to think about other than how much I miss your mother and how awful my life has been since she passed on. And I've got Hattie to thank for it.'

Sara wrinkled her nose.

'She was the one who made me see how good my toys were. She was the one who persuaded me to set up the shop. She also gave me the idea of giving all the profit to charity.'

'I'm worried that it will be too much for you.'

'It's only until Christmas – the shop will close its doors on Christmas Eve.'

There was a pause, then Sara said, 'That's another thing I'm worried about now – when it's all over and there's nothing for you to get up for in the morning again, what will happen to you?'

Unfortunately. Alfred couldn't answer that particular question, because he had been wondering the same thing, too.

CHAPTER 27

HATTIE

'No one is coming,' Hattie said, pacing up to the door and peering around the blind. The posters had been taken down, and the only thing that remained to be done as soon as the shop was officially open was to remove the fabric from the window, which would only take a second. Zoe had already been instructed that this was her responsibility, and Hattie tried not to tell her again, but she was so nervous.

Alfred, on the other hand, was utterly calm. 'They'll be here,' he said, for the fourth or fifth time. 'It's only nine-thirty. You can't expect people to stand outside for hours in the cold.'

'At least it's not raining,' Hattie said, staring anxiously up at the sky. It was quite a nice day as far as November days went – cold and bright, with a weak sun hanging in a pale blue sky. A good day for it

– *if* anyone turned up.

Her tummy was in knots and her head was starting to ache with the stress of it all. Why, oh why, did she have to act on her idiotic idea to open a toy shop? What did she know about setting up and running a business? That it wasn't technically her business was neither here nor there. Everyone who'd had a hand in it felt the same way. And none of them, apart from Zoe, had arrived either, except for Maddison, who'd delivered the yummy cookies and cakes earlier. And had then had to leave.

Hang on, were the couple standing on the pavement with their two children loitering or were they here for the opening? It was difficult to tell.

A few more people arrived, then Hattie spotted Logan on the edge of what was quickly becoming a crowd. Juliette was with him, and Hattie opened the door a crack, causing a surge of interest, and hissed, 'Come in!'

Logan shook his head. 'We'll stay out here – there'll be enough people inside when it officially opens.'

Hattie saw the sense in that, especially when Benny, Marge, Father Todd, and Nell all joined them. The shop needed paying customers, not helpers, right now.

A bloke with an impressive camera with the largest

lens Hattie had ever seen, pushed his way to the front of the crowd, together with another man, and she wondered if they were a photographer and reporter from one of the regional newspapers, here to capture the image of Cllr Taylor snipping the ribbon.

'Scissors!' Hattie yelled, making Alfred jump.

'Here.' Zoe pointed to the edge of the window, near to where she was kneeling in readiness to remove the black fabric.

Alfred, showing the first sign of nerves, shuffled forwards and glanced down at the few words he had written. That she'd made him write. It was his shop, she reasoned, so it was his job to say something. To be fair, they had worked on it together, and she thought it was short and to the point. Anyway, she had no doubt in her mind that the mayor would have enough to say. That one liked the sound of her own voice far too much, but publicity was publicity, and as long as she said good things about the shop, the mayor could stand there all day and pontificate.

'If the mayor has a big black car and a massive chain around her neck, then she's here,' Zoe called.

Hattie and Alfred exchanged a quick look and nodded, then they stepped forward together to slip through the door and greet their honoured guest, leaving Zoe to secure a ribbon across the open door behind them.

There was a disturbance in the force as the waiting people craned their necks to try to peer inside, and Hattie smiled to herself. There was nothing like a sense of mystery to raise curiosity levels, and the assembled children were bouncing in anticipation. Hattie hoped it was due to the toys and not the free cookies.

Hattie stood aside to let Alfred take centre stage as Cllr Taylor made her way to the front of the shop, where she took her rightful place as the "celebrity" who was opening the premises.

Alfred cleared his throat.

There was no discernible drop in decibels.

He cleared his throat again, louder this time.

The noise level remained the same, so Hattie took things into her own hands.

'Oi, you lot! Quiet!' she yelled.

Silence (more or less) descended and Alfred shot her a grateful look. For a grumpy old git, he was rather sweet.

'Ladies and gentlemen, boys and girls,' he said. 'I am delighted to welcome you today to the opening of Ticklemore's very own toy shop – called, funnily enough, the Ticklemore Toy Shop.'

Good-natured tittering rippled through the crowd and as Alfred continued his speech Hattie scanned the expectant faces with pleasure. More people had turned up than she could have imagined; she guessed that most of the village was here, plus many faces she didn't recognise. But one face stood out, and Hattie did a double-take when she saw it.

Sara, Alfred's daughter was standing there with her husband, together with a young couple; the girl was the spitting image of her mother, but she had Alfred's soft brown eyes. The four of them hadn't taken their eyes off Alfred, and both Sara and her daughter wore proud expressions.

Hattie blinked in surprise; Alfred had informed her during his usual evening phone call that he'd told Sara about the shop and his involvement in it, and that they'd reached a sort of impasse where Sara wasn't convinced that Alfred was doing the right thing, and Alfred intended to carry on regardless. Hattie hadn't expected the woman to turn up, yet here she was. Well, well, well…

By the time Hattie had tuned back in again, the mayor was making her speech, and thankfully appeared to be coming to the end of it.

Hattie, in the hope of hastening things along even further, stepped forwards and handed her the scissors. With a flourish, the mayor took them from her, said, 'I declare the Ticklemore Toy Shop well and truly open,' and snipped the ribbon.

Clapping and cheering filled the air, and Hattie

found herself beaming and clapping along with the rest of the crowd.

The next hour or so passed in a flash, beginning with Zoe swiftly removing the fabric hiding the window from prying eyes, and the response from the people outside the shop was heart-warming as everyone exclaimed over how eye-catching it was. She heard several comments about how it reminded them of a living room from days gone by, and she made a note to pass the comments on to Zoe who, Hattie knew, would be thrilled with the praise.

The reaction of the customers as they filed inside was even better, and Hattie saw Alfred's flushed and happy face as they marvelled over the craftsmanship and the details. The prices didn't put people off either, which had been another of Hattie's worries. But hats off to Nell, the woman certainly knew her onions – and she had advised on the optimum prices to charge for each of them. Alfred hardly had a chance to draw breath as he was approached time and time again by people wanting to talk to him about the toys, and congratulate him.

Hattie had to admit that seeing the shop full of customers was a joy to behold, as were the happy faces of children and adults alike. A warm glow of contentment spread through her chest as she watched Zoe ring up sale after sale. Hattie had Marge in charge of the cookies and drinks, and she was delighted to see that the free refreshments were going down a treat, especially the milk and carrot-shaped cake, as everyone loved the idea and the sentiment behind it.

Hattie had given herself the task of making sure everything ran smoothly, so Alfred didn't have to. This was his day, and she intended to make sure he was free to enjoy it. From the expression on his face, he was loving every minute and Hattie wanted nothing more than to go up to him and give him the biggest hug in the world.

'You're Hattie, aren't you?' a male voice asked, and Hattie looked around to see Sara's husband standing by her elbow. He had a mulled wine in his hand. 'Hi, I'm Sara's husband, David.'

'Pleased to meet you,' she sing-songed, not entirely sure whether she was pleased or not. Alfred had confided in her that David had had an inkling about the toys going missing from the shed well before Alfred had filled his daughter in, but until Hattie knew what David thought about the shop and Alfred's involvement in it, the jury was out on him as far as she was concerned.

'Pleased to meet you, too,' he said. 'The place looks good. More than good – wonderful in fact. I can't believe Alfred is responsible for all this.'

'Why not?' Hattie's tone was sharp. 'Don't you

think he's capable of it? Let me tell you, sonny Jim—'

David chuckled. 'That's not what I meant at all. Alfred is eminently capable, but he hasn't been himself since his wife died, and, well…'

'Is he himself now?' she demanded, casting a look in Alfred's direction.

'I should say so; just look at this place. I thought when I first saw them, that it would be a shame to dispose of all these lovely toys, but it seemed the right thing to do at the time, because seeing them upset him so much.'

Hattie felt like telling David that what had really upset Alfred was his daughter's thoughtlessness, but she didn't want to cause an atmosphere or risk spoiling Alfred's special day, so she held her tongue and forced her mouth into a smile.

Her smile became even more forced when Sara joined them.

And when Alfred stepped over to them, Hatti guessed she must be looking positively manic as she tried to keep her opinions to herself and not let her dislike of the woman show.

'It's fabulous, Dad. I must admit I had my doubts, even after I saw the shop yesterday, but now…' She gazed around at the people making purchases and Hattie's attitude softened slightly. The woman hadn't apologised as such, but at least she had the decency to give Alfred credit for what he'd achieved.

It was slightly annoying that Sara hadn't acknowledged the part Hattie herself had played, but never mind, she could live with that.

'It doesn't stop me from worrying, though,' Sara continued. 'I'm scared you're taking on more than you can cope with.'

'We'll manage,' Alfred said, and Hattie glowed when he put one arm around her shoulder and hugged her to him. Despite his slight stoop and the walking stick, the silver hair and the lined face, he felt solid and dependable.

'If it gets too much for you, I can always help,' his daughter said, and Hattie felt him stiffen.

'That's very kind of you, Sara. We'll bear that in mind,' he said.

He let go of Hattie, but for some strange reason it felt as though he was still hugging her, and she felt all warm inside. Hattie gave the woman a side-eyed look, and filed her offer away for future reference – the closer they got to Christmas, the busier she anticipated the shop being, and although she hadn't taken to Sara on a personal level, Alfred might need her help at some point, whether he wanted it or not.

Eventually, the refreshments were all consumed and the people who had only come to be nosey left, and the shop steadied down to a more manageable stream of customers. By the time it shut for the day, Hattie was nevertheless exhausted. And Alfred looked positively drained; so much so that she was worried about him.

He perked up when Zoe closed the door behind the final customer, and the takings were counted.

'That's a lot,' Hattie said, quickly tallying up the amount, and the three of them stared at each other in awe.

Alfred had a tear in his eye, and even Zoe was lost for words for a change.

'I can't believe my whittling made all that,' Alfred said, gazing at the figure.

'I can.' Hattie's voice was firm.

'But for people to pay money for them…' He trailed off and dabbed at his eyes.

Hattie moved closer and put her arms around him. 'I told you they were good,' she said. 'Do you believe me now?'

He nodded.

'Do you believe in yourself?'

The second nod was more hesitant, but Hattie thought they were getting somewhere.

Zoe had left them to it and was busily tidying up. In no time at all, the shop was ship-shape again, although it needed to be restocked as there were a few empty places on the shelves, but that could be done in the morning. For now, it was time for the three of them to go home for a decent meal and some well-earned rest.

Hattie was about to go to bed, her body knackered but her head swirling with visions of the day, when Alfred made his usual nightly call to her, and it was only after she'd spoken to him did she realise just how important hearing his voice last thing at night, had become to her.

Closely followed by the realisation that it wasn't only the phone call that was important to her – it was the man who had made it.

CHAPTER 28

ALFRED

Alfred had never been one for a fayre, Christmas or otherwise, not since Sara was small. To him, the atmosphere had always seemed strained, as though people were determined to enjoy themselves no matter what. Rain, muddy fields, soggy cakes, grizzling children, too many crowds, too much noise. And Christmas fayres were not much better, apart from the fact that they were never held in fields, and the temperature usually hovered around freezing.

Ticklemore's Christmas Fayre was an altogether different kettle of fish, though, because Alfred had a vested interest in its success, and he was delighted to wake up to a still, calm day. It was cold, admittedly, but it wasn't raining (which was a bonus) and as the morning went on, the weather was reminiscent of last Saturday, when the shop had its official opening.

Zoe was opening up this morning, and he had planned on having a leisurely breakfast before heading into the village, but for some reason he felt excited, so he gobbled down his cereal and toast, dressed as hastily as he was able, and headed out of the door as fast as his gammy leg would allow.

He'd barely reached the end of the high street when the atmosphere hit him. It was the music that reached him first, the sound of a fairground, that unmistakable tinny music which issued forth from a merry-go-round. As he turned the corner, there it was, slap bang in the middle of the cordoned-off street, all flashing lights and dancing horses.

He was immediately transported back to his own childhood, and a wave of nostalgia swept over him. He used to love a merry-go-round, always choosing a black horse and pretending he was a highwayman.

Where had those days gone? One minute he had been a boy, fizzing with the sheer excitement of being alive and having Christmas to look forward to – the next, he was walking with a stick and feeling jaded and stale. Except, he wasn't feeling that way today, and he hadn't felt that way for a good few weeks now.

It was all down to Hattie.

She'd been like a female Prince Charming to his Snow White and had woken him from his sleep with her sheer zest for life.

Smiling to himself, he vowed to steal a couple of hours and spend some time with her at the Christmas Fayre. She deserved to be treated and spoiled, and he was just the man to do it.

With a quick call to Juliette to ask if she'd take his place in the shop for a while today, they arranged a time, and then he went into Bookylicious to put the second half of his plan into motion. With Maddison on board and agreeing to give Hattie the time off, Alfred spent the next couple of hours in his shop, chatting to customers and selling his toys.

He was enjoying himself so much (*who'd have thought it a few weeks ago?*) that he almost forgot the time, and stared blankly at Juliette when she appeared in the shop, handed him his stick and his coat, and steered him out of the door.

'Shoo, go and enjoy yourself. This place will be here when you get back,' she said, and winked at him.

As he skirted and dodged his way along the pavement, the wink preyed on his mind. What had she meant by it? Was she reading too much into him taking Hattie to the fayre? Did she think they were on some kind of a date?

The thought stopped him in his tracks and a woman behind bumped into him. He apologised absently, his mind on the wink and dating. And Hattie.

Nah, the idea was absurd. They were friends going out together for a couple of hours, just enjoying each other's company for a bit. How could that be construed as a date?

But suddenly, it felt like it was, even though Hattie didn't know anything about it, because it was a surprise. He had the same feeling now as he had when he'd appeared at Dorothy's house with a picnic basket on his arm and hope in his heart; they'd only just started courting and everything was new and uncertain. That's what they called dating in his day – courting.

Was he courting Hattie?

Could he?

Should he let himself feel something for someone other than Dorothy? Or would it be a betrayal of her memory? Did he even want to allow himself to love again?

And if he did, what could possibly come of it? They were pensioners for God's sake; far too old for all this courting nonsense.

Nevertheless, a spark flared in his chest and he realised that his brain might insist he was too old but his heart had already gone ahead without him. He cared for Hattie. Deeply. She was more than a friend to him, and the feeling he had for her had crept up on him without his permission and without him being aware of it.

He supposed the question was, was he prepared to do anything about it? And if so, what?

Hattie's face broke into a smile when she saw him, and she beamed even wider when he explained why he was there. 'You're taking me to the fayre? But what about—?'

'I've squared it with Maddison, and Juliette is standing in for me at the toy shop. So get your coat—'

'—because I've pulled?' Hattie finished, chortling, leaving Alfred to think that perhaps she had, as she darted behind the counter to take her pinny off.

'What's the plan?' she asked as soon as they emerged from Bookylicious. 'Ooh, smell that.'

Alfred sniffed, the mingled aromas of hot spiced wine, candyfloss, doughnuts, roasting chestnuts, and frying onions assaulting his nose all at the same time. Despite the substantial breakfast he'd enjoyed, his mouth watered.

'I thought we could have a wander around, soak up some of the atmosphere, and take a gander at the competition,' he replied.

'There isn't any – not for the toy shop, although Bookylicious has some stiff competition from a fella selling hot chocolate with a shot of Bailey's Irish Cream.'

Alfred grinned. 'It sounds delicious.'

'It does, doesn't it? Shall we be naughty and have one?'

So they did, Alfred laughing at the froth coating Hattie's top lip as she took an experimental sip before declaring it as yummy as it sounded.

He lifted a gloved hand and gently wiped away the chocolatey foam, his attention focused on not missing any. But before he'd finished his task, he glanced up and his eyes met hers.

What he saw in them made his heart skip a beat.

Bloody hell, not here, not now. Not a bloody heart attack? For God's sake—!

His pulse steadied and he realised he wasn't going into cardiac arrest; his skipping heartbeat was a result of something else entirely.

However, his sudden panic had killed the mood (he wasn't certain whether to be pleased or sad), and he held out his arm to her. She took it, and they sipped their hot chocolates and strolled around the fayre, taking it all in.

'I love this time of year,' Hattie said, and when Alfred grunted she hastily added, 'Of course, it's different for you, what with your Dorothy not been gone all that long.'

'This is my third Christmas without her,' he said. 'So, it has been a while now.' It didn't feel nearly as raw as it once had. His grunt hadn't been because he didn't like Christmas (he didn't mind it – it just wasn't his most favourite time of year) but because he was enjoying himself far more than he'd expected. And he wasn't sure how to deal with it, as the enjoyment was linked directly to the woman whose arm was linked through his.

'Shall we go on the merry-go-round?' he asked abruptly and Hattie looked at him in surprise.

'Are you sure?'

'I'm game, if you are. Or are you too much of a scaredy-cat?' he teased.

'Huh! I'm not scared. Race you.' And she was off, scuttling up the road in her haste to beat him to the carousel.

'That's not fair,' he panted when he caught up with her trying to skirt around a man on stilts. Now that was an idea – he'd never thought of making stilts; he reckoned they'd go down a storm in the shop. Oh, hang on, the shop was closing on Christmas Eve, and his toy-making days were behind him. Oh, well… It was nice that he still had the ideas, even if he didn't intend to do anything about them.

Alfred insisted on paying for their ride. He also insisted that the man collecting the money held onto his walking stick, and with the practicalities out of the way, he headed for the nearest black horse. It had red-painted flared nostrils and wild eyes, and he thought it was perfect. Hattie chose the one next to him, which was far more garish and considerably more feminine. He hoisted her on, pushing her backside while she screamed with laughter, then had to wait for the man to come around again to ask him to help him onto his own horse.

Dear God, it was high. The gold-coloured floor of the carousel seemed very far down, and Alfred clutched the pole with both hands and prayed he wouldn't fall off. If Sara could see him now, she wouldn't half give him a telling off for being silly and reckless, and she might have a point.

The merry-go-round began to move, and the horses started a slow dip and rise in time to the music, and Alfred's heart soared along with his flying horse as the carousel picked up speed. He was dimly aware of Hattie's wild infectious laughter, and then he was laughing and yelling along with her, and life was full of fun and light once more.

Having to get off soon brought him back down to earth, as Alfred once again had to enlist the help of the bloke who collected the money, and he seemed to have stiffened up considerably between getting on and getting off, but it had been worth it, he saw, when he took a look at the joy on Hattie's face.

Some of her hair had escaped its bun and was

framing her face, her cheeks were pink and glowing, and her eyes sparkled. 'How about the helter-skelter next?' she asked, and he groaned.

What the hell had he let himself in for?

A go on the helter-skelter (he was terrified he was going to fall over the side), was followed by him winning a teddy bear for her on the hook-a-duck stall, which he presented to Hattie. Then they ate a hotdog each (made from speciality wild boar sausages), and Alfred bought a bag of roasted chestnuts for dessert, and they ate them whilst mooching around the various craft stalls.

There were so many lovely things on sale and hundreds of people wanting to buy them, that he was worried that his little shop wouldn't be noticed, but as they walked past it he saw that it was full. He was also delighted that so many people stopped to admire the window display, and he knew for a fact that Zoe's skill and creative eye were making a mark.

'I'd best get back,' he said reluctantly when his allotted two hours were up. 'I'll walk with you to Bookylicious.'

'Yes, I suppose I need to do some work, too. After all, it's one of the busiest days in Ticklemore's calendar. Thank you for bringing me,' she said, when they reached the café. 'I really enjoyed myself.'

'As did I.' Alfred couldn't help himself. He

303

reached out to tuck one of Hattie's stray strands of hair off her face and behind her ear. She had lovely eyes – forget-me-not blue – and the skin of her cheek was surprisingly soft despite the wrinkles.

She rested her head against the palm of his hand and gazed at him.

He gazed back for a moment, before dropping his hand and nodding gently, acknowledging the growing feeling between them.

When she kissed him briefly on the mouth, he'd half been expecting it and a thrill shot through him as her lips touched his.

Then she was gone, hurrying through the café door as if the hounds of hell were after her.

He stood there for a moment, the fingers of one gloved hand raised to his lips, wondering what to make of what had just happened and hoping to God that the fleeting contact hadn't damaged their friendship.

But when he made to leave, he spotted her through the glass heading for the counter at the far end of the café and as he did so she half turned, saw that he was watching her, and gave him a radiant smile.

All through the day, the swift kiss lingered in his mind and thoughts of her kept popping into his head. And when he phoned her later that evening to bid her a customary goodnight, the delight in her voice when she answered his call, made his heart miss another beat.

'Alfred… you called,' she said softly.

'Of course I did. I call you every evening.'

'I thought maybe you're regretting—' She broke off.

'The only thing I'm regretting is letting you talk me into going down the helter-skelter.'

'Oh, good. I was worried…'

'Don't be.'

'We're still friends, then?'

'I hope we are more than that.' It was his turn to be worried. Was she regretting kissing him? Had he read more into it than she had meant?

'We are.' Her reply was decisive.

'Goodnight, Hattie, sleep tight.'

'Goodnight, Alfred.'

He hesitated, waiting for her to end the call, but he could still hear her soft breathing over the airways. 'Hang up,' he told her.

'You first.'

'No, *you* first.'

She giggled and the sound made him go all gooey inside. 'On the count of three – one, two—'

She was gone; the little madam had hung up on him, and he chuckled softly to himself. Hattie

Jenkins's unpredictability was one of the many things he loved about her.

CHAPTER 29

HATTIE

Hattie wrapped her arms around herself and squeezed. That the whole weekend had been a roaring success was agreed by everyone she'd spoken to in the village, and Hattie was delighted the toy shop had done so well, as she totted up the figures after she called in to the shop before closing.

Alfred had already left, but Zoe told her that he had a fair idea of how much they'd made, and the last couple of hours had been quiet as the fayre had wound down and people had begun to make their way home before the night closed in.

'Is Alfred OK?' Zoe asked.

'Why do you ask?'

'He looked wacked. I mean, really done in.'

'Oh, dear, I'll give him a call.' Worried, she pressed his number, and waited anxiously for him to answer.

'Hattie, hello.' Alfred's voice was warm, and she couldn't detect any hint of weariness in it.

'I'm fine, but more importantly, how are you? Zoe thought you looked tired.'

'I'm OK. Zoe must be mistaken.'

'Alfred, this is me you're talking to.'

'I know.' He paused. 'OK, I am rather tired. Are you happy now?' He didn't sound cross, despite what he said – he sounded amused. 'It's been a busy weekend.'

She had to agree. She was shattered too, and for the first time ever she wondered whether it would be prudent to give up work. But if she did, she'd soon get bored and the thought of sitting at home staring at the four walls for hours on end, or watching drivel on the television, filled her with dread. Besides, it was just until Christmas, she told herself. Surely she could last until then?

Satisfied that it was only tiredness he was suffering from and nothing more serious, she said she'd speak to him later (she wasn't sure she'd be able to go to sleep these days if he didn't call), and helped Zoe lock up before heading for her little cottage and some rest and recuperation.

As soon as she got home, she fed Puss who was winding around her ankles and threatening to trip her up until she did what he commanded, then she toed off her shoes and dumped them in the cupboard under the stairs. Her coat, hat, and scarf quickly joined them.

Her last act before she began the task of making a meal, was to unpin her hair and let it tumble down her back. Once upon a time she would have shaken her head and maybe even bent forwards at the waist and tipped her head upside down to let her hair fall in front of her face, before flicking herself upright again. These days she daren't risk even a gentle shake in case she lost her balance and fell over. Instead, she raked her fingers through it, feeling the wonderful relief of loosened hair.

Dinner was a simple cottage pie that she'd prepared a while ago, had frozen, and had taken out of the freezer this morning. Now that it was suitably defrosted, she popped it in the oven and threw a couple of florets of broccoli into a saucepan to go with it, along with a handful of peas.

But all the time she was working, she was conscious of a feeling of unease. There wasn't anything she could put her finger on, but something was bothering her – she could feel it in her water, although the sensation wasn't as strong as the first time she'd met Alfred.

Was it to do with him? Was he more tired than he had let on, or was it something more serious?

She could hardly turn up at his daughter's house and demand to see him in order to check for herself (although she was sorely tempted) and if she phoned him again it might seem like she was stalking him.

She ate her meal in the kitchen, the sound of Radio 2 keeping her company, and when she was done she washed up her dinner things and set them on the drainer to dry. Then she went into the living room and switched the TV on and tried to settle down.

Her mind was still going nineteen to the dozen and, in order to distract herself from her own silly thoughts, she heaved her aching body out of her chair and decided to visit the shed to see how many toys were left. Zoe had been restocking the shop – which was logical since she was there most of the time and therefore she was the one who'd have a better idea of what was needed to refill the shelves. But it wouldn't hurt to check on how many toys were in there, and from that she might be able to guesstimate whether they'd run out of things to sell before Christmas Eve.

Leaving a light on in the kitchen which shone down the path, Hattie made her way slowly down the garden, feeling every one of her (nearly) eighty years. She should go to bed and try to sleep, but the restlessness hadn't abated; it was getting worse, and she couldn't shake the feeling that something was afoot.

Having no idea what it was, all she could do was to pray that it didn't have anything to do with Alfred. He had become far too important to her for anything to happen to him.

She unlocked the shed door and groped around on the wall until her questing fingers encountered the light switch. Flicking it on, she was relieved to see that there were still some boxes of toys on the shelves, as well as some larger pieces on the floor. Zoe appeared to have gradually worked her way from the front, and now a large space had been cleared. However, Hattie was fairly certain that they probably did have enough stock to see them through, Hopefully…

She closed the door behind her in a vain attempt to keep some of the cold night air out and, wanting to see for herself what toys were in those boxes, she stepped towards them and almost tripped over, her hand darting out to grab hold of the edge of the former dining table.

'Puss! You silly creature! If you trip me up who is going to feed you, or give you cuddles?'

The cat glared balefully at her for a second, then promptly sat down, stretched out a back leg with all the grace of a world-class ballerina, and began washing himself.

Stupid cat.

Her ladder was still at the toy shop, so Hattie decided to improvise, and she dragged the stool which Logan had commandeered from the Tavern on that night back in November when they had spirited Alfred's toys out of his shed and into hers, nearer to the shelving unit and positioned it carefully on the somewhat uneven floor. Ted, bless him, had built the shed years ago and he'd laid the concrete base too, but although the shed was as sturdy as the cottage, the floor wasn't the best. He'd promised more than once to re-lay it, but he never had, and Hattie knew she'd go to her grave with the floor in her shed as wonky as the day it had been made.

Ah well... It served to remind her of Ted whenever she entered, although, with all the toys in it and with Alfred's tools and various pieces of equipment as well as enough lengths of wood to stock a small branch of B&Q, it now reminded her more of Alfred than her late husband.

Steadying herself with one hand on the table and the other on the shelving unit (which she knew was secured to the wall) she clambered onto the seat, one shaking wobbly leg at a time, until she was kneeling on it. It was at this point that she realised this was probably as far as she was going to get, because she didn't have the strength to lever herself up from a kneeling to a standing position, and now her legs were going numb.

She hadn't thought this through, had she?

There was no option but to wriggle her reluctant legs out from underneath her, and clamber back down again. Tomorrow she'd ask Benny if he'd be kind enough to pop into the shop and fetch her ladder back, but for now she was stumped.

And her one leg was so numb she was going to have hell to pay when the blood flowed into it again – pins and needles were simply horrid.

Carefully, she raised her body up as far as she was able, while hanging onto one of the shelves with both hands, and yanked her foot out as hard as she could.

Too hard, she realised, as the stool wobbled precariously with the abrupt redistribution of her weight.

She tried her best to maintain a firm grip on that pesky shelf, but her hands and fingers didn't work as well as they used to, and as the stool toppled sideways, Hattie, to her horror, went with it.

She landed on the hard concrete floor with a bang, and felt her head crack against the trunk-like leg of the old table.

Her last coherent thought was of Alfred and the phone call she was almost certain to miss later.

CHAPTER 30

ALFRED

Alfred stared at his mobile phone in consternation. This was the third time he'd called Hattie, and there was still no answer. Which was most unlike her. She always, *always* answered on the third or fourth ring.

Several thoughts popped into his mind in rapid succession. Maybe she was having a bath. She might have fallen asleep – preferably not in the bath. Maybe she was fed up with him ringing her every night at ten; she might be sick of him, despite the fact that she always sounded so pleased to hear his voice. And she didn't seem to mind the "you hang up first" game which they'd taken to playing. Or maybe she did mind playing it, and this was her way of letting him know.

If so, it was unkind of her – surely she knew he'd be worried if he didn't get an answer?

Which brought him neatly back to why she wasn't

answering in the first place, and that maybe she *was* in the bath…

When he dialled her number for the fourth time and she failed to answer, he slipped his dressing gown on and went downstairs in search of his son-in-law.

David was watching the news and Sara was knitting (knitting? he hadn't realised she knew how) when he stuck his head around the door.

'I'm worried about Hattie,' he announced.

'She's enough to worry anyone,' his daughter replied in a dry tone.

'No, seriously, I'm worried about her.' He stepped inside the room and stood in front of them, his phone in his hand. He waggled it. 'She's not answering.'

'Perhaps she's in bed?' Sara offered. 'Why are you bothering her at this time of night anyway?'

'I always call her at ten.' When Sara raised her eyebrows, he added, 'To wish her goodnight.'

'Might she be in the bath?' David asked.

'She might.' Alfred could hear the doubt in his voice, and David heard it, too.

'Try calling her again, and if there's still no answer would you like me to pop around to her house and check on her?'

'Yes, please. But I want to go with you.'

'I'm sure it's nothing to worry about,' Sara said, but Alfred was sure it was. This wasn't like Hattie at all.

The pair of them watched and listened as Alfred called Hattie yet again, and when there was no answer David got to his feet.

'Get dressed, Alfred, and put your coat on. I'll go and warm the car up.'

Sara was waiting for him at the bottom of the stairs when he came back down. 'Careful,' she warned, watching him scuttle down them. 'I'm coming with you. She might need another woman.'

Alfred's eye's widened at the implication, and he hurried past her and out to the car, Sara hot on his heels.

They completed the short journey in silence, Alfred wrapped up in worry which wasn't alleviated when David pulled the car up to the pavement outside Hattie's house and Alfred saw the downstairs lights on.

David reached Hattie's front door first and rang the bell.

By the time Alfred had freed himself from the confines of the seatbelt and the passenger seat, his son-in-law had rung again and was now peering through the living room window.

'I can't see anything,' David said, and Alfred shoved him out of the way in order to take a look for himself.

No Hattie, but the TV was on.

It was feasible that she'd gone to bed and had forgotten to turn it off, but he doubted it, and by the expression on David's face, his son-in-law didn't think it likely, either.

'We can go round the back,' Alfred suggested, so all three of them traipsed to the end of the little row of cottages and down the lane.

It was very dark, but there was just enough light to allow Alfred to identify which garden gate belonged to Hattie, and they filed through it and up the garden path.

'There's a light on in the shed,' David remarked.

'Let's try the house first,' Sara said. 'I very much doubt she'd be out here at this time of night. She's probably put it on for security.'

The kitchen light was also on, but once again there was no sign of Hattie as they looked through the window, so David tried the door.

When it opened, David sent Sara a meaningful glance.

'I'll take a look upstairs, shall I?' she suggested and darted inside, Alfred and David following more slowly.

'Hattie? It's Sara, Alfred's daughter. Hattie? Are you up there?' Sara called, as she reached the bottom of the stairs, then Alfred heard her footsteps as she climbed the staircase, and he held his breath, listening to his daughter's quick, sure tread above.

He let it out in a whoosh when she came back down and shook her head.

Where the hell was she? With dawning comprehension, he stared out of the kitchen window. The light in the shed could only mean one thing.

David was already dashing out of the door, having come to the same conclusion, and Alfred, dread clutching his heart, followed him, almost tripping over his own feet in his haste.

When he reached the shed door, it was already open and David was inside kneeling on the floor, a motionless figure on the ground in front of him.

Hattie!

'Is she…?' Alfred couldn't finish the sentence.

'She's still alive,' David said, his fingers pressing into the side of Hattie's neck. 'Sara, ring for an ambulance.' He stripped off his padded jacket and draped it over her, tucking it in around her.

Alfred simply stared, wishing there was something he could do, and took in the scene, trying to make sense of it. An overturned stool lay next to her, and he stepped forwards to move it out of the way. Puss, Hattie's ginger tomcat, stalked past him, tail held high, without giving his mistress so much as a cursory glance, and Alfred wondered if the cat had played a part in Hattie's accident.

'They're on their way,' Sara said. 'Is there anything I can do?'

David said, 'Not at the moment, but Alfred, you might like to talk to her. I think she's unconscious, but she might be able to hear you.' He got to his feet and moved to the side.

Alfred shuffled over to her and, with considerable effort, knelt next to her. Hattie's hair splayed out around her head, and he gently lifted some strands off her face.

'Hattie, my love, stay with us. Please stay with us. Stay with *me*; I'm not ready for you to leave me, not when I've only just found you. Please, Hattie, please,' he begged, tears trickling down his face and plopping on her cheek as he bent over her.

He brushed them away, wanting nothing more than to scoop her into his arms and cradle her head to his chest, but he was terrified to move her in case he caused her any further damage.

'Hattie, my darling, my love, open your eyes,' he pleaded.

His heart leapt when her lids fluttered. She didn't open her eyes, but he was certain she could hear him.

'You can't go,' he told her. 'I won't let you.'

Another flutter, and hope flared deep inside him. Please God, don't take Hattie, too, he prayed, because he didn't know what he'd do without her.

He didn't think he'd survive.

And he knew he wouldn't want to.

CHAPTER 31

HATTIE

'Thank God,' Hattie heard Alfred mumble when she forced her reluctant eyes open, and she smiled to herself as, when she lifted her head, she was immediately gathered up into Alfred's arms, her cheek resting against the crook of his elbow.

'Dad, don't! You shouldn't move her. The ambulance will be here any minute.' Sara hoved into view and draped her coat over her, and Hattie was grateful for the additional warmth it provided.

'Stuff it,' he muttered, then he said a little louder, 'She's conscious.'

Hattie certainly was conscious, but only just. She was pretty sure she had knocked herself out, but for how long she couldn't tell.

Alfred cried, 'What the hell were you doing? If we hadn't… if I hadn't… Sod it!'

'Good to see you,' she croaked.

'Hattie, are you OK? Have you broken anything?' he demanded.

Hattie gingerly wiggled the toes of one foot and then the other. When those extremities appeared to be working, she moved her legs. Her ankles, knees, and hips ached, but those were old hurts and had more to do with a long life of wear and tear and the steady creep of arthritis, than anything to do with the fall.

Next she tried out her arms and both of them worked as well as they usually did. Her shoulders were sore, her neck was stiff, and the back of her head ached like hell, but she'd heal. Eventually.

'Nothing is broken,' she confirmed, struggling to sit up, and wincing when her head felt like it was about to explode.

'Don't move,' Sara warned. 'Let the medics check you over.'

Hattie subsided back into Alfred's arms, the uppermost thought in her mind being that it felt very nice to be held by a man. A hug off Logan didn't count. This was a proper hold, with Alfred cuddling her to his chest and cradling her head with one hand as he pressed her to him.

'Ouch!' she cried.

'Oh hell, you are hurt. I knew it.'

'Shush.' Hattie lowered her voice. 'I think I've got a lump on the back of my head,' she whispered, 'but don't mention it. I'll be damned if they are going to cart me off to hospital. Once you're in one of those places, you don't come out again unless it's in a box.'

'Did you knock yourself out?'

'I might have done,' she admitted, 'but if you say anything Alfred Miller, I'll never speak to you again.'

He loosened his grip on her, and shifted her weight a little, until she was balanced in the crook of his one arm. 'How many fingers am I holding up?'

'Three, and I'll be holding up two if you don't stop this nonsense.'

'What day is it?' he persisted.

'That depends on how long I was out for. It could be Sunday, or it could be Monday.' She kept her voice low, hoping Sara and David wouldn't hear.

'It's Sunday. Who is the Prime Minister?'

Hattie sighed. 'That stupid one. I can never remember his name. You know, the one who looks like a camel. What's he called?' She pulled a face as she tried to dredge his name from the depths of her mind.

Alfred pulled a face in response. 'I can't remember it either, but I know it if I hear it. They change so bloody fast – there's a new one every five minutes, so how we're supposed to keep up, I don't know.'

'Gosh, that's quick, the paramedics are here,' David announced, sticking his head around the door.

Thank God for that. Perhaps she could get up off this freezing floor now. She was rather enjoying lying in Alfred's arms, but the cold was starting to get to her and she was shivering even with two coats over her.

The paramedic burst into the shed, all one of him, and he knelt beside her. Taking over from Alfred, he popped something on the floor underneath her head and eased her back down until she was lying almost prone.

Damn it, but that concrete was blimmin' cold.

'Your son-in-law filled me in on the details,' the bloke said, 'but can you tell me what happened, love?'

'I stood on a stool and fell, that's how it happened,' Hattie said. 'I've got no one to blame but myself. You'd think I'd know better at my age.'

'Let's get your vitals checked, then we'll have a good look at you and see what's what. You fell from quite a height.'

'It was two foot. I don't call that high,' she retorted.

'It is when you get to your age, love. You could have broken something.'

'Stop calling me "love". My name is Hattie.'

'She's as sharp as a tack, isn't she?' the paramedic

said to everyone but her.

'Oi. Don't talk about me when I'm still in the room. I don't care what you say about me afterwards, but I can hear every word. And I haven't broken anything.'

'That's where I come in; I need to make sure,' he told her.

'Get on with it then. I want a cup of tea, my bed, and a hot water bottle.'

'Um, we'll see, shall we? You might have to go to hospital.'

'I won't go and you can't make me,' Hattie retorted, but she allowed him to examine her without making any more fuss. The sooner he was done, the sooner he'd be gone and she could go to bed. She was more tired than she could ever remember being in her life and that included the time she'd walked a nineteen mile stretch of Offa's Dyke in one day.

She endured his prodding, poking and questioning to the best of her ability, the only sticky point being when he asked if she thought she'd lost consciousness at all. Thankfully Sara and David were huddled in the corner talking amongst themselves, so neither of them heard the question.

With a warning glance at Alfred, she said she hadn't. She could tell that her friend was uncomfortable with her lie, but at least he didn't contradict her.

She guessed she was being rather silly and that she should tell the paramedic the truth, but she really, really didn't want to go to hospital because they'd probably keep her in for observation and they might also want to run a barrage of tests.

She felt fine. Or as fine as one could be at her age, after a shock like the one she'd just had. The headache was still there, but it had settled into a throb rather than a pound and she was sure a couple of painkillers would take the edge of it.

'Right, shall we get you to your feet?' the man asked eventually, and called to David to fetch the offending stool so she could perch on it for a few seconds until everyone was certain she wasn't going to keel over again.

She had to admit to herself that she did feel rather dizzy as she was being hauled unceremoniously to her feet before tottering a few steps to the stool. David positioned himself behind her to ensure she didn't topple backwards and do herself even more damage.

'Nothing appears to be broken,' the paramedic declared. 'Your heart rate is a little fast and your blood pressure is a little lower than I'd like, but it's nothing to be alarmed about. Now, are you sure you won't go to hospital? I'd like to get you checked over properly.'

'I'm sure. I know my own body, and when I say it's fine, it's fine.'

'Have you got someone to stay with you tonight? Ideally for a couple of days?' he asked.

Hattie caught the exchange of looks between Sara and David as Alfred immediately said, 'I can stay with her. If she'll let me.'

Hattie hesitated. Apart from the plumber, she hadn't had a man upstairs in her cottage for many years. And she'd been married to the last fella who had stayed overnight. Yet, she did have a spare bedroom and there was a fully made-up bed in it, although it would probably need some airing before it was fit to sleep in, so if the only way to get rid of the paramedic was to agree to have Alfred stay, then so be it.

'I think you've had enough excitement for one night, Dad,' Sara piped up. 'I can stay with Hattie. She'd probably be happier having another woman in the house, rather than a man.'

It depends on the woman, Hattie was about to retort, when Alfred said, 'Shall we let Hattie decide?'

'I'll leave you to it,' the paramedic said, then went on to warn her about the danger of standing on stools or anything else, including ladders.

Sara's stare was full of meaning, and Hattie glared defiantly back at her.

'I'll put up with Alfred,' Hattie said, and Sara shook her head.

'I don't bite, you know,' Alfred's daughter said.

'It's your barking that'll get on my nerves,' Hattie grizzled, but she allowed Sara and David to help her get into the house, one either side of her, and the arrangement continued until she was settled in her favourite armchair.

Sara lifted a throw off the back of the sofa and tucked it around Hattie's knees then went into the kitchen to make them all a much-needed cup of tea.

'Thank you, all of you,' Hattie said when everyone was sitting down with a mug in their hands. She was disconcerted to see that hers were trembling ever so slightly. The fall had shaken her up more that she liked to admit. 'If you hadn't arrived, I might have been there a while.'

Sara shuddered. 'It doesn't bear thinking about.'

It most certainly did not, Hattie silently agreed. When it was her time to go she didn't want to have to face her maker whilst lying on the floor of her own shed, on a cold December night. She was planning to go when she was snuggled up in bed. Preferably in her sleep, so she wouldn't know a great deal about it.

'Why were you phoning Hattie anyway?' Sara wanted to know.

'I told you, I phone her every night, just to say

goodnight.'

David grinned, but didn't say anything, and Hattie would have given her eye teeth to know why he was smiling and shooting her and Alfred such pointed looks. Sara, on the other hand, wasn't as pleased, if the expression on her sour face was anything to go by.

Alfred noticed his daughter's disapproval too. 'If I hadn't...' He trailed off and swallowed. Hattie saw that his eyes were moist.

'I, for one, am delighted you did, Alfred,' David said, earning himself a sharp look from his wife.

Just what was that woman's problem, Hattie wondered. She was as miserable as sin and twice as grumpy, and she didn't deserve a nice man like David for a husband, or an even nicer man like Alfred for a father. Hattie would swap places with her in a flash if it meant she had someone as caring as that in her life.

'You don't need to stay,' Hattie said to Alfred. 'I'll be fine. Honest.'

'You need someone with you, for tonight at least,' David insisted.

'Isn't there anyone you can call?' Sara asked.

'Of course, there is,' Hattie said, pouncing on the idea. 'You get going and I'll just finish my tea, then I'll call them.'

'Who?' Alfred asked.

'My, er… niece and her husband.'

Alfred narrowed his eyes at her and shook his head. 'Phone them now, we can wait.'

David sank back into the sofa and folded his arms. He was enjoying the spectacle.

'I'll do it in my own good time,' Hattie insisted.

'It's five past twelve in the morning. How much good time do you need?' Alfred said. 'Give me the number and I'll phone them for you.'

'No.'

'No?'

Hattie shook her head.

'You don't have a niece, do you?' he demanded.

'I do!'

'What's her name?'

'Phoebe.'

'Where does she live?'

'York.'

'That's miles away,' David said. 'It'll take them all night to get here.'

Alfred was regarding her suspiciously. 'Hmm, I think you might find it's a bit further away than that. Which York are you referring to, the one in Australia or the new one in America?'

Hattie shrugged. He'd seen right through her. 'Does it matter?'

'No.' Alfred got to his feet with some effort. That

was why Hattie rarely sat in that chair – it liked to suck you in and not let go. 'It's settled then. I'm staying the night.' He caught Sara's disapproving expression. 'I'll see you tomorrow. I'm not sure when, because I'm going into the shop for a few hours.'

'After being up half the night? You've got to start taking care of yourself,' Sara objected.

Hattie bit back a giggle when he retorted, 'You don't know much about getting old, do you? You try sleeping all night when you get to my age. Getting up to pee a couple of times a night is par for the course. And once you're awake, it's not easy getting back off to sleep.'

Hattie nodded, wished she hadn't when the top of her head felt like it was about to come off, and said, 'I always make a cup of tea.'

'Does that help?' David appeared genuinely interested.

'No, but it gives you something to do other than think of things you should have said to Cissy Blake when she made fun of you in infant school.'

'What did she used to say?' Alfred asked, but Sara getting swiftly to her feet derailed the conversation.

'Come on, David. We can't sit here all night. You've got work in the morning and I need my beauty sleep.'

'Don't you just,' Hattie mumbled, before

plastering a smile on her face. She was starting to feel a little under the weather and Sara was seriously getting on her nerves.

Suddenly Hattie wanted nothing more than for everyone to go, so she could sink into her bed and pretend that the last couple of hours hadn't happened.

Except for the part where she'd been held by Alfred; she was very glad that had happened, despite the circumstances and the fact that he had only been holding her because he'd thought she'd half-killed herself.

She was also glad he was staying tonight to look after her. Not that she needed looking after, but it was reassuring to think someone else was in her house if she needed them. And she couldn't think of anyone she'd prefer to need than Alfred.

CHAPTER 32

ALFRED

Alfred hadn't been joking when he'd told Sara that he didn't sleep much. And what sleep he did manage was usually in two to three hour blocks.

Last night he'd hardly slept at all. The thought that kept him from slumber was, what if he hadn't phoned Hattie? In fact, he could take it back a notch – what if he'd never started calling her in the first place? He most definitely wouldn't have phoned her tonight, if that was the case. If he took it back even further again, to when he'd asked her for the phone number for a storage facility, he could beat himself up even more.

Anyway, in his mind, what it boiled down to was that he was ultimately responsible for Hattie falling off a stool.

She could have died.

That was what was bothering him and preventing him from sleeping. And if Hattie had died it would have been his fault.

He didn't know how he would have lived with himself.

If he was honest, he didn't know whether he would have wanted to – and not solely because of the crushing guilt he would have felt – *did* feel. Hattie had given him back his will to live, and for him to have taken her own life from her would have destroyed him. Not only that, he wasn't sure he'd have wanted to carry on in a world without her in it.

This revelation had surprised him earlier, and he found he couldn't let go of it.

Although he had already started to think of her as more than a friend, and she'd inveigled herself into his life and his affections without him noticing, he hadn't been truly aware of the depth of his feelings for her until now. In the beginning he'd found her incredibly annoying, then one day he realised he liked her. He certainly admired her, and he was rather in awe of her determination, drive and sheer zest for living. She was a force of nature and he, along with the majority of the village, was helpless to stand up to her; what Hattie wanted, Hattie got, and if she set her mind on something nothing was going to stop her from getting it.

Life would be very grey without her in it.

As he lay there, debating whether he should get up and check on her yet again (he'd done so three times already, anxious to make sure it was sleep she had slipped into and not unconsciousness), he understood that the fear he had felt when he'd seen her still form lying on the floor of the shed had been vast and all-encompassing. He also understood something else – something incredibly surprising and not at all welcome. He had an awful feeling that he had fallen in love with Hattie Jenkins.

How could he have let that happen?

Dorothy had been his life. He'd been devastated to the point of incapacity when she'd died. Now here he was, having done away with all the things she'd held so dear and was in the process of selling the home she'd lived in for all her married life, having feelings for a woman he barely knew and hadn't long met.

Did that make him disloyal and fickle?

Or did it mean that he still had some life left in him and he should live it to the full and embrace it, because God only knew how long he'd have left on this earth.

He knew what Hattie would say if he asked her.

Not that he intended to.

Unable to fight it off any longer, he swung his legs out of bed and padded across the landing, dressed only in his socks and underpants, and wearing a borrowed dressing gown. It was baby pink and fluffy, and didn't suit him in the slightest, but he'd be damned if Hattie was going to see him in his undercrackers.

Gently, so as not to disturb her, he pushed Hattie's bedroom door open and peered around it. The last time he'd checked on her, she had been lying on her side. This time she was on her back and he could see the rise and fall of her chest under the bedclothes.

Deliberately he made a small noise and watched for any reaction.

Hattie grumbled and shifted slightly, and he was relieved that she hadn't slipped into a coma. Because that was another thing he was feeling guilty about. Not only had he been the cause of her fall in the first place, he had also colluded with her in her claim that she hadn't been knocked out, when both of them were well aware she had. He understood and respected her decision not to go to hospital, but if she had a bleed on the brain (God forbid!) then that would be his fault too, for not calling her out on her lie and for not insisting that she went to A and E and got her head looked at.

The way he was acting, he believed he needed his own head examined, too. Not only had he been as irresponsible as she had been (although it looked like the pair of them had got away with it), he had begun to care for Hattie far more than was sensible.

However, he had no intention of doing anything about his feelings. He'd carry on the way he was, and nothing would change. And when Christmas Eve arrived, he'd probably not see a great deal of Hattie afterwards. Fact.

The little kiss she'd given him didn't count for anything. She was simply being friendly, he told himself. It meant nothing.

He spent the rest of the night mulling everything over and castigating himself for being so silly and for letting it happen in the first place – all of it, not just his burgeoning love for her – and by the time he eventually gave up, got dressed, and went downstairs, he was in a right old mood.

'What's up with you?' were Hattie's first words as she entered the kitchen a little while later. 'You've got a face like a slapped arse.'

'You, that's what's up with me.' Alfred turned the switch on to reboil the kettle.

'Me? What have I done?' Hattie's eyes were wide and innocent.

'Where would you like me to start?'

'I don't know – you tell me!'

'What the hell were you doing in your shed at that time of night. And do you know how stupid you were

337

standing on a stool? A ladder would have been bad enough, but a blasted stool! For God's sake, woman, you could have broken a hip. You could have died!' The last came out as a wail, and Alfred hastily coughed and cleared his throat.

'I know that,' was Hattie's mild reply. 'But I didn't break anything and I'm still alive, so what are you whining about?'

Alfred wasn't sure that taking it out on Hattie was the best idea he'd ever had, but he couldn't seem to stop himself. He'd spent a couple of hours last night thinking the worst, then, when he'd realised she was OK, he'd spent the rest of the night berating himself for being so silly, on at least two fronts. Three if he included opening the damned toy shop in the first place. Why had he let himself be talked into it? The fact that it was doing brilliantly was neither here nor there.

Reluctant to leave her, but aware that he had to go into the toy shop, he said, 'I hope you're not thinking of doing anything silly like going into work today?'

'Stop nagging,' Hattie grumbled.

'If you don't promise me you'll stay home and rest, and phone Maddison to let her know you won't be in, I'll tell her myself.'

'All right. Anything to stop you going on at me,' she agreed, and Alfred knew he was right, and that she wasn't in any fit state to wait on tables today. The fact that she'd given in with very little fuss gave the game away.

Wishing he could stay to keep an eye on her, but knowing that she'd resent the inference that she needed someone to watch over her, he left her to it.

But throughout the day, his mind was taken up with thoughts of her. She was already in his heart, and now she was in his head, too.

There wasn't any hope for him. He was well and truly smitten, and he wasn't sure what he should do about it.

CHAPTER 33

HATTIE

Hattie stood behind the living room curtain window and watched Alfred tap his way up the path, as he planted his stick firmly with each step.

When he was out of sight, she let out a sigh and her shoulders sagged. Not only was every part of her aching, some parts were aching worse than others, like her head, neck, and shoulders, for instance. There was also an impressive bruise developing on her right hip (she was lucky she hadn't broken it) and she'd wrenched her wrist.

It had taken all her determination and will power not to let Alfred know the extent of her injuries, but now that he'd gone she allowed herself to have a little cry.

'Don't be so silly,' she muttered under her breath

when she'd finished spluttering and snivelling into what had once been a clean handkerchief and was now a disgusting, sodden, crumpled mess. She wasn't completely sure why she'd bawled her eyes out in the first place. She was physically under the weather and that accounted for some of it, but her crying jag wasn't solely the result of a few aches and pains that a couple of painkillers would take the edge off.

It was deeper than that, and more encompassing.

It was to do with Alfred and how she felt about him.

It was also to do with her stupidity (she should know better than to climb on stools at her age – she did know, but she'd done it anyway).

It was to do with an awful lot of things, beginning with her embarrassment at having worried him and his family; shame at being seen to be so reckless; despair over her growing love for him. And sorrow at her realisation that she was lonely. She'd never admitted it to herself before – she'd never allowed herself to acknowledge it. But having Alfred in the house last night had brought it starkly home to her.

She'd relished him being in the bedroom across the landing from her, and she loved that he'd crept into her room to check on her throughout the night. She knew that he had because she hadn't been sleeping much either, and she was incredibly touched by his concern.

Now that he'd gone, though, the house felt empty without him. Which was daft. She was used to her own company, she thrived on it. She liked company but only on her terms. Or so she'd told herself. So she'd believed.

To try to distract herself, Hattie's thoughts focused on how many toys were left in the shed. Probably just enough to last until Christmas Eve. She didn't know what she'd do when the toy shop closed its doors for the last time. How she'd cope.

Her life would be easier, but she'd miss it. She'd miss Alfred. Would he still want to bother with her as much once the thing that had brought them together had disappeared? She was sure she'd still see him (Ticklemore wasn't a big place at all) but it wouldn't be the same.

And what if he fell back into his old ways? With the shop gone, there wouldn't be anything for him to do, and she dreaded the thought of him reverting to the depressed and morose chap she'd met all those weeks ago. Especially now that she knew the real Alfred, the one who'd been buried beneath a tonne of despair and shrouded in a blanket of sorrow. He had so much life left to live, and she was terrified of the thought of him wasting it.

But she had no idea how to prevent it from

happening. Alfred was the type of man who needed to be doing something. He needed to be occupied, to have a purpose, but she was fresh out of ideas.

The pat on the back she could give herself for succeeding in her mission to draw him out of himself was tempered by the knowledge that her water was right – it had been trying to tell her there was a danger he might return to his old ways.

Thinking furiously, she wondered if she should have a chat with Benny about giving him a plot on the allotment – even though Alfred had never shown the remotest interest in gardening.

At a loss, Hattie took herself back to bed. She was tired, her head still hurt, and now her heart ached as well.

CHAPTER 34

ALFRED

With his mind on other things and with his body complaining about the lack of sleep, Alfred wasn't in the mood for the shop today. For once, the sight of it didn't fill him with delight, and he didn't feel up to bantering with the customers either.

'What's wrong?' Zoe asked, as he went out to the little room in the back for the third time in under an hour.

'Tired,' he replied shortly.

'Join the club,' Zoe muttered. 'Can you come and help serve, because I'm trying to wrap a farm set for a customer and other people are waiting to pay.'

With a deep sigh, Alfred struggled to his feet and shuffled after her. He wasn't up for this today – the work was relentless from the minute the shop opened

344

to the second the last customer was ushered out of the door.

Not everyone bought something, obviously, but they all still needed a certain amount of attention, and it wasn't wise to leave Zoe short-handed.

When there was a lull, Zoe drew him to one side.

'Alfred,' she said, 'I know you're old and you can't help that, but I can't do everything by myself. I love working here, but it's hard work when I'm on my own.'

'Are you asking for a pay rise?'

Zoe looked shocked. 'No, I'm not!' she cried indignantly. 'What I need is some help.'

'Sorry.' Alfred hung his head. He'd been as much use as a chocolate fireguard today, and he wasn't that much better on the days when he wasn't so knackered. He didn't know how Hattie managed it.

Thinking about Hattie led him to wonder how she was, and he took the opportunity to give her a quick call.

'How are you feeling?' he asked, as soon as she answered.

'Better for hearing your voice,' Hattie said, and his innards did a little flip of happiness.

'Good, good… I hope you're not overdoing things, because if you are, Hattie—'

'Is that Hattie on the phone?' Zoe interrupted.

'Tell her we need her because you're knackered and you need to go home. When is she coming in?'

Alfred glared at Zoe and she said, 'What?' back at him, her eyes wide as she tried to work out what she'd done wrong.

'What did Zoe say?' Hattie wanted to know. 'What's going on?'

'Nothing.'

'Did I hear Zoe say that you need to go home?'

'No—'

'Yes, I did. I'm coming in.'

'You're not! I forbid it.'

Hattie cackled so loudly that he had to hold the phone away from his ear.

'OK, I'll say it another way,' he said hastily. 'Please don't. You're not in any fit state to.'

'Neither are you, by the sound of it. But I have got an idea,' she said, once she'd stopped laughing. 'Ask your daughter.'

'Sara?'

'The very same.'

'But she… she's… I mean…'

'She offered on Saturday, so take her up on it.'

'She's probably busy,' he objected.

'You won't know until you ask.'

Hattie had a point. There was the glaring reality that things couldn't go on as they were, and if she was able to help at least it wouldn't be for long. There were less than three weeks to Christmas and Sara wouldn't be expected to work every day, only now and again.

But, and this was the real reason he didn't want to ask for Sara's help – she'd say "I told you so" and she'd be right. Although setting up the shop and the subsequent running of it had done wonders for his mental health, he was starting to suffer physically. Last night had merely hurried things along. He was finding it too much, but he didn't want to give his daughter the satisfaction of hearing him say it.

'If you suggest that she covers my shift for a couple of days, you can always tell her that I'm doing more hours than I actually am,' Hattie suggested.

'That's a bit dishonest.'

'No more than setting up a shop and not telling her about it,' she pointed out reasonably.

'Hmm. I'll think about it.'

'Don't take too long. I'm going to check in an hour, and I'll be speaking to Zoe not you, because I don't trust you to be honest with me.'

'I'll always be honest with you,' he promised.

'The way you're honest with Sara?'

It was his turn to laugh. 'Point taken. Seriously, Hattie, I'll always tell you the truth.'

'Always?'

'Yes.'

'Did you mean it when you called me "my love"?'

Mindful of his promise, the only thing he was able to say in reply was, 'Yes.'

'I'm glad. You're *my* love, too,' she said, and with that she ended the call, leaving him amazed and perplexed, and feeling rather giddy with happiness.

The feeling didn't dissipate despite Sara arriving to take over from him, and continued long into the evening, by which time he'd had a nap and was refreshed enough to prepare dinner for everyone. Sara, being terribly organised, always put a menu on the fridge for the week, so she could tell at a glance whether she needed to get anything out of the freezer, and he saw that tonight's meal was going to be hotpot. He'd seen Dorothy make it enough times, so he'd set about browning the lamb in a pan, and slicing potatoes, dredging his memory to make sure he got it right.

He'd brought it out of the oven and was checking it when his daughter arrived home.

'Mmm, something smells nice,' she said, coming into the kitchen and giving him a peck on the cheek.

'Hotpot,' he said. 'It'll be ready in half an hour.'

'Thank you, that saves me a job. Zoe's quite a madam, isn't she?' Sara took off her coat and slung it over the back of a chair.

'If you mean she's in charge, then yes.' Alfred had made it clear when he'd asked Sara to step in, that Zoe was responsible and that Sara was there merely to help. Alfred hadn't had any choice, because Zoe had threatened to walk out if Sara had tried to take over or became high-handed.

'I thoroughly enjoyed myself today,' Sarah said as she rolled up her sleeves to stack the dirty dishes into the dishwasher. 'And have I told you how proud I am of you, Dad? Your toys are amazing and the fact that every penny you make is going to charity is mind-blowing.'

'Aww…' He felt heat creep into his face which had nothing to do with the oven he was carefully returning the hotpot to.

'I've got something for you.' She pulled out a newspaper from her handbag, and handed it to him.

'It's this week's Tattler,' he observed, reading the headline.

Would you look at that, he thought. Juliette had run a two-page spread on Ticklemore's Christmas Fayre, and the centrepiece was the toy shop.

Last week the Tattler had carried an article on the grand opening, featuring the mayor and her part in it, but this weeks' article expanded on the toy shop's success and urged people to spend, spend, spend, because it was in a good cause.

Alfred's heart swelled with pride. He couldn't wait to phone Hattie later and share it with her, because she deserved as much praise as him – without her, the toy shop would never have existed.

CHAPTER 35

HATTIE

Hattie paused for a while to catch her breath. She loved Christmas but every year it seemed to start a little earlier and was a little more frantic. She'd never known Bookylicious to be so busy, and although her shift flew by as a result, she was doubly exhausted at the end of it. And she'd been even more tired lately in the three days since her fall. The shock had taken it out of her, and she guessed it would be a little while yet before she was back to her old self.

She hadn't informed Maddison of what had happened the other night, but her employer had been able to tell that she wasn't firing on all cylinders after her unprecedented day off sick and was being extra easy on her. So when Juliette appeared in the shop sometime later and asked to have a quick word,

Maddison waved to an empty table and told Hattie to take a seat.

'I'll bring you a caramel and hazelnut latte each and some gingerbread wands,' Maddison said. 'If that doesn't get you in the mood for Christmas, nothing will.'

'Sounds divine,' Juliette enthused, sliding onto a chair.

She was wearing a cream woollen coat, a huge fake fur hat, and leather gloves with the same fur around the cuffs. She pulled them off and placed them on the table. Her hat followed next and she unbuttoned her coat to reveal a bright red jumper with Father Christmas emblazoned on it. When Hattie looked closer, she saw he was rather the worse for wear and was clutching a bottle of wine in one hand and slurping from a half-full glass with the other.

'Very festive,' she commented, enviously.

'So is the smell in here.' Juliette sniffed the air. 'Cinnamon, chocolate, orange, coffee, vanilla... Yummy.'

'Have you seen how many people have bought something from the toy shop?' Hattie asked, jerking her head at a nearby table, where a threesome of middle-aged ladies was sitting. Two of them had carrier bags sporting the toy shop name. 'I do worry there won't be enough stock to see us through to the end,' she added.

'That's the reason I wanted to speak to you.' Juliette took a sip of the latte that Maddison had just placed in front of her and closed her eyes. 'My, this is good.'

'It is, isn't it? It captures the essence of Christmas perfectly. Now, what was it you were saying?'

Juliette's eyes flew open. 'Oh, yes! Have you thought about organising an official "handing over of the cheque" ceremony to the two charities, once everything is settled?'

'What a marvellous idea!' Hattie lifted her mug and took a mouthful of the delicious coffee and Christmas exploded on her tongue.

'I can discuss some dates with them, if you like, and maybe get the press involved again. Both you and Alfred deserve as much recognition as you can get for what you've achieved.'

'Not me,' Hattie mumbled, her mouth now full of crunchy sweetness as she chewed the gingerbread wand. Ooh, she really did love this time of year – the edible goodies were astonishing.

'The toy shop has certainly captured people's imagination,' Juliette continued. 'The Tattler had a call from one of the nationals this morning. The Newsday Post wants to do a piece on Alfred and the shop.'

'That's marvellous! He'll be thrilled.'

'I think everyone in Ticklemore will be. The number of shop owners who've told me that this is one of the best Christmases so far in terms of trade, is exceptional. The toy shop has certainly brought more people into the village than would otherwise have come here, and I think the fact that profits are going to charity also appeals to the general public. It's such a shame it has to end.'

Hattie was thrilled for Alfred, but she had to agree with Juliette – it was a pity it all had to end on Christmas Eve.

CHAPTER 36

ALFRED

Hattie had broken the news to him about the Newsday Post as soon as she heard it yesterday, and there he was, just one day later, being interviewed by a chap fresh out of school by the look of him.

How bizarre. If someone had told him he'd be in the paper, Alfred would never have believed them. He still couldn't get his head around it, as Shelley would say.

'Can we get a shot of Alfred standing in front of the window?' the reporter whose name was Liam, instructed the photographer he'd brought with him. 'Then I think we'll have a close up of him, and after that if you can do some artistic shots of the toys, that would be fab. Ta.'

Alfred allowed the photographer to tell him where

to stand and how to pose, feeling like a right plonker as he did so. And when that ordeal was out of the way, Liam asked if they could go somewhere quieter to talk, so Alfred took him into the little room out the back and offered him a seat and a cup of tea.

'The toys are ace,' the young man said when they were both settled. 'I can't believe you made them all yourself.'

'I didn't make them overnight, young man. It took me years. And you should have seen the first few things I made – they were only fit for the scrap heap.'

'Why did you decide to make toys in the first place?'

'I dunno. I'd retired, you see, and my wife, Dorothy, God rest her soul, had her own things to be getting on with, and I needed something to do to keep me out of mischief. I'd always liked woodwork at school, and the college was running courses in all kinds of things aimed at OAPs, so I enrolled on one, and the rest is history so to speak.'

'What happened then?'

'Nothing. I kept making toys in my shed.'

'You didn't sell any of them?'

Alfred chortled. 'I didn't think they were worth selling, lad. Anyway, I didn't make toys to make money. I made them to keep myself occupied.'

'What changed your mind? I mean, the idea of

opening a Christmas shop and selling everything off with all the profit going to charity is admirable and hats off to you for that, but why now? Was it that you finally had enough toys to make opening a shop worthwhile?'

'Hattie Jenkins, that's what changed my mind.'

'Excuse me? Who is Hattie Jenkins?'

'She's… she's… just Hattie. You must have read about her – she was mentioned in that article in the Tattler. You'll have to meet her. What happened is that I had a fall in my kitchen. No, hang on, even before that, Sara, she's my daughter, thought I might be suffering from dementia.'

'Are you?'

Alfred saw the man's eyes light up at the thought of this extra-juicy nugget to add to the human interest story. 'I don't think so. Depression is the most likely explanation. Anyway, after my latest fall, she insisted I went to live with her. She can be very domineering can my Sara.' A bit like Hattie, although Alfred wouldn't dare tell either woman that. 'Moving in with her meant that my house, the one I'd lived in with my wife, has to be sold. But before that, Sara wanted it cleared, so she got a house clearance company in to empty it.'

'And they gave you the idea to open a shop?'

'Are you going to shut up and listen? That's not

what happened at all.'

'Sorry. Carry on.'

Alfred stared at him for a few seconds and the reporter shifted uncomfortably. 'As I was saying, the house clearance people were due to empty it, and I hated the thought of all the things me and my wife had loved being sold off, or sent to landfill, or whatever, so I asked Hattie Jenkins if she could help me find a man with a van and one of those storage places you can rent. She and Logan – he owns the Tavern – came up with a better plan, and that was to put everything in her shed until I decided what to do with it.'

Alfred took a sip of his tea to wet his dry mouth, before continuing.

'They quite rightly told me that most of it wasn't worth hanging on to, and that I'd never have any use for it ever again. So we came from there emptyhanded. But, and here's where the story really starts, unbeknown to me, the silly blighters went back that night and nicked all the toys and all my equipment out of my shed and stashed it in Hattie's.'

'Did you call the police?'

'You're doing it again.'

'Sorry. I'll let you tell it in your own way.'

'Good idea. No, I didn't call the police, because I didn't know they'd done it. Not until they came to

Sara's house in the middle of the night and started throwing pebbles up at my bedroom window. When I went downstairs to ask what they were playing at, they took me to Hattie's place and showed me what they'd done.'

He took another sip of his tea and pulled a face. It was tepid and he hated cold tea.

'I was extremely touched that they'd gone to all that trouble, because they could see what the toys meant to me. But I didn't have any use for them, and I hadn't so much as lifted a saw since my Dorothy passed away, so I told her and Logan to get rid of them.' He paused and smiled. 'Opening a shop wasn't what I had in mind, but when Hattie told me that they were too good to throw away – Nell from the Treasure Trove said the same thing – one thing led to another, and the idea of opening a shop, selling everything off and raising money for children's charities was born. It took a lot of work by a lot of people to get it off the ground, but it's all in a good cause, eh?'

'It most certainly is, and what a marvellous story. You must be very proud of what you've achieved. I must admit that I fancy a few things for my kids. And you're definitely going to close on Christmas Eve?'

Alfred nodded, his thoughts not on closing the shop, but on the fact that this young man, who was barely out of short trousers, was old enough to be a dad.

'What happens to the toys you don't manage to sell?' Liam asked, breaking into his musing.

'I don't know.' Alfred shrugged. 'Auction them off, maybe.'

'Or you could hang onto them and open another shop next year; I'm sure our readers would love to hear that you intend carrying on.'

'No, definitely not.'

'Do you mind me asking the reason? Is it because of your age? I can understand if this is all a bit much for you, despite the help you're getting.'

Alfred snorted. Cheeky blighter. His age, indeed! Then he smiled to himself; he was beginning to sound like Hattie. 'It's because there won't be any stock to open a shop with.'

'But if you don't sell everything off, surely you can hang onto what's left and add to it throughout the year?'

'I told you, I haven't picked up as much as a saw since my wife died. Besides, all those toys took me years to make. If you think I can rustle up several hundred items in a few months, you've got another think coming.'

'I can see that they must take a great deal of skill. It's a pity you couldn't pass your expertise on to the next generation.'

'The next generation down from me are probably your grandparents' age,' Alfred scoffed.

Liam smiled. 'I meant today's youth.'

'Nah, all they're interested in is computer games and their bloody phones.'

'You'd be surprised.'

No, Alfred thought – he wouldn't.

But as he was saying goodbye to the reporter, he caught sight of Zoe rearranging the display in the window because the rocking horse had been sold earlier in the day, and he remembered his very first conversation with her.

Maybe, just maybe, that reporter had a point.

CHAPTER 37

HATTIE

Hattie took the newspaper off the shelf and rifled through it. It was probably too soon for the article to appear, the reporter having interviewed Alfred a mere three days ago, but she was scared she might miss it.

'I hope you're going to buy that,' Mrs Cromwell who owned the newsagents said, and Hattie pulled a face at her. 'Only if Alfred is in it,' Hattie retorted. 'There's no point otherwise because I never read a newspaper. Except for the Tattler, and that's only because it's local.'

She kept turning the pages. He'd not be near the front (that was too much to hope for) but maybe he—

She let out such a squeal she made Mrs Cromwell shriek. 'It's in here!' Hattie cried, shaking the newspaper violently in her excitement.

'You're going to have to buy it now,' Mrs Cromwell said firmly. 'Look at the state of it – I can't sell that.'

'Oh, I'm going to buy it, all right; and this one, and this.' Hattie grabbed a handful of copies, marched over to the counter and plonked them down.

'What do you want them for, anyway?' the woman asked, ringing them up on the till.

Hattie snatched one off the top of the pile, hastily opened it to the correct page and jabbed a finger at the photo of Alfred standing outside the toy shop and looking uncomfortable despite the smile on his face.

Never mind, the shop window behind him looked fabulous and the article was glowing, full of praise for what he'd achieved and how much he hoped to raise for charity. Not only that, there was a considerable amount of column inches (if that was the right phrase), given over to Alfred himself, and how he'd begun making toys by hand, and how it was a pity that these old crafts were being lost to modern manufacturing techniques.

Hattie had read the article once, but she was more than happy to read it again, and as she did so, an idea began to form.

She paid for the newspapers and hurried outside, trying to phone Juliette and walk at the same time, and wondering how youngsters today could do both things without walking into a lamp post or stepping in front of a car.

'Juliette? It's Hattie – the article is in the Newsday Post today, and it's given me an idea. Can you round everyone up for a quick meeting of the Toy Shop Team?'

'Of course. When are you thinking of holding it, and where?'

'Now, in the next few minutes. I know it's incredibly short notice, but hopefully most people will be able to make it, especially if you tell them it's being held in Bookylicious and the cake is on me.'

'You do realise it's only seven-thirty?'

'Meh, time is relative. Will you do it, or not?'

Juliette sighed loud enough for Hattie to hear. 'I'll do it, but this had better be worth it – I haven't even brushed my hair yet.'

Hattie didn't care if Juliette looked as though a family of birds had set up home in her barnet as long as she rounded everyone up and put in an appearance herself.

'One more thing,' Hattie said, before she ended the call. 'Not a word to Alfred or Zoe.'

'Okaaay. May I ask why?'

'I'll tell you at Bookylicious.'

Maddison was already in the café, although it

wasn't open yet, when Hattie arrived breathless and red in the face and started to drag a couple of tables together.

'It's for a meeting of the Toy Shop Team. Don't worry, I'll put the tables and chairs back afterwards. We won't be long.'

'Take as long as you need,' Maddison told her. 'It's usually only take-away trade at this time of day. Why are you in so early?'

Hattie dropped a newspaper in front of her boss as she hobbled behind the counter to select the cakes. 'Alfred is in it, and I've got an idea.'

'Oh, dear…' Maddison shook her head.

'It's a good idea,' Hattie protested. 'You'll see.'

To her surprise, everyone arrived within thirty minutes, and Hattie, conscious of the time and that people had other things to do, began the meeting by handing out copies of the newspaper.

'Don't read it now,' she urged. 'But Alfred is in it, and I wanted to share something with you. Shoot me down in flames afterwards if you want, but hear me out first.' She took a deep breath. 'I have a proposal that we club together to keep the toy shop going after Christmas.'

She saw mouths open ready to speak, but she held up a hand and glared.

Silence descended and Hattie chewed at her lip.

Ah well, they can only say no, and if she didn't put it out there they wouldn't have an opportunity to say yes, either. 'I'm thinking that the shop doesn't just sell hand-made toys. It can sell lots of other hand-made things as long as they are up to scratch and of a suitable standard. It'll be a sort of outlet for individual craftspeople?'

'A bit like Etsy?' Silas said.

Hattie had no idea what Etsy was, but before she could ask, Juliette jumped in with a question.

'What about the charity part? Will the proceeds still go to charity, and if so, I can see a problem right away, because you can't expect people to make stuff, then give all their profits away.'

'How about a percentage?' Father Todd suggested. 'It can run as a cooperative – the craftspeople take turns to man it, they pay something towards the upkeep like the rent and electricity for example, and a small percentage of what they make is given to charity. It would be self-funding before too long.'

'What a great idea! Father Todd, you're a genius!' Juliette exclaimed, throwing her arms around him and giving him a resounding kiss on the cheek, which made him blush.

Benny spoke up. 'What about the toys? Would Alfred be agreeable if only a percentage was to go to charity?'

'We'll need to speak to him about that,' Hattie said – she'd need to speak to him about all of it! 'But I hope so. Any profits he makes can go back into toy making.'

'Someone will need to manage it – it's a big undertaking. What about your Zoe? I know she's young but she's proved herself to be very capable,' Marge said.

She would have been Hattie's first choice too, but for one thing. 'I think her true passion is working with wood. Which is one of the reasons I didn't invite her along this morning – I didn't want to get her hopes up, because I think she should be Alfred's apprentice. I know from Zoe that there is a distinct lack of apprenticeship places and Alfred needs to make more toys. He can't do it on his own, but he can teach Zoe, and in that way his toymaking skills won't be lost.'

'Why doesn't Alfred know about this?' Nell asked.

'Because I wanted to see if you thought it was a good idea. And now that you do, I want to make sure the interest is out there – because if we can't get any craftspeople on board, then the whole thing is dead in the water.'

Juliette said, 'I can run an ad in the paper – it can go out in this week's edition which is tomorrow. I've probably got more time than anyone else, so I can collate any responses.'

'I'll speak to the letting agents and I also know a few people who may be interested,' Nell offered.

Silas said, 'I know a glassblower and a jewellery-maker who might also be up for it.'

'Now that's sorted, please be aware that time is of the essence, so shall we meet again in three days?'

Hattie was under no illusion that if this was to happen (assuming there were enough people out there to make the shop viable), there was an awful lot to organise.

And with that in mind, she also realised that she needed to have a quiet word in someone's ear.

CHAPTER 38

ALFRED

Alfred closed the newspaper and uttered a deep sigh. The article had only come out today, so maybe it was a bit too soon to digest it properly and perhaps he ought to give himself more time for the reporter's words to sink in, but he couldn't help feeling guilty. He knew Liam probably hadn't meant it to sound like it did, but the tone of the article made Alfred feel as though it was his fault that his carpentry skills would be lost to future generations when he met his maker.

The idea was quite absurd – anyone would think he was the only fella on the planet who knew how to use a wood chisel. Carpentry was hardly a dying art, but maybe making toys from scratch by hand was...

And it was this fear that made him say to Zoe as the shop was about to shut, 'Fancy a quick coffee?

I've got something I want to talk to you about.'

She sent him a questioning look. 'OK, but I think Bookylicious shuts at five.'

'I was thinking we could lock up, turn the lights off, and hide out the back.'

'Hide?' She was staring at him as if he'd lost his mind.

Which is exactly what he was thinking himself, but now that this idea was in his head, he couldn't seem to shift it.

He watched Zoe add up the day's takings, while he shut the shop door and made a half-hearted attempt to tidy up. Then as soon as she had finished her task, he switched off the lights and gestured for her to walk ahead of him.

'What's this about?' she demanded suspiciously. 'Why are we hiding?'

'I don't want Hattie or any of the others to know about what I'm going to ask you, not yet anyway. I've been thinking… How would you like to learn how to make wooden toys? You won't come out of it with any formal qualification, of course, but I promise to teach you to the best of my ability.'

Zoe froze, then her eyes widened and she let out a shriek and threw herself at him. His arms came around her to steady them both as she hugged him with all her might.

Crikey, for such a slender girl she was incredibly strong.

'I can't breathe,' he forced out.

'Sorry.' She released him and stepped back. Her eyes were shining and her face was full of excitement. 'I'd love to!'

'I wouldn't have guessed,' was his dry response.

'If I speak to the college, maybe they'd let me be your apprentice?' she suggested.

Alfred was doubtful, but he went along with it. 'Great plan.' He had no clue about apprenticeships apart from the fact that they didn't pay the poor kid who was learning the trade much. He'd already decided to give her an allowance out of his own pocket and it wouldn't be a trifling sum, either. He would have plenty of money once the house was sold, and his pension covered his contribution to Sara's household (he insisted on paying his way). He had a fair bit left over every week, and he didn't have anything to spend it on. Investing in Zoe and her future was as good as anything else, and better than most. The girl deserved it.

Zoe's face was flushed and her eyes were bright with unshed tears. 'I'll work hard, Alfred, and I'll be a good learner, you'll see.'

Alfred smiled, and patted her hand. He didn't have any doubts about that — what he did have doubts about was his ability to pass his knowledge on, and where he was going to find a suitable workshop, if Hattie wasn't too happy about him taking over her shed permanently.

Maybe that should be Zoe's first task?

But for now, he was content that his plan was taking shape, and he had to get through the next ten days.

'Let's keep this just between us for the time being,' he said to Zoe. 'You know what Hattie's like – if she knows about it, she'll blab and Sara will get to hear about it. My daughter wasn't happy about the shop, and the only thing stopping her from going on about it, is that it's closing on Christmas Eve and that it's for charity. God help me when she finds out I've taken on an apprentice and I'm going to carry on making toys. We'll tell everyone after Christmas.'

'If she loves you, you'll want you to do what makes you happy. That's what my mum says.' Zoe's expression was earnest.

Alfred sincerely hoped Sara felt the same way, but he wasn't going to hold his breath.

CHAPTER 39

HATTIE

'Zoe, can you hold the fort for half an hour? I want to have a quick chat with Sara,' Hattie said three days later, after a very fruitful second secret meeting of the Toy Shop Team earlier that morning. Her plan was taking shape and it was time to move things to the next level, which was why she'd popped into the toy shop this morning. With Zoe in charge and Sara helping her, Hattie hadn't felt the need to be there every second she was free.

'Can't it wait? I'm rather busy,' Sara said.

Hattie glanced around. It was ten minutes past nine – the shop had one customer and was looking spotless. If Sara was busy, then whatever she was doing didn't need to be done immediately.

'No. It's about your father.'

Sara's hand went to her chest. 'Oh my God! What's happened? Is he all right?'

'He's fine. Stop being a drama queen,' Hattie said and saw Zoe roll her eyes behind Sara's back. 'But I still want to talk to you. We'll go to Bookylicious and you can have a coffee.'

'I've just had one.'

Hattie bit back a retort. There was no point in rubbing the woman up the wrong way; they'd already started off on the wrong foot, and Hattie wasn't just referring to today. 'Please?'

'If you're sure you can manage, Zoe?'

'I'm sure,' Zoe said with a hint of impatience.

Hattie grinned at her. The girl was more than capable, and had proved it constantly since Hattie had made the wise and executive decision to take her on.

'Well? What did you want to talk to me about?' Sara demanded the minute they were seated.

Hattie made her wait for a few moments while she caught Teresa's eye and ordered two cappuccinos and a plate of Danish pastries.

'I've had my breakfast,' Sara said once Teresa was out of earshot.

'They are for me,' Hattie retorted. 'But I suppose I could let you have one.'

'Hmph' Sara tapped her fingers on the table. 'I'm waiting.'

'What for—? Oh, yes, the shop.'

'What about it. Golly, but this is worse than dealing with a child in reception class.'

'I want to keep it open after Christmas,' Hattie announced. 'Hear me out before you jump in with your size sevens.'

'Six, actually.'

'Whatever.' Hattie took another deep breath. 'The Toy Shop Team have been looking into the possibility of keeping the shop open but operating it in a slightly different way. We propose that a variety of different crafts are represented, not just toys—'

'Good, because there's not many more to sell.'

Hattie ignored the interruption and carried on. 'Each crafter will do a shift in the shop as a condition of being allowed to display their wares, and a small percentage of their profits will be taken by the shop to cover rent, rates, and utilities, and a portion of that will also go to charity.'

Sara tilted her head to the side and Hattie saw the first spark of interest. 'Like a form of cooperative?'

'I suppose.' Hattie wasn't entirely sure what a cooperative was – the only one she knew of was the little Co-op on the edge of the village, where she shopped for the bits and pieces that she couldn't get elsewhere on Ticklemore's high street.

'But as I just said, my father doesn't have a lot

more to sell. What role will he play? And for the record, can I say that I'm not too happy about him playing any role at all.'

'He won't be in the shop.'

Sara narrowed her eyes. 'So why are you telling me this, if it doesn't affect him?'

'Because it does, in a way. He'll carry on making toys in my shed. I'll cover his day in the shop.'

'He'll do what?' Sara spluttered.

'Carry on making toys. It's what he loves and what he's good at.'

'It took him years to make enough to sell! He's an old man, in case you hadn't noticed; he's not going to make enough in a year to fill a single damned shelf.'

'Keep your knickers on – that's where Zoe comes in. He's going to teach her to make them.'

'Dad's happy with this arrangement, is he? I can't believe he hasn't said anything, and has sent you to do his dirty work.'

'He doesn't know.'

Sara barked out a laugh. 'He doesn't know? That's ridiculous. How can he not know?'

'Because we haven't told him. I wanted to make sure it was doable before we got his hopes up.'

'Is that why you wanted to speak to me? Because you want me to give you my blessing or something?'

'No. I want you to manage the place.'

'You're winding me up.' Sara's eyes were wide and she was shaking her head in disbelief.

'I'm serious. You'll be good at it and Alfred will be happier knowing his baby is in safe hands.'

Sara sat back in her seat, her face slack. 'I'm not sure my dad is up to it.'

'What? Teaching a kid to nail some wood together?' Hattie scoffed. 'He could do it in his sleep. And it won't be all day every day. He can suit himself as to the hours he puts in. He'll be able to do as much or as little as he feels able.'

'I'm not sure he'll feel able to do a great deal, going forward.'

'Are you referring to his so-called dementia?'

Sara worried at her lip. 'It's no laughing matter. I've been going out of my mind with worry.'

'I'm not trivialising it,' Hattie insisted. 'It's a terrible disease, but I don't believe your father has it.'

'You're not a qualified doctor – what do you know?'

'I know that he's been grieving. That he'd lost his way for a while. But not anymore. Not the grieving part, that's still there. I'm talking about the losing part.'

Hattie watched the woman carefully, wondering what she was going to say as she thought hard. Hattie could almost see the smoke coming out of Sara's ears.

'He's a different man since he's come to live with me – actually, that's not true.' Sara paused. 'He's a different man since he became involved in the toy shop.' She smiled wryly. 'I must admit that at first I thought the whole thing was ridiculous, but when I came in this morning and looked around the shop, I felt quite sad to think it'll close down in a week's time.'

'This way it doesn't have to.'

'I don't know…' Sara shrugged. 'I have to say I've been somewhat bored since I retired, which is probably why I've been micro-managing my father, and I've thoroughly enjoyed the time I've spent in the shop. In a way I can see how my dad lost his purpose when my mum died, because I lost mine a bit when I retired.' Her chuckle had a cynical edge to it. 'For some reason I thought it would be more exciting than it has been, but I officially left the school on 31st August, and I've felt at a loose end ever since.'

'There you go then; this will be perfect for you.'

'It would, but I'm sure Alfred has told you that my daughter, Shelley, is pregnant and I'm going to be minding the baby two days a week.'

'Won't she have maternity leave?'

'Yes, but—'

'When is it due?'

'May, but—'

'No buts, this is made for you. Get the shop operational—' Hattie loved that word – she'd heard it on the news yesterday morning when some politician was talking about a new factory being opened, '—it'll take a fair bit of organising what with deciding what stock goes where. I mean that'll be between you and the craftsperson concerned – the rota, all the running costs, reconciling the takings and making sure everyone gets what they are entitled to. Then there's the advertising, liaising with the charities themselves, and loads of other stuff I can't think of off the top of my head – it'll be right up your street. Anyway, once you've got it running the way it should be run, then you can do a day or two in the shop yourself, and everything else is paperwork, so you can do that at home.'

Hattie could tell Sara was tempted.

'I'm still not sure about my father's involvement. He's not getting any younger.'

'That applies to all of us, but if you want him to slip back into feeling worthless, then so be it.' Hattie was beginning to lose her patience.

'That's not what I'm saying,' Sara retorted.

'You've got some serious trust issues, haven't you? Your father will do as much as he feels able to and nothing more – mainly because he doesn't want to be a burden to you and doesn't want you on his case every five minutes. Anyway, I'll make sure he behaves himself.'

'Can I think about it?'

'Don't take too long. I've got loads of people who would jump at a chance like this.' She hadn't but Sara didn't know that. 'By the way, please don't mention anything to your father just yet, whatever you decide.'

'You do realise all this might be a waste of time and effort. What if he says no?'

'He won't.' Hattie grinned cheerfully.

'How can you be certain of that?'

Hattie tilted her head to the side and studied the woman sitting opposite her. For all her highfalutin education, she could be a bit dim sometimes, bless her.

'Men need something to keep them busy, otherwise they just get under your feet and grizzle a lot. Your dad needs to get back to making stuff and if we couch it in terms of not letting his toymaking expertise die when he does... What's up? You don't like me talking about dying? Get over yourself. We've all got to go sometime, and when he pops his clogs it'll do him good to think he's passed his knowledge and skill onto another generation. And, if we stress that he'll be doing the likes of Zoe a favour – giving youngsters a chance and keeping them off the streets – then I'll bet my right arm he'll go for it.'

Sara was nodding thoughtfully all the way through Hattie's little diatribe. 'OK, I'll do it, but on a trial basis. Things might have to change when my grandchild is born.'

'Deal.' Hattie shoved out her hand. 'There's something else I need to you do for me,' she added, once the agreement had been shaken on. 'Tell your father you're dead against it'

'Why?'

'Because that's one sure-fire way to make sure he agrees to it.'

Sara snorted. 'Shelley wasn't this much trouble when she was a teenager. Can I ask you a question?'

'You can – that don't mean I'll answer it though.'

'Why are you doing this?'

'You've worked with Zoe. She and others like her deserve a chance—'

'Why are you really doing it?' Sara interrupted.

Hattie stared at her. How could she tell this woman that she had developed feelings for her father?

'You like my dad, don't you?

'Of course I do, otherwise I wouldn't be doing this, even though he can be as grumpy as hell at times, and downright annoying. And he winds me up a treat.'

'You know what I mean.'

Hattie didn't say anything.

'It's OK, you know. I don't mind,' Sara said.

'There's nothing to mind. I respect your father, and I hope he respects me. He's a decent fella.' She paused again. 'There's nothing going on between us.'

'I didn't think there was.'

Hattie scowled at the inference. 'And why wouldn't there be? Hmm? Tell me that? It's not as though either of us are in a relationship. Or are you referring to our age? Because, let me tell you, my girl, age is meaningless when it comes to love.'

Hattie froze.

Sara froze.

The two women stared at each other.

Neither of them spoke for several minutes, then finally Hattie said, 'This is as much of a surprise to me as it is to you.'

Sara's touch was light as she patted her on the hand. 'No, it's not. And I have a sneaking suspicion that my dad feels the same way about you. But I suppose the important question is, are you going to do anything about it? Because as sure as God made little green apples, my father won't, so it will have to be down to you.'

CHAPTER 40

ALFRED

There was something going on – Alfred could feel it in his water. Sara was acting a bit off; every time he tried to talk to Hattie about the arrangements for the toys that hadn't sold by the end of Christmas Eve, which was only one day away, she muttered something incomprehensible under her breath and changed the subject. Logan was avoiding him – yesterday Alfred had seen the man scoot out the back as soon as he entered the pub and he failed to emerge the whole time Alfred was there, despite the place heaving with customers. Juliette wasn't answering her phone and neither was Silas. And all Nell said to him when he popped into the Treasure Trove was that she was too busy with her own shop to think about his, and that there was plenty of time to deal with it after

Christmas.

Eventually, he made his own arrangements with Zoe for her and a friend to come in the day after Boxing Day and take whatever was left back to Hattie's shed.

Thinking of Hattie's shed reminded him that he had yet to tell her about his plans for him and Zoe. And he also needed to ask her if she minded letting him use her shed as his workshop. He would prefer it, but Zoe was already looking for somewhere else, just in case Hattie objected.

If he was honest, Hattie's shed would be fine if it was only him working in it, the same as his shed in his old house had been perfect for one. Having two or even three people trying to work in there would be a bit of a squash.

But Hattie's shed was familiar and convenient and he was reluctant to move, and when he examined the reason why he felt that way, he realised that part of it was because he wanted to be close to her.

Which was utterly ridiculous.

Why on earth would he want to be close to Hattie? If he thought she was odd before, she was being even odder now. And grumpier. And he had no idea why.

'What's up?' he asked Sara over breakfast. 'It's only three days to Christmas – I would have thought you'd be full of the festive spirit by now.'

'Stress, that's what I'm full of,' Sara grumbled.

'What do you have to be stressed about?'

She shot him a funny look and seemed to be about to say something but she changed her mind because she said, 'How do you feel about inviting Hattie for lunch on Christmas Day?

Alfred blinked. He hadn't been expecting that. He guessed that the two women had garnered a bit more respect for each other now that Sara was helping in the shop, but he didn't think his daughter liked Hattie enough to want to have her visit them on Christmas Day.

'I think it's a grand idea – if she'll come. She mightn't want to,' he said.

'Oh, of course she mightn't. Silly me! She's probably going to spend the day with her own family.'

That wasn't what Alfred meant, but he let it go. There was no point in prodding a wasps' nest. 'You can ask her,' he replied mildly. 'The worse she can do is say no.'

'I thought the invitation might be better coming from you.'

Sara was probably right. Although whether Hattie would want to spend any more time than she had to in Sara's company was another thing. He'd love to have her there, though, so he made a vow to pitch it to her as appealingly as possible.

With that in mind, he decided to catch Hattie before she started work at Bookylicious, and he hurried upstairs to get changed. Tracksuit bottoms and a fleece were great for lounging about the house, but he wouldn't dream of stepping outside the door unless he was properly attired, and that meant trousers, a shirt, and a pullover.

It was a pity it took him so long to wrestle one lot off and put another lot on, and he had to stop and catch his breath for a second before he attempted to do his shoes up.

Finally ready, he picked up his keys and phone, stuffed his arms into his padded winter coat and did the zip up on the second attempt.

Stick, where was his stick?

Ah, there it was, propped up in the corner next to the front door. Hat on, scarf on, and gloves in hand, Alfred yelled, 'I'm off out,' and listened for an answer. When it didn't come, he guessed Sara had already left, probably off to fuss some more about the food for the holidays. She didn't need to because the fridge was packed, the freezer was stuffed full, and every time he opened a cupboard something fell out. A large bag of nuts had clonked him on the head yesterday. Living in his daughter's house was dangerous. But he had to admit that she put on a jolly good spread at Christmas so maybe the extra fussing was worth it, and he was pleased she was pulling out all the stops, especially with Hattie as a guest.

The high street was quiet this early in the morning, although there were a few people about, hurrying off to work presumably. Bookylicious, he knew, opened at eight to catch the pre-work crowd, providing them with a much-needed caffeine and croissant hit, and Hattie should already be hard at it.

From the outside, the café-cum-bookshop was the epitome of festive cheer, and he stopped for a moment to admire the display of Christmas titles in the window, which had been stacked on a table alongside a teapot in the shape of Father Christmas (the handle was one of his arms and the spout was the other, with the lid being his head), and chunky round mugs in the shape of snowmen. Each one was different, and he particularly liked the one with a walking stick.

He was about to enter when he looked past the display and into the café beyond.

What he saw made him freeze.

The Toy Shop Team were gathered around a couple of tables which were loaded with mugs and plates, and were talking seriously.

Darn it – had he been invited to the meeting and forgotten? He hoped not, and he had a quick think, frantically trying to remember. He knew he could be forgetful sometimes, but he was sure he'd have remembered this.

Nope. He was certain nothing had been mentioned to him.

Shuffling sideways a bit so the display semi-hid him, he peered in again and his heart sank to his shiny shoes. Sara was at the table with them, looking as serious as the others, and it was then that he knew for sure they deliberately hadn't told him about this meeting because they didn't want him to attend.

Gutted, that was the word that leapt into his mind. He'd guessed something was going on – his instinct hadn't been misleading him – and here was the proof.

What could they possibly be discussing? Him?

They must be, otherwise why wouldn't they have invited him along?

Oh God! They didn't believe he was capable of winding the shop up. Maybe they'd had concerns all along about him being able to run it, which was why Zoe had been brought in.

But the question playing on his mind was, were they right to worry? Was he starting along the frightening and lonely path to dementia? If he was, maybe he'd be the last to realise it? Was that how it worked? That the poor souls who suffered from it didn't see that their faculties were gradually being eroded, and if they did, they put their forgetfulness and confusion down to simply being old and not quite as sharp as they once were.

Was he that person?

The walk from Bookylicious seemed to take forever, and he was glad when he stepped out of the cold and into the relative warmth of the toy shop. Zoe had only just arrived and had put the heating on, but Alfred suspected that no matter how warm the place became, it would fail to drive out the chill in his heart and the ice in his mind.

'You're early,' Zoe said, offering him a bright smile.

Alfred grunted. Speaking seemed too much of an effort.

'Are you OK?'

'Fine,' he forced out, and headed out the back to make a cup of tea.

When he emerged carrying two mugs, he'd had a chance to gather his thoughts while the kettle was boiling. 'Have you managed to find a workshop?' he asked her.

'Not yet, I've been looking, but there's not much around.'

'Keep trying,' he urged. There was no way he could continue to operate out of Hattie's shed, not after she'd betrayed him like this.

He wasn't sure he could continue to live with his

daughter, either. Once the sale of his house was finalised, he wouldn't be short of a penny or two, so there was nothing stopping him from renting his own place. A bungalow perhaps, where he could do what he wanted, when he wanted, and how he wanted, without his bossy, interfering daughter breathing down his neck. There was nothing wrong with him. He'd know if there was.

The worst thing was, he'd thought his relationship with Sara had turned a corner and they had a better understanding of each other. Cleary this wasn't the case at all.

And he couldn't believe his so-called friends would do that to him.

Tomorrow was Christmas Eve and Alfred couldn't wait to close the shop for good and put an end to all this. He was stupid to have entertained the idea in the first place. He might have known it would all end in tears, and if it wasn't for Zoe, the charities, and any last minute customers who were depending on the shop being open, he'd be tempted to close right now.

He should have stayed in his own house and not let Sara's nagging drive him out of it. He'd been happy there. OK, maybe not happy – not since Dorothy had died – but at least he'd been alone with his misery. It had been familiar. Not like this new, sharp pain that he had no idea how he was supposed to deal with.

Oh God, what a sodding mess.

CHAPTER 41

HATTIE

'Alfred? Are you OK?' It was coming up for quarter-past ten and Hattie was worried. Alfred always phoned her at ten o'clock, without fail.

Apart from tonight.

Mindful that if he hadn't raised the alarm when she'd had her fall, things might have been a lot worse, she called him, fully prepared to ring Sara if he didn't answer.

Her relief when he picked up her call was overridden by his terse tone.

'I'm fine. What do you want?'

'Um, nothing. You usually phone me at ten, and you didn't tonight, so I was worried.'

'I'm sick to death of people worrying about me,' he shouted, and Hattie nearly dropped her phone in shock.

'I'm sorry you feel that way,' she replied stiffly. 'If I'd have known that having people care about you annoyed you so much, I wouldn't have bothered.'

'I wish you hadn't.' He'd stopped shouting but his voice was cold.

'What's happened, Alfred?'

'You tell me.'

'I haven't got a clue what you're talking about.' Oh, my God... could Sara be correct, and Alfred actually was in the first throws of that dreadful disease?

'Don't lie. I saw you.'

Hattie was none the wiser. 'Saw me?'

'This morning in Bookylicious.'

'Oh.' Bugger; no wonder he was upset.

'Yes, "oh". What have you got to say for yourself?'

'I wasn't going to tell you until tomorrow.'

'Tell me what? That you all think I'm a fruitcake and can't be trusted?'

'*What?* Is that what you think? You're nuts.'

'Ah ha!'

Hattie gritted her teeth in exasperation. 'You utterly ridiculous man! If you must know, we were discussing a new venture for the toy shop, and for you.'

Silence.

'Alfred, are you still there?'

'I'm here.' His voice was so faint, Hattie had difficulty hearing him.

'You'll have to speak up. My hearing's not as sharp as it used to be.'

'Your tongue is,' he muttered.

'I heard that!'

'I thought you might. What is this new venture and why didn't you include me in this discussion of yours? Is Sara in on it?'

'Don't blame her or any of the others – it's my fault. I asked them not to tell you, because I wanted to make sure it would work.'

'*Wha*t would work? For pity's sake, tell me.'

'No.'

'Hattie…' he growled, and his voice sent a shiver through her. Bless him, he was trying to be masterful and he was succeeding a little.

Not enough, though.

'No,' she repeated. 'We've got a small closing ceremony at one o'clock tomorrow. You'll know then.'

'I thought we were closing at three?'

'Change of plan.'

'Hattie?'

'Yes?'

'I will like this venture, won't I?'

'I bloody well hope so!'

'Hattie?'

'What now?' The man was starting to get on her nerves.

'Would you like to come to ours for Christmas lunch?'

Bloody hell. The shock stole her breath. She wondered how Sara would feel about it. Not too pleased, she guessed, despite them having made some progress with regards to their relationship.

'Hattie? Did you hear what I said?'

'I heard. You'd better not let your Sara know you've asked me to lunch – she'll have a hissy fit.'

Alfred's low chuckle made her pulse soar. 'It was her idea. Please say you'll come.'

She'd planned a nice steak and ale pie, with some creamy mashed potato, a couple of sprouts (even though she wasn't too keen on them, but it wasn't Christmas without sprouts, was it?) and a handful of green beans. She'd also planned to eat it on her own, and have finished her meal and the washing up in time for the traditional royal speech, which she'd also planned on watching alone.

That Sara had been thoughtful enough to ask her, touched her heart.

Over the years, she'd been asked to spend Christmas Day with a whole host of Ticklemore's residents. Each year, she'd been touched, and each year she'd politely refused, not wanting to intrude. She'd considered it enough to have been asked.

'Thank you, but—' was all she managed to say before Alfred jumped in with, 'If you don't come to mine, then I'll come to yours and I'll bring your Christmas dinner with me.'

'I've got plans,' she said, loftily.

He asked her gently, 'Have you, honestly?' His disbelief was evident.

Hattie hesitated. If there was one person she would choose to pull a cracker with and wear a silly hat for, it was Alfred.

'Will there be sprouts?' she asked.

'I expect so.'

'Then I'll be honoured to have lunch with you. Bye!'

CHAPTER 42

ALFRED

Alfred had been convinced that he wouldn't be able to sleep last night, but he'd managed a solid seven hours – which was a record for him these days. He'd had to do a hasty scuttle to the toilet as soon as he'd opened his eyes, but he could handle that.

It was amazing what a good sleep could do for both the body and the mind, because after he'd done the necessary, he was pleased to discover that the anxiety of yesterday had faded, and he had far fewer aches, pains, and stiffness to contend with. His gammy leg was an ongoing annoyance, but that was to be expected, but even that wasn't as bad as it had been. They said soft tissue damage took a long time to repair, but it was healing slowly, and so was the rest of him – and by that, he meant his grief wasn't as overwhelming. It was still there – it always would be and he welcomed it because it made him feel nearer to Dorothy – but he could live with it, not in spite of it.

Despite his intense curiosity about this venture Hattie had teased him about, Alfred's mind was constantly diverted by the steady influx of people into the shop; some of them were hoping for a last minute bargain and were disappointed when they realised that nothing was reduced. Others came in to congratulate him on the shop's success and to enquire whether he could tell them how much had been raised.

He could take a guess, because he knew what the sales figures were up until yesterday, but he had yet to factor in the expenses the shop had incurred, and it might be a few weeks before the final figure was known. So he rounded it down to the nearest thousand and added the words, 'There or thereabouts,' at the end, which seemed to satisfy them.

'You're not going to believe this,' Hattie said, pushing her way inside and brushing at the shoulders of her woollen coat. 'It's snowing'

'Squee!!' Zoe scampered to the window and peered out, clapping her hands when she saw it was true.

Alfred looked at Hattie ruefully. Once upon a time they might have felt the same way, but these days snow meant decreased mobility outside the house with an increased fear of slips and falls, together with the worry of obtaining bread and milk should supplies run short.

'It's certainly pretty,' Hattie said.

'I suppose it's a fitting end to the Ticklemore Christmas Toy Shop,' Alfred agreed, sadly. Despite the hard work, he'd enjoyed the experience immensely. The delight on his customers' faces as they gazed around the shop had made it worthwhile. He just wished he could see the children's expressions when they saw what Santa Claus had brought them.

At the stroke of one o'clock Hattie closed the door on the Ticklemore Christmas Toy Shop for the very last time, and as Alfred watched her turn the little sign which hung on the inside of the door from open to closed, he had a lump in his throat.

He'd miss the place more than he ever thought possible and he had to look away and blink hard to get rid of the threatened tears.

At least he'd still have Zoe to keep him occupied, and he reminded himself again that he must ask Hattie if he could continue to use her shed, for the time being at least. He'd pick his time with care – maybe at lunch tomorrow when she was enjoying one of those sprouts.

One by one the Toy Shop Team trickled in, all of

them carrying a bottle or two. He noticed that Hattie had already stashed some glasses in the kitchen part of the back room, along with a bottle opener. The woman had thought of everything.

Once everyone had arrived and they all had a drink in their hand, Hattie asked them to raise a toast.

'To Alfred, who made this shop possible and whose vision will bring joy to countless children, and whose generosity in giving the profits from the shop to charity is an example to us all. To Alfred.'

'To Alfred,' the rest of them chorused and he dipped his head in acknowledgment, feeling more pleased and embarrassed than he could ever remember being in his life.

'Before we make an announcement...' Hattie stared meaningfully around at the others, 'I just want to thank everyone for all their hard work and support. Without you this wouldn't have been achievable. As for how much Alfred has made, I'll have a guesstimate for you after Christmas and a final figure...' She paused. 'Actually, there won't be a final figure at all if Alfred is happy with our proposal.'

'About time,' he muttered.

'We've had an idea,' she began, but was interrupted by Juliette who called out, '*You* were the one who had the idea, so don't blame us!'

Hattie blushed and Alfred thought how endearing

she looked.

'Anyway, as I was saying,' she gazed around the room as if daring anyone to contradict her, 'we want to keep the toy shop open. And before you say there aren't many more toys left, Alfred, we know. What we are suggesting is that we ask other craftspeople to join us by displaying their stock. The shop will take a percentage of what is sold to cover the running costs and another percentage will go to charity – the rest will be kept by them. We have seven people on board, and they have all agreed to sign up to a rota system to run the place, and your Sara will be setting it up and managing it in the first instance.'

His Sara?

He couldn't believe it. So that's what all the weirdness had been about.

'That's not all. Zoe, we don't think you should work in the shop anymore.' Hattie paused, giving Alfred time to focus on Zoe's reaction. 'We think you should work with Alfred to make toys, and that he should train you.'

Alfred's mouth fell open. Bloody hell – that was exactly what he'd been planning on doing. He shot Zoe a look, realising the shock on her face was mirroring his own. He grinned, his heart leaping with joy.

'Now that you come to mention it…' he said, and

proceeded to tell the others what he and Zoe had planned.

By the time he fell into bed later that night his head was whirling and he was so excited he felt like a kid again, waiting for the man in red to wriggle down the chimney.

'Merry Christmas, Hattie, and thank you for the best Christmas present in the world,' was all he said to her during his nightly phone call. Apart from, 'I love you and I'll see you tomorrow.'

CHAPTER 44

HATTIE

That Alfred had told her he loved her was the final thing on her mind before she dropped off to sleep last night, and it was the first thing that popped into her head when she'd opened her eyes on Christmas morning.

It was all she could think about as she ate her breakfast, despite the fact that it had snowed a little more overnight and that Ticklemore was coated in a blanket of sparkling, crisp whiteness.

She could think about nothing else as she rummaged around in the spare room for a Christmas jumper and it was still on her mind when she heard a knock on the door a little before noon, indicating that David had arrived to pick her up.

Therefore, it was no surprise to her to blurt out

what she was thinking as soon as she clapped eyes on Alfred, despite her vow not to mention it.

'Do you really love me?' she hissed in his ear when he moved in to give her a kiss on the cheek.

'I most certainly do.'

'Then I suppose I'll have to tell you that I love you too,' she said.

They beamed at each other.

'Out of the way, love birds, I've got a table to lay,' Shelley said, squeezing around the pair of them as they hogged the hall.

'How are you feeling?' Hattie asked her. 'You're looking well.'

'I feel great, thanks. By the way, Mum asked me to set up a website for the toy shop. Let me put these in the dining room and I'll show you.' She waved a handful of assorted cutlery in the air.

Alfred showed Hattie into the sitting room and she gazed around curiously. It was very modern and minimalist, and she could see how Sara thought Alfred's old furniture would have looked out of place. It wasn't to Hattie's taste at all – she preferred oddments and unusual things, and the idea of having everything matching went against the grain. Houses were just houses, but it was the picture that you picked up on a spontaneous trip to the Norfolk Broads, or the rug you saw in a boot sale and whose bright colours and interesting pattern spoke to you – those were the things which turned a house into a home, and gave it colour and personality. Not orchestrated, matching blandness like Sara's house. The only redeeming feature that Hattie could see was a large bookcase stuffed full of hardbacks and paperbacks in all sizes and colours, depicting a variety of subject and genres.

'I've brought my laptop,' Shelley said, dragging Hattie away from trying to read a title sideways. 'Sit on the sofa and I'll squash in the middle.'

Hattie wasn't too bothered about seeing a website – she was more interested in the mouthwatering smell wafting from the kitchen.

'Hattie, I'm so pleased you could join us,' Sara said, appearing in the doorway with her husband close behind her. 'David, have you offered her a drink?'

'What would you like?' David asked. 'How about a nice glass of sherry?'

'I prefer gin.'

'Gin it is. Tonic?'

'Nah. Got any Earl Grey tea? You'll have to let it go cold.'

'Gin and Earl Grey tea…?' David shuddered.

Hattie said, 'Don't knock it until you've tried it,' and cackled as he didn't look convinced but went off to make the drink for her anyway.

Shelley opened the laptop, and clicked onto the page. 'Here you go. It's not published yet because it's still in the creation stage, but it'll give you an idea of what it will look like. What do you think?'

Hattie thought it looked perfect – professional without being too slick, attractive without being too arty. Shelley had got the tone just right, as far as Hattie could tell; not that she was an expert or anything, but if the site appeared on her phone screen it would make her want to click on it.

'I've set up a Facebook page, too. Grandad, you might want to take a look at this.'

'Aw, you know me and modern technology…' He waved a hand in the air.

'Grandad, look.'

And there on the screen was photo after photo of small children holding one of Alfred's marvellous toys, and every child wore a massive grin.

'I sent out a request for anyone who had bought a toy from the Ticklemore Toy Shop to post a photo on the Facebook page, and this is the result.'

Hattie had a quick glance at the screen, then turned her attention to Alfred, love swelling in her chest at the sheer joy on his face. This was what his toys were meant for, she saw – to be played with, and not buried in the dark, dusty depths of a shed. If this new venture didn't get off the ground for whatever reason, Hattie knew that the Ticklemore Christmas Toy Shop had served its purpose.

Her water had been right – Alfred Miller had needed saving.

Now all she had to do was to sit back and watch him bloom.

EPILOGUE

'I've forgotten my best tie,' Alfred told Hattie as he came out of the bathroom dressed in a nice shirt and a pair of smart slacks, and holding his overalls at arm's length.

'For goodness' sake! I'll ask Sara to bring it with her – you'll have to put it on later.' Hattie took the overalls from him and shooed him downstairs. 'I don't know why you felt the need to play in the workshop this morning, anyway. You know how important today is.'

'I told you, I wanted to see if the glue had set on Buttercup.' Buttercup was the rocking horse he and Zoe were making especially for the imminent arrival of his great-granddaughter.

'That was a five-minute job. You were in there for three hours.'

'You know what it's like... one thing leads to

another and before you know it, the whole day has gone – whoosh!'

'I'll whoosh you in a minute, if you don't get a move on.'

'Stop nagging. You always nag. Anyone would think we're married.'

'We bloody should be, the amount of time you spend in my house,' Hattie said.

'So why aren't we?'

'You haven't asked me, that's why.' Hattie was about to step past him, when he reached out a hand and caught hold of her elbow.

'Would you say yes if I did?'

'I might.'

Creakily, Alfred got down on one knee. There was some concern on the minds of both parties as to whether he'd manage to get back up again.

'Hattie Jenkins, will you do me the honour of being my wife?'

'What will your Sara say?'

'I'm not asking *her*, you goose, I'm asking *you*.'

'Where will we live?'

'Here? Somewhere else? I don't care – you decide. You love me, I love you, and we're not getting any younger. Hattie, my little dragon, you're going to have to give me an answer soon, because my knees are killing me.'

'In that case, yes, I will marry you. Do you need a hand to get up?'

'I think I'm going to need more than a hand…'

As Hattie helped haul Alfred to his feet, he lurched upright and knocked against a side table, sending the newspaper which was sitting on it sliding to the floor.

The pair of them were too busy sharing a kiss to notice.

Besides, they'd read the Tattler's headline so many times, they knew it off by heart and a copy of it was already stashed in Alfred's memory box for safe keeping.

It said…

ROYAL VISIT TO TOY SHOP

On Friday, Ticklemore's Toy Shop founder, Alfred Miller, will be presenting the first in what he hopes will be many cheques to two children's charities, after the success of his Christmas toy shop. The ceremony will be witnessed by one of the charity's patrons, Prince—

'Hattie?' Alfred pulled away for a moment.

'Yes, Alfred?'

'Do you think we'll be happy?'

'Of course we will! I can feel it in my water.'

More from Liz Davies

We hope you enjoyed reading Cynthia Smart's Midwife Crisis. If you did, please leave a review.

If you'd like to gift a copy, this book is also available in paperback.

Acknowledgements

Husband, of course, because he sees more of the top of my laptop than he does of my face most days (mind you, he might say that's a good thing!)

Catherine Mills, as always, for her unstinting enthusiasm for my stories and her willingness to gently put me right when I've drifted off course.

Mum for reading my stuff, Daughter for promising to (and for listening to me wittering about formatting when she has no idea what I'm rabbiting on about)

And my readers. Thank you for loving my books and making all the blood, sweat and tears – OK, coffee, sleepless nights and snivelling – worth it.

Liz x

ABOUT THE AUTHOR

Liz Davies writes feel-good, light-hearted stories with a hefty dose of romance, a smattering of humour, and a great deal of love.

She's married to her best friend, has one grown-up daughter, and when she isn't scribbling away in the notepad she carries with her everywhere (just in case inspiration strikes), you'll find her searching for that perfect pair of shoes. She loves to cook but isn't very good at it, and loves to eat - she's much better at that! Liz also enjoys walking (preferably on the flat), cycling (also on the flat), and lots of sitting around in the garden on warm, sunny days.

She currently lives with her family in Wales, but would ideally love to buy a camper van and travel the world in it.

Social Media Links:
Twitter https://twitter.com/lizdaviesauthor
Facebook: fb.me/LizDaviesAuthor1